Where the Heart Is
and other stories

Where the Heart Is
and other stories

Jim Bates

Bridge House

British Library Cataloguing in Publication Data
A Record of this Publication is available from the British
Library

ISBN 978-1-917854-03-0

This edition published 2025 by Bridge House Publishing
Manchester, England

for Sheila

Contents

Introduction

In this eclectic collection, Jim introduces the reader to everyday people whose lives are seemingly uneventful on the outside but are deep, rich and interesting nevertheless. Starting with Lindsey, a young girl who enjoys wrestling in *Gold,* and continuing to the final story, *The Lock Ness Monster* where Elizabeth makes a momentous decision, these stories are filled with captivating characters who will entertain and delight.

Many of the stories in this collection have appeared before in *CaféLit,* the *Pure Slush Lifetime Anthologies, Periodic Stories Volumes Two and IV,* and various Bridge House Anthologies. They are noted at the end of each story.

Gold

Wearing a pink tank top and tights, Lindsey Copeland danced out of her corner into the center of the ring. Her opponent, a kid named Frankie she knew from her seventh-grade art class, approached her confidently. She could see him smirking and she knew exactly what he was thinking. *You're going down, little girl.* Or something like that. He was a bully in school and thought he was tough stuff. Too bad for him.

Lindsey was fighting in the first round of the first fight of her life. Without stopping she danced right up to him and belted him square in the forehead. Even though he was wearing a boxing helmet, his head snapped back and tears came into his eyes. He blinked them away, but it didn't help. She grinned to herself. *Just like Uncle Sid taught me. Take 'em by surprise.*

In a matter of seconds, she hit him twice more, a left in the stomach and then a right cross to the jaw. For a skinny wisp of a thing, Lindsey had muscle, and her punches were like being hit by cement blocks. They were also unexpected, and Frankie stood stunned before reeling into his corner.

The ref put her hand on Lindsey's shoulder to stop her from stalking him. "Hold it a minute, sister." Lindsey looked at her. Her name was Skeeter, a well-respected former boxer, retired now for nearly ten years. Skeeter winked. "Nice couple of shots there." She raised Lindsey's arm. "The winner! Technical knockout." The crowd of about fifty or so cheered and applauded. Then Skeeter guided the young boxer to her corner and said to her uncle. "Well done, Sidney. You've got a good little fighter there. See you in the next round."

Uncle Sid helped Lindsey out of her gloves and gave

her a high-five. He grinned. "Excellent work. Next time remember to keep your right up a little more. But that first left jab to the forehead was awesome."

Lindsey spit her mouthguard into her hand and said, "Thanks, Uncle Sid." Then she took a long drink from her water bottle. Her heart was pounding, adrenalin running through her like a freight train. Man, that was fun!

Uncle Sid wrapped a towel around her shoulders and prepared to lead her out of the ring. She glanced at Freddie's corner, hoping he was okay. He was. He had his gloves off and gave her the thumbs-up sign. Good. She liked to box; she just didn't want to hurt anyone. Not too bad at least.

She was fighting in the U12 class, twelve years old and under. It was a round-robin tournament, and she was the only girl fighting. She was sure all the guys thought she'd be a pushover. Ha! Too bad for them. Talk to Frankie. He still looked a little crossed-eyed.

At five feet two inches, Lindsey was tall for her age. And skinny. "You're like a broomstick," her Aunt Claire had told her when she'd first come to live with them a year ago. "I've got to put some meat on those bones."

So began meals of pancakes and eggs in the morning, roasted chicken and mashed potatoes at noon, and roast beef and gravy and garden-fresh string beans at night. Or some variation thereof. Lindsey ate it all, happily, because she was always hungry. But she never gained an ounce.

Uncle Sid smiled six months later when his wife complained about their niece's lack of weight gain. "Don't worry about it, Claire." He turned to Lindsey. "Show her what you've got." Lindsey proudly flexed her arm, showing off her newly developed muscle. "See," he winked at his niece and gave Claire a one-armed hug. "It's all muscle."

"Humph!" Then she grinned good-naturedly. "Well, I guess that's okay, then." She really did want her niece to

11

succeed after all, her life hadn't been a bed of roses up until then.

Claire's mother, Brittany, was a sales rep for a medium-sized publishing house. She was a free-spirited woman who traveled the country meeting with clients and was only home maybe twenty percent of the time. She'd had Lindsey when she was thirty-five, telling her younger sister when she told her she was pregnant, "I think I'll give it a try. You know this mother thing."

Claire was aghast. "Brit, you can't approach being a mother like that." She'd raised three sons and knew what it took. Plus, all the time she'd been raising the three boys she'd had a full-time job doing bookkeeping for Willard's Construction, the company her husband, Lindsey's Uncle Sid, worked for.

"Sure, I can, little Sis," Claire had said, uncorking a bottle of wine. "Watch me." She'd poured two glasses. "Here's to us."

Claire had dealt with the alcohol demon off and on for years until she'd quit on the day after her thirtieth birthday. That was twenty years ago. She picked up the glass and poured it down the drain. "No thank you."

They were in the kitchen on the twelfth floor of Brittany's townhouse in downtown Minneapolis. Brit paid dearly for the million-dollar view of the Mississippi River and Saint Anthony Falls and the Stone Arch Bridge. Which was a shame, Claire thought, because her sister was hardly ever there. Claire poured a glass of water. "I wish you'd reconsider."

Brittany guzzled her White Zinfandel and poured another. "I already have, Sis. The light is green for go."

Claire had had all she could take. "Well, fine. It's not you that I'm concerned about," she said, walking to the door. "It's your unborn child."

12

Brittany laughed. "My child?" She drank from her glass and walked toward her sister, swaying slightly. "You mean my daughter, don't you?"

Claire's eyes went wide. "Daughter?"

"Yeah, sis. I've been checked. It's a she. I'm calling her Lindsey."

In spite of her anger toward her oldest sister's irresponsible behavior, Claire had to smile. After raising her three boys, it'd be nice to have a daughter in the family.

It was good she felt that way, because she became a surrogate mother right off the bat, driving downtown nearly every day from her and Sid's home in Orchard Lake, twenty miles west of Minneapolis.

Pretty soon, it was clear that Brittany was more than willing to turn over bringing up Lindsay to Claire. Sleepovers at her aunt and uncle's became long weekends which became a week, then two. Then a month. Then an entire summer.

Finally, Sid said to Claire, "Why don't we just have her live with us full-time? She could go to school up here. She's already got a bunch of friends." He smiled at his wife and gave her a hug. "She could be the daughter you never had."

Claire laughed and kissed him on the cheek. "She already is."

Sid grinned. "My point."

At first reluctant, Brittany finally relented. "Go ahead," she finally said after relentless pressuring by Claire. It was the summer Lindsay was just starting fourth grade. "It's for the best."

Years later, Claire would always remember how happy both sisters seemed. For entirely different reasons. Brittany wasn't cut out to be a mother. Claire was. And she loved her niece. Even to the point of indulging her desire to become a boxer.

13

"I just don't get it," Claire told her when she'd first broached the subject. "Why boxing?"

"Why not?" Lindsey pointed at her uncle who had just come home from work. "Uncle Sid did." Which was true. Sid had boxed right up through high school and into college when he'd hung up the gloves for good, saying to everyone he was sick of getting beaten to a pulp. Plus, he was starting to get headaches and boxing wasn't helping them any. Besides, he'd met Claire.

"I don't mind you boxing," she'd told him. "I just mind seeing you get your ass kicked."

She had a point. Truth be told, Sid had more enthusiasm for the sport than skill. But at least he was smart, smart enough to listen to Claire anyway. He quit soon after.

But he still liked the idea of fighting, especially the one-on-one aspect of it. He watched fights on YouTube and when Lindsey joined him in watching he didn't think anything of it. Claire didn't mind. Too, much. Except for occasionally shaking her head and muttering, "I don't see the point."

But there was something in Lindsey that attracted her to the idea of proving herself in the ring. She watched a lot of women boxers and had Uncle Sid teach her the rudiments. So, when her high school announced over the summer that it was going to field a boxing team, Lindsey begged and pleaded to be allowed to join. Uncle Sid was overjoyed, Claire less so. But she reluctantly went along saying, "As long as she doesn't get hurt." She poked a finger in Sid's chest. "Train her well." To Lindsey, she said, "I only want you to have fun. When it's not fun anymore, tell me, and that'll be that."

"Okay, Aunt Claire," Lindsey had said. She was thrilled.

Over summer she'd trained with Sid and by the time fall came around, it was apparent she was a natural. She was fast on her feet and skillful with her punches. She caught the eye of her coach, Soren Blackstone, a history teacher and former boxer himself. He took her aside that first month and said, "There's a tournament in Minneapolis in November. Talk to your folks. I think you should be in it."

She'd talked to Sid and Claire and they'd agreed to let her box. She was ecstatic.

And she'd won her first round.

The second round was against a kid named Bucky. He was tall and thin like she was. He was also as skillful as Lindsey and hit her hard four times to every one of hers. Fortunately for Lindsey, one of her punches bloodied Bucky's nose and the fight was stopped. They bumped gloves when it was over. "Sorry about that," Lindsey said, pointing to the towel Bucky was holding up to his nose. It was turning red.

Despite the blood, Bucky grinned. "That's okay. It was fun."

Lindsey went back to her corner and drank from her water bottle thinking that Bucky seemed like a good guy.

Sid gave her a high five. "Way to go Tiger. You're in the finals."

The next day, Lindsey found Alex Young. He was a short, muscular kid who hit Lindsey without mercy. She took every hit and gave him more back, punching with four or five left and right jabs to every full-blown swing. She also kept moving. In fact, she wore him out. By the end of the third and final round, after boxing for nearly six minutes, Alex was exhausted. Lindsey could see it in his eyes. He even had trouble holding his arms up. Finally, the moment she'd been waiting for happened. He dropped his guard. Lindsey hit him with a hard one-two punch to the head that sent him stumbling backward. He fell into the ropes and pitched forward, falling to the mat, too tired to get to his feet. She'd won.

Lindsey was awarded a gold medal and a blue ribbon for first place.

That night at home she sat down with Sid and Claire. They were celebrating with pizza and ice cream. When she was finished, she said, "You guys, I've been thinking."

"About what?" Claire asked.

"About the next tournament?" Sid asked grinning. "You're quite the fighter, you know."

Lindsey smiled. "I know. I love boxing."

Claire could tell something was up. She reached over and rubbed her niece's shoulder. "What's up, honey?"

"Well, I have to say that I like boxing. I just don't like hurting those guys."

"It's part of the sport, though," Sid said.

"I know. It just doesn't seem right."

Claire looked at Sid. "We promised to let her decide."

"I know." Sid looked at Lindsey and smiled. "Do whatever you want, sweetheart. Your aunt and I will support you."

Lindsey smiled, relieved. "Good." She told them and when she was done, her aunt and uncle couldn't have been happier.

Lindsey continued to box. She also became an assistant coach and helped Soren Blackburn train hundreds of boxers. She went to college and got a degree in physical education and teaches at Orchard Lake High School.

And she has a gold medal she keeps hanging on the wall in her bedroom to remind her of that one tournament. The tournament which she not only won, but also where she met her future boyfriend and then husband and father to her two girls, both pretty good boxers themselves.

Originally published in *Periodic Stories* Volume IV

Flapjack Johnny and Sourdough Slim

The biggest Lutheran Church in Minneapolis was packed for the funeral. Men were dressed in their nicest suits and women were decked out in their finest dresses and jewelry, everyone looking rich and well off, everyone coming together to show respect for the likable man who was my Uncle Don. He'd been a successful grain futures salesman for Cargill. He was also a people person. Maybe that's why he was so good at his job. He seemed to have hundreds of friends, all of them now pouring into the church. At least that's what it seemed like to me, a kid of twelve who idolized the man who'd died unexpectedly from a rare blood disease.

It was the last week in July 1959, and the church was stifling hot and muggy. I was trying to talk to a friend of my mom's with little success. "You must miss him so much, honey," Mrs. Dayton was saying, her perfume wafting over me like a pungent tidal wave, causing my eyes to water. No, it wasn't tears. Well, maybe just a little. I was raised to be polite and was racking my brain for a suitable response when a flurry of activity caught my attention. I turned and saw that Flapjack Johnny and Sourdough Slim had just entered the back of the sanctuary. Nobody had made a move to greet them although many were certainly giving the two out-of-place men a stern eyeball. They were standing up against a wall, feeling, I was sure, more than a little uncomfortable. Me? My mood brightened considerably now that Uncle Don's two best friends had arrived.

"Excuse me, Mrs. Dayton," I said, moving toward them, "I've got to say Hi to some friends of mine."

I made my way through the crowd. My heart went out to the two north woodsmen because I knew what it had taken for them to get to the funeral. They'd have to have gotten up before dawn to make the six-hour drive from Finland, a small town in the forests of northeastern Minnesota, to get to the church in time.

I hurried up to them. "Hi guys," I said, tears welling up in my eyes for real now, "I'm so glad to see you."

Flapjack enveloped me in a big bear hug. He was a huge man, standing six and a half feet tall and weighing at least three hundred pounds. He was dressed in what looked to be brand new OshKosh B'gosh bib overalls, relatively clean work boots, and carried his ever-present green John Deer cap awkwardly in one hand. His kind face, walnut tanned from being in the sun, was lined and he was cleanly shaven for the occasion.

"Stevie, my boy," he said, "how are you holding up?"

I tried unsuccessfully to hold back my tears. "Okay," I said, my voice cracking. Then I broke down in a flood of emotion.

Sourdough moved closer and started rubbing my shoulder affectionately. "We'll all miss him, son." Coming from him was a lot, he being a person prone to, and comfortable with, long periods of silence. He was the opposite of his friend, a short, wiry man, dressed in clean blue jeans and a black shirt with white snap buttons. He held his straw cowboy hat in his left hand. Like Flapjack he'd done his best to spruce himself up for the occasion. His white, full beard was clean, and I could tell he'd trimmed it. His blue eyes were sad, though, like Sourdough's. Uncle Don's death was as hard on the two of them as it was on me. Maybe harder, because, besides being extraordinarily close, my uncle had once saved their lives.

In addition to being a successful salesman, Don was a member of the Minneapolis Jaycees and a deacon in the church. He was also the older brother to my mom, a single mother ever since my father left home when I was only five years old. Uncle Don deeply loved me and my two younger brothers, and after Dad left he filled the void by saying, "Don't worry, Cathy, I'll do right by those boys of yours."

And he did, too. His true love was being outdoors, and he took it upon himself to teach us how to hunt and fish. I showed more of an interest than my brothers and he picked up on that. Over the years he taught me the ways of the woods: how to track an animal, how to build a lean-to, and where to find edible plants saying, "If you know what to look for, you'll never starve." He taught me how to tie ten different kinds of knots and how to identify a bird by its call. He easily could have lived in the eighteen-fifties with Jim Bridger and other mountain man, or so I thought all the time I was growing up.

Uncle Don met Flapjack Johnny and Sourdough Slim long before I was born. He'd been working at Cargill for a few years when his boss told him to take some time off. So, he did. He packed his fishing pole and drove north with no particular place in mind. "I was just following my instincts," he told me whenever he was in a story telling mood, which was often, especially if he'd been sipping his favorite drink, Jack Daniels, neat. He found a tiny resort, "Bob's by the Bay", and rented a small one-room cabin on the shore of Lake Superior for a week.

Bob also rented him a sixteen-foot aluminum fishing boat with a twenty-five-horse Evenrude motor on it.

"What about bait?" my uncle asked.

"For that, I'd suggested the two Finnish boys," he pointed arbitrarily further north, and smiled, "Onni and Veeti, but everyone calls them Flapjack Johnny and Sourdough Slim."

"Why's that?" my uncle asked.

Bob grinned wryly. "Why don't you head on up there? You'll see for yourself."

Onni and Veeti ran a bait shop north of the Temperance

River. It didn't have a name, everyone just called it "The Finnish Boys Place". In addition to fishing supplies, the two of them also enjoyed cooking and they sold the best pasties on the entire north shore. People would drive for hours to purchase them. Uncle Don found their shop, bought a bunch of flathead minnows and, on a whim, decided to try one of their meat and potato and vegetable-filled delights. He didn't eat it until he was trolling along the shore of Agate Bay. He didn't catch any fish that day, but he did catch something better: a love of pasties, a food traditional to the Cornwall Coast of England and nurtured by those with a love of simple, yet filling fare, like Flapjack and Sourdough's Finnish ancestors. And with that, a friendship was born.

My uncle hit it off immediately with Onni and Veeti and continued to visit the north shore every year, sometimes staying a week, sometimes longer. Once, when I was around six or seven, I asked Mom why Uncle Don wasn't married. She'd been doing the laundry and I was helping her fold a sheet. She said, "Well, your uncle just never found the right person to be with, you know, someone that he liked a lot." I was about to let it go at that when I had a thought. "What about Onni and Veeti? Doesn't he like them a lot?"

Mom squatted down, looked me in the eye, and said, seriously, "Your uncle has a special kind of relationship with Onni and Veeti, one that not many people are ever fortunate to find. We should be happy for him. In fact, he's never happier than when he's up north with his two friends."

That seemed fine with me. I had friends, too, and I was glad that Uncle Don was as happy with his as I was with mine. I let it go at that.

The story of my uncle saving Onni and Veeti's lives came out a few years before he died, the first time he took me fishing with him on Lake Superior. I was nine. It was also the first time I met Flapjack and Sourdough formally even though my uncle had told me about them for years. We drove up in early spring and dropped off our gear at Bob's. By now my uncle's friends had decided to formalize their store with a name, and we made our way to it: "Onni and Veeti's Bait Shop and Pasty Palace".

We drove up and parked in the gravel parking lot. It was packed with customers. As my uncle put his arm around my shoulder and ushered me inside, I felt like I was entering another world. The place was filled with wall-to-wall displays of every kind of fishing paraphernalia you could imagine: poles and reels, colorful lures, tackle, nets, clothing and foul weather gear, and even a few outboard motors. It smelled of fish from the live bait kept in tanks along one side of the store. It also smelled of the fresh pasties that were cooked in a kitchen in the back. (Something they never would have gotten away with these days.) I was awestruck. I also loved everything about the old place.

"Hey there, boys," Uncle Don called out to his friends, "I'd like you to meet my nephew."

They welcomed me with open arms, huge Flapjack and skinny Sourdough, but they were busy in the store and couldn't join us that day for fishing. Uncle Don took me out alone, and it was then he told me the story of how he had rescued his two friends.

"We had planned to make a day of it," he began, both of us casting our lines out into the deep, gunmetal-blue water. "It was a few years before you were even born. I used to come up here once a year after that first time. Usually, I stayed for a couple of weeks, fishing the whole time. Flapjack and Sourdough came out on the water with me as often as they could."

He set the motor to the lowest trolling speed possible and we slowly made our way along the rugged, pine tree studded granite coastline just north of Gooseberry Falls. He told me that the three of them were fishing for lake trout. It was late April, and the ice had just cleared from the lake. They were about five miles from shore when a sudden storm came up out of the northeast, pounding them with near-gale force winds and swirling, blinding sleet and snow. They were completely caught off guard. My uncle gunned the motor and raced for the nearest land, a rocky outcropping called Seagull Island a half mile away. They didn't make it. The boat capsized and for the next eight hours, Uncle Don kept ahold of both men (who couldn't swim), fighting the waves and the freezing conditions, making sure they didn't slip off the overturned boat and drown in the icy water. It wasn't until just before sunset that they were rescued by the Coast Guard.

Onni and Veeti were forever in my uncle's debt, which he always brushed off saying, "Anyone would have done the same thing."

To which Flapjack always replied, "Maybe, but it was you who did it."

Which was true.

To me, the interesting thing about the whole rescue was how my uncle downplayed it all. Nowadays, people are given an award, it seems, for just showing up.

Uncle Don saved the lives of two men from the icy waters of Lake Superior and none of his friends or business associates ever knew one thing about it. My uncle must have had his reasons, but he never told anyone. It was his secret along with a small group of people who lived on the north shore. (And my mom and me, of course.) I wondered if today, at his funeral, it would be a good time for me to tell the story of his heroic rescue. For some reason, I felt everyone should know about it.

As if reading my mind, Flapjack took me aside and said, "I know what you're thinking, Stevie. I know you want to tell all these good people gathered here about what your uncle did. You're proud of the man, and want others to be, too. I get that, and I respect you for wanting to do it, just like I've always respected Don's wish for not wanting to make a big deal out of it."

I stood near these two men who not only were my uncle's best friends but who were also so much different from everyone else at the funeral. They were the salt of the earth, hard-working and honest. They cared about my uncle and they cared about me. "What do you think I should do?"

Sourdough stepped close and softly spoke, "Do what your uncle would have done."

That's all he said, and that was all he needed to say. It sealed the deal. If my uncle hadn't wanted to make a big thing out of his rescue, who was I to disrespect his wishes? I kept my mouth shut.

When the service was over, I was having a hard time saying my goodbyes to my two friends. Mom had let me sit with Flapjack and Sourdough, which I appreciated, but I had to get back to her and my two younger brothers and get ready for the drive home, twenty miles to the west. Flapjack gave me a big hug and so did Sourdough.

"You take good care of your mom and brothers," Sourdough said, wiping a tear from his eye.

"I will," I managed to say, my tears welling up.

Flapjack added, "Before you go home, I want to tell you something. Something I think will serve you well as you get older."

"What's that?" I asked, wiping my eyes, not wanting to leave the company of these two good men just yet.

"Whenever you're faced with a tough decision in your life, do me a favor. Always think about what your uncle would do. He was the best person Veeti or I ever knew. You live that way, you'll be doing the man proud."

Mom came up just then and I made the introductions. We all tried valiantly to make conversation, but it was hard because everyone was so sad. Finally, Mom said that it was time we left. She graciously thanked Flapjack and Sourdough for attending the service, and I hugged them each one more time. Then we left and I began the long journey, not just home, but of learning how to make my way through the world without my uncle in it.

After all these years, I will say this, when my uncle died in 1959, no one talked about him being gay or what kind of relationship he had with Onni and Veeti. But I'm glad I respected his wishes and didn't bring up the rescue at the funeral, even though it's too bad he had to keep not only the rescue but the depth of his friendship with Flapjack and Sourdough under wraps. It must have been hard, but times were different back then; close, loving, relationships between men were made more complicated by society's stigmas. It wasn't right, but that's just the way it was.

For me, after all these years, having my uncle gone from my life has been hard, especially in the beginning. But it was made easier by remembering what Flapjack had said about always keeping what Uncle Don would do in any given situation in my mind. I haven't always been successful, but I've always tried. I think my uncle would have been happy about that.

One other thing. Flapjack Johnny and Sourdough Slim sort of became surrogate uncles to me, taking over Uncle Don's role. They took me fishing every summer and even had me stay with them at their store from time to time. They told me it was something Don would have wanted them to do. They even laughed and said, "We don't mind having you around bugging us in the least," making a joke of it.

They died within a year of each other in the middle '80s from complications due to HIV.

I appreciated them so much. They taught me that even if you lose a loved one, you can gain something in return: you can grow up a little and you can learn that life goes on. I might have learned that lesson eventually on my own, but my friendship with Flapjack and Sourdough just made it a little easier. They were wonderful human beings, among the best men I've ever known. Just like my Uncle Don was.

Hitchhiking to California

It was a frigid five degrees and ice crystals were drifting past the street lights early that morning when we left our south Minneapolis duplex. It might have been pretty if it hadn't been so bone-chillingly cold.

The night before my friend Kyle had said to me, "Screw it. I'm sick of this winter. Let's get out of here." He'd been shuffling through our records looking for the new Creedence Clearwater album. We were twenty years old. It was January of 1970 and one of the coldest winters we could remember.

I was curled up on the couch wrapped in a blanket. Our duplex never seemed to have any heat. "I'm with you," I said, taking a sip of tepid hot chocolate. Nothing stayed warm for long in that place.

Kyle turned to me and grinned for the first time in days. "Really? Far out, man." He walked across the threadbare carpeting and sat next to me, blowing on his hands to try and breathe some feeling back into them. "Where should we go?"

I didn't have to think twice. "San Francisco," I said. "We can wear some flowers in our hair."

Kyle laughed. "I dig it. You bring your wooden flute and I'll bring my spoons."

"We'll be street musicians," I said, finishing his thought.

"Right on."

So, at 5:00 a.m. the next morning we shouldered our backpacks, stepped outside into the winter darkness, and started for the interstate. Our breath curled from our lips as we tried to keep from slipping on the icy sidewalks. By the time we got to Interstate 35W, we were so cold we could barely feel our fingers. Our toes were like blocks of ice inside our boots. But if you thought we might have been discouraged, you'd have been wrong.

"Let's get this show on the road," Kyle said, almost scampering down the entrance ramp to the interstate. He wore a red knit stocking cap and had a dark blue scarf wrapped around his face.

"Let the good times roll," I added, following close behind. I was wearing a black watch cap and a dark green scarf my mom had knitted. Plus, of course, a heavy winter coat and boots with wool socks. Just like Kyle.

I joined my friend and we put out our thumbs. Kyle looked and me and smiled a frozen smile and said, "California, here we come."

I laughed and added, "Let's kiss this cold goodbye."

Despite the frigid conditions, we were having fun. Kyle and I had been best friends since grade school. We did everything together, even working at the same restaurant in Minneapolis as dishwashers. We'd lived on the bottom floor of our duplex for nearly a year with two other guys and life was pretty good. Now if we could just get out of town.

The sun had been up for about an hour when we got what we called "a good ride". It was a young guy about our age who looked the worse for wear. "I can take you a little way," he told us, rolling down his window and letting out a cloud of pot smoke. "Out of town, anyway."

Sounded good to us. We got in and he drove us about twenty-five miles south, down to Faribault.

Well, outside of Faribault would be more accurate. The interstate bypassed it by a mile, so we were let off where the ramps leading into and out of town were located. We waved goodbye to the pot smoker and assessed our situation. Technically, it was against the law to hitchhike on an interstate in Minnesota. Standing on the entrance ramp was usually okay. We had hitchhiked lots during the past year and never had any trouble.

I turned to Kyle. "What do think?"

"I think I'm freezing," he said, stomping his boots to warm up.

I pointed up the entrance ramp to the interstate. "Should we chance it?"

He started walking. "You bet."

So, we walked up to I-35W and put out our thumbs.

The first hour wasn't so bad. Our spirits were high. "Next car will be the one," Kyle said, every so often. "I can just feel it."

"It won't be long now," I'd add, jumping up and down to stay warm.

After a while, I didn't say it so much.

Don't get me wrong, there was lots of traffic. Semi-trucks and cars were driving by almost non-stop. Some would slow down and look at us, but then speed off. I guess picking up two long-haired guys with backpacks didn't seem like a good idea to them.

Toward late afternoon, our enthusiasm, once so high, had faded to just about zero, and the reality of our situation had started to creep in.

I looked at Kyle. "I don't get it," I said, turning my back to the north wind which had picked up, probably bringing colder weather. "We should easily get a ride."

"What's wrong with these people? They should take pity on us," Kyle said, pointing to the traffic speeding by, trying to make a joke. He looked at me, his eyes were watering in the wind, tears streaming down his face. Finally, he admitted, "Man, I'm freezing out here."

He looked cold, like a human icicle. There was a real possibility we'd be stuck here overnight. Not a pleasant thought.

"You know what?" I said.

He turned stiffly toward me. "What?"

28

"Let's go home."

"Really?"

"Yeah."

He smiled through frozen lips. "Excellent idea."

We walked across to the other side of the interstate and got picked up right away. It was a guy and his young family. He and his wife took pity on us and brought us right to our duplex.

We thanked them and went inside, happy to be home. And you know what? It was good to be there. It even felt warm. That night we made a vow never to hitchhike again. And we never did.

———————

Originally published in *Pure Slush 25 Mile Anthology*

Drowning

"You kids be careful," my aunt called to us as we raced out the door. "I'll be down in a minute after I finish…"

My guess was that she was going to say, "After I finish taking the last tray of cookies out of the oven." But me and my brother were too excited to go swimming to find out. Too fired up, even, to wait for a warm, melty, chocolate chip cookie to sink our teeth into. Nope. The lake awaited.

"Race ya!" Eric called.

He was already three strides ahead of me, plus three years older. Still, I wasn't going to give up that easily.

"I'm right behind ya!" I called.

He glanced over his shoulder and taunted. "You'll never catch me."

The race was on.

I have to admit I stayed close as we ran down the path and onto the dock. Our bare feet pounded across the wooden boards, thump, thump, thump. At the end, Eric stopped. "Beat ya!"

"Not by much!" I panted, coming up behind him. Although he did. By a good ten feet or so. I punched him in the arm. Kind of good-naturedly, kind of not.

"Ow," he said, grinning, and rubbing his muscle pretending like it hurt. He grabbed me around the neck and held me tight while mussing up my buzz cut. "Don't ever let anyone tell you you're a wimp, ya' wimp."

"Let go!" I yelled.

He did and we stood and looked at each other. Do we fight or not? It could go either way, but just then a motorboat sped by not a hundred feet from the dock distracting us. Believe me, our attention span was like that of a gnat. On a good day. Forgetting our standoff, we watched the boat. It had two men in it with fishing poles poking out over the side.

Eric pointed. "Going fishing, ya' think?"

"Duh," I said. "See the poles?" I pointed. "Doesn't take a genius."

Eric laughed. "Surprised you figured it out."

My brother and I had a relationship, I suppose, like most brothers. Sometimes I liked him; sometimes I hated him. Like the time five years ago when he'd been bugging me so much, I'd thrown a glass of orange juice at him. He'd ducked and the glass had slammed into the wall shattering into a million pieces. He ran out the door to escape the wrath of our father. Me? I was a wimpy five-year-old. I sat unable to move from my chair, frozen in place by the incredible insanity of what I had done. Dad ran in, took one look at the glass on the floor and juice running down the wall, and marched me downstairs to the basement. I got ten lashes from his belt for my punishment and couldn't sit down the rest of the day.

But generally, we got along well, and today we were pretty excited. Normally, growing up, we celebrated the Fourth of July by going to a firework show down along the Minnesota River at the Hidden Valley Golf Course, twenty-five miles southwest of where we lived in Minneapolis. I guess Mom and Dad had friends who were members there. Anyway, it was a huge display culminating with thundering rocket explosions and showers of brilliant red and green and golden cascades of falling sparks. From the point of view of me and Eric, it was not only exciting but defined the holiday, if not our entire summer.

However, this summer in 1958 when I was ten and Eric was thirteen, we didn't go to that huge display. My aunt had invited us up to spend a month at her home on a lake in northern Minnesota. I think Mom thought it'd be a good idea to get away, so we did. Dad had started working extra hours and was gone a lot, but when he was home the two of them weren't always getting along that well.

Frankly, I was looking forward to taking a break from all the bickering and fighting even though I was going to miss my best friend, Randy. We'd built a tree house in an old oak tree in his parent's backyard and it had become sort of a clubhouse for us and our other friends, Al and Jason. We'd nailed boards to the truck to use to climb and we'd go up there and read comic books, eat candy, play cards and generally stay away from adults. It was very cool.

Randy and I would never say things like, "I'll miss you," or mushy stuff like, "You're my best buddy in the whole wide world." But we did seal our friendship before I left by using our pocketknives to slice our thumbs and press them together becoming blood brothers. So that was something.

"See you in a month, four eyes," I told him the last day we were together. He wore glasses.

"Later alligator," he responded. Then he gave me a stick of juicy fruit gum which I broke in half and shared with him. He was a pretty good guy.

The next day we left. Mom drove the Oldsmobile and we talked her into having the top down all the way to the lake. It was fun! She even stopped at a drive-in along the way for burgers and malts which I swear to you was the best food I'd ever tasted.

As Mom drove, she had the radio on and we sang along to songs by Buddy Holly and Jerry Lee Lewis, and I have to say, by the time we got to Aunt Ellen's house, all thoughts of missing my friend Randy were gone. Not to mention my dad. We piled out of the car, carried our suitcases inside, put them in the spare bedroom like my aunt directed us to do, and ran down to the dock. Already, I felt like this was going to be a great adventure.

Aunt Ellen was my mom's sister. She was in her late fifties and a secretary for an insurance agent in town. She was taking time off to be with us. As she put it to my mom, "My boss owes me. I hardly ever take vacation time."

So that was good because I really liked Aunt Ellen. She was a sturdily build woman about as tall as Eric. She had long brown hair she kept rolled up in a bun and pined to her head. I honestly don't recall ever seeing her wear it down. Anyway, she was what mom called "no-nonsense" which meant we had to mind our manners and watch what we said or did around her. We couldn't slam the screen door. We had to take our shoes off before going inside. When we were inside, we had to keep our voices down. We couldn't argue and fight. Stuff like that. "Rules of the house" is what she called them. We liked that we knew exactly what we could and couldn't do.

One thing we couldn't do was go swimming without supervision. So why we decided that day to swim from our dock to the next dock over, about one-hundred yards away, is still beyond me.

But we did.

After the fishing boat went by, we watched as it motored out into the big part of the lake. I glanced down the shore at the house next to Auntie's. They were the Jorgenson's, a retired couple who were off visiting their son in Seattle for the Fourth of July holiday weekend. I was a little pissed I'd lost the footrace with Eric and was wondering how I could get back at him. Without thinking the entire idea out too clearly, I pointed to their dock and said, "Okay, big shot. How about this? How about we race to Jorgenson's." I was a pretty good swimmer. "I'll clean your clock."

Only one problem. Mom had driven into town for some last-minute groceries, so it was just Aunt Ellen and her rule: No swimming without supervision.

Eric glanced back at the house. It was about one hundred feet from the shore, maybe a hundred and fifty feet away all total from where we were standing. I knew what he was thinking. *Should we wait for Aunt Ellen or not?*

I jabbed him in the arm. "Come on," I said. "Ya chicken?"

Now of the two of us, I a.m. by far and away the most cautious. Here's the way I'll compare us: Eric is kind of a jock and likes sports and thinks nothing of jumping off the roof of our house in the winter into a snowbank after a snowfall. Me? I'm into music and like to read. No jumping off anything. Anytime. Get the picture?

So, I'm sure that me bringing up a swimming race was shocking to my older brother. For a moment, maybe. He might even have thought to himself, *you know, we really should wait until Aunt Ellen comes down like she wants us to do.* I never asked because the question got lost in what happened next.

"No, I'm not chicken!" he said, pushing me aside and diving in. "You're on!"

Damn! "No fair!" I yelled, diving in after him. "You cheated."

Up ahead of me, he laughed. "Tough!" Then turned toward the Jorgenson's dock and began doing the crawl, swimming for all he was worth.

God, sometimes he made me so mad!

"I'm coming for ya!" I yelled and started swimming after him. I soon found my rhythm and evened out my strokes and my kicking. As I said, I was a pretty good swimmer. I liked being in the water. My brother and I rode our bikes down to Lake Harriet in the city about a mile from our house and swam there as much as we could.

But Eric was bigger, taller, stronger than me, and as good a swimmer as I was. Still, I was pissed and full of adrenaline. After cutting through the water for a minute, I realized that I was gaining on him. Yea!! Maybe I could catch him. I focused on the task at hand and settled in to chase him down. I was doing the crawl, my best stroke. Head in the water. Stroke, stoke, stroke. Head out of the water. Take a breath. Head in the water. Stroke, stroke, stroke. Head out of the water. Take a breath. Head in the water. Stroke, stroke, stroke... As I swam furiously, I kept an eye on Eric. I was gaining! Head in the water. Stroke, stroke, stroke. Head out of the water. Take a breath. Head in the water. Stroke, stroke, stroke.

A minute later, I was close behind him; close enough to catch. I dug in and swam with my last ounce of strength. Stroke, stroke, stroke. But I must have gotten too close. Eric's kicking and splashing was causing massive turbulence, and as I turned my head to breathe, I took in a big mouthful of water instead of air. *No problem*, I thought to myself. I'd swallowed more than my fair share of lake water in my time and felt I had the situation under control.

Wrong! I had taken in more water than I thought. I tried to swallow but couldn't get it down. I choked and started coughing. Then I tried to breathe but couldn't. I choked again and started coughing some more. And with each cough, I sucked in more water while Eric kept swimming, getting further and further away from me, oblivious to what was happening behind him.

Panicking, I stopped swimming and started treading water, coughing, and trying to clear my throat. It was then that things got really bad. I had stopped over a submerged weed bed and they started entwining themselves around my legs. I swear those weeds must have had a mind of their own because they started pulling me down. I went below the surface to try and pull them off but there were too many of them. When I tried to swim to the top I couldn't. The weeds held me tight. I was trapped underwater and in my panicky state of mind, I coughed again and sucked in a ton of water. I was drowning!

Do you know how they say your whole life passes

before your eyes when you are dying? Well, I'm not sure about that. Maybe I hadn't lived long enough for anything important to have happened. All I remember was struggling, fighting the weeds and the water, and choking to death. A massive amount of bubbles escaped from my lungs. I began to pass out as everything went black. My final thought was this: I'm too young to die!

But I didn't. Thank God for Eric.

I was losing consciousness when, like in a dream, I felt his strong hands grab me tightly under my arms. Before I knew what was happening, he yanked hard and in one strong motion pulled me free of the weeds. A moment later my head broke above the surface and I gasped for air. I coughed and gagged and coughed some more. And, in my terror, I struggled with Eric, too, not understanding what was happening. But his strong arms held me, keeping my head above the water, and all I remember was his calm voice saying, "It's okay, Ben. I've got you. It's okay."

While holding me close to his chest, he kicked with his legs and got me near enough to shore that he could stand. He got me on my feet and kept me stabilized and let me catch my breath. By then Aunt Ellen had heard my screams and run down into the water where she waded in and helped Eric walk me the rest of the way to shore. All three of us collapsed next to the lake, me thankful I was alive and Eric and Aunt Ellen panting with the exertion of saving me.

When she caught her breath, Aunt Ellen got to her feet and tore into us like a drill sergeant at a marine boot camp, berating me and Eric for at least five minutes. "What'd I tell you boys about swimming unsupervised? There're weeds out there! A boat overturned last week and two people drowned!" And on and on. I have to say, we deserved it. When she was done, she gave us a steely eye. I thought for sure she was going to lite into us again, but she didn't. In fact, she surprised both of us when she said, "Well, anyway, I'm just glad you're both safe."

What a nice thing to say. It didn't escape me that despite breaking one or her cardinal rules, she honestly did care about both of us.

Then she hugged me and Eric together, and I have to say that it felt pretty nice.

"I'm sorry, Auntie," I told her.

"Me, too," Eric was quick to add.

And we were. Now that I realized I was going to live to see another day, I not only was happy to be alive but feeling bad about causing Aunt Ellen to worry so much.

She hugged us again and said, "You boys come up to the house and change before your mother comes home." Uh-oh Mom. For a moment I'd forgotten about her. Aunt Ellen saw the worried look in our eyes and said, "You boys have a decision to make. I'm not going to tell her about what you did. I'll leave that up to you. I'll abide with whatever you decide to do." She looked at us. "Think about it." Then she headed up to the house. When she was halfway there, she turned and said, "Don't stay down here too long. I've got a plate full of cookies and some Kool-Aid for you." Then she left us to our decision.

To make a long story short, we told mom. We really didn't have any choice. Aunt Ellen would always know what we'd done and that was bad enough. Lying to Mom and not telling her? That would make it even worse. So, we told her. She grounded us from swimming for a few days.

Her exact words were, "I appreciate you boys telling me what happened. But you still broke Aunt Ellen's rule. Today's the Fourth of July. I'm going to ground you from swimming for two days. Tomorrow's the fifth and then there's the sixth. You can go swimming on the seventh."

"Aw, Mom!" I said, for some reason thinking I could

argue with her. She gave me even a steelier look than Aunt Ellen had given us and that's all it took. "Okay, Mom. Two days. That's fair," I was quick to say. Plus, it suddenly dawned on me that it was way better than if my dad was there. I could envision him drawing his belt slowly through the loops of his trousers in preparation for administering his preferred form of punishment. Especially for me. The thought wasn't a pretty one.

Later that day, Eric and I were sitting on the dock, our feet dangling in the water, watching sunfish nibble our toes. They tickled. After a minute I looked at Eric and said, "You know, you saved my life. I guess I should thank you."

He grinned. "Yeah, I did. And you are welcome. You owe me, buddy. Big time." Then he looked at me. He was wearing one of my uncle's old fishing hats to keep the sun off his face. "How are you feeling?"

I have to say, after nearly drowning a few hours earlier, I wasn't feeling too bad. "I'm okay." I had a baseball cap on for the Milwaukee Braves, my favorite baseball team. I pushed the brim up. "Sorry that we can't go swimming for a few days."

He nodded but didn't appear very upset. "That's okay. Maybe we can build a fort out back in the woods."

I smiled. "Fun! That sounds good to me."

We looked out over the lake. Fourth of July activity was starting to pick up. Firecrackers were going off and there were a lot of boats out pulling water skiers. People were starting to get into the celebrating mood.

I watched a boat speed by and suddenly thought about my friend Randy. I wondered what he was doing. Then I got what I considered a great idea. Maybe Eric and I could become blood brothers like me and Randy. But when I asked Eric about it, he just laughed. "No way, José. No way in hell. It's bad enough just being brothers, let alone sealing it with blood."

When he put it that way, he kind of had a point.

Later that night we all sat on the front lawn looking out across the lake. My Uncle Al had grilled hamburgers and we had corn on the cob with them and it all tasted great. He'd also bought some sparklers and bottle rockets which we shot off over the water. It wasn't like the fancy fireworks at the golf club but that was okay. It was me and Mom and Eric and Aunt Ellen and Uncle Al and, I have to say, it was pretty memorable. Maybe nearly drowning and surviving had something to do with it.

Later that summer when I got home and told Randy about almost dying, he didn't believe me. "Almost drowned? You? No, way!"

"Cross my heart," I told him. "Promise."

He didn't believe me until Eric told him. "Yeah, your friend here was going down for the count," Eric said pointing at me. "Thank goodness his big brother was there to rescue him."

I knew that he was right, but I wasn't going to let him get away with it. I made a move to slug him in the arm and he dodged out of the way. He took off running and I chased him. Both of us laughing like crazy.

_____

Originally published in *Holiday Stories*

39

Winterfest

It was Tuesday morning, January 17, 2023. Clark rolled over and said to Ethan, "Good morning, lover. Happy 25th anniversary."

Ethan smiled and kissed Clark. "Good morning yourself." Then he smiled. "I can't believe it's been this long." He hugged Clark. "You look just as good to me now as you did back then."

Clark smiled at the compliment. Slightly paunchy, thinning hair and liver spots forming on his hands, he appreciated Ethan's ability to look at sand and see a sandcastle.

But a compliment was a compliment. "So do you, lover. So do you."

And Ethan did look good. He was a runner, and though he didn't run races anymore due to bad knees, he still liked to jog and work out in the gym. Clark counted himself lucky that Ethan still cared for him like he did. But he did. This trip to Quansettville was proof of that. It was their first real vacation since Covid. They were staying at the historic Kellogg's Butcher Station Hotel and were in a lovely room on the third floor. Their four-poster bed was soft and comfortable, and the cotton sheets felt wonderful. They slept with the window open, savoring the wintery fresh air while they slept soundly under a thick handmade quilt with a green, white, and mauve wedding ring design. The rest of their room was adorned with antiques and tasteful artwork. There even was a photo of the hotel taken in the early 1900s at its heyday.

The two of them were there for a few days to participate in the week-long Winterfest celebration that had been the weekend before and last through the next Sunday. They'd arrived last Sunday night and would be leaving Wednesday.

It was to be a getaway of pleasant surprises, the first being Monday morning when they turned on the bedside radio. It had been tuned to a local station WVOC 91.3FM. At 7:05 a.m., just after the 7:00 a.m. news, the host, Brendalee Benard, an eighty-five-year-old lady with a love of Maurice Ravel's *Bolero*, played that lovely song, much to the delight of Clark and Ethan.

The two men had been lying in bed talking quietly and planning their day when the song had begun. They'd smiled at each other. *Bolero* was considered "Their Song". Ethan had put it on the CD player the first night they'd spent together twenty-five years earlier and it had had a special place in their hearts ever since. The fact that they'd heard it that first Monday morning promptly at 7:00 a.m. they looked at it as a good omen.

And it had been. They'd spent Monday walking around the town getting to know the place. Clark taught American Literature at nearby Montpelier Junior College and Ethan was a potter who made solidly functional pots and mugs that he sold locally and online. Some of his work was even carried at the local Potty Mouth Studio. They had a good life.

Now it was Tuesday morning. They'd set the alarm so they were awake for today's broadcast. During the 7:00 news, Clark sighed wondering if he should tell Clark his bad news. He'd recently been diagnosed with macular degeneration, a potentially debilitating eye disorder that could result in blindness. He'd scheduled his first treatment to the end of January. It would be a shot administered to his eye. He wasn't looking forward to it at all.

Well, he might as well get it over with.

Ethan was pouring them a cup of steaming caffe latte they'd had sent to the room at 6:45 a.m. He brought it to the bed, handing Clark his cup before climbing in. "Here you go. Fresh coffee for the broadcast."

"Thank you."

Clark took his cup and held it warming his suddenly chilled hands.

Ethan looked at him. "Hey there, guy. What's up?"

Clark looked at the clock. He still had a few minutes. The

news was just starting. He took a sip. "I've got something to tell you."

Concerned, Ethan set his cup down on the night stand. Clark did the same. Ethan took Clark's hand. "What is it, lover? Tell me."

"I will in just a minute. Let's listen to this recording first."

So they did.

Brendalee's Bolero broadcast that day was by recording of Herbert von Karajan conducting the Berliner Philharmoniker, originally released on Deutsche Grammophon in 1966. Clark and Ethan lay in each other's arm listening to every note of the 13 minutes recording. They loved it.

When it was over, Clark told Ethan about his eyes and Ethan didn't hesitate. "Don't worry, guy. I'm with you forever. Never forget that."

Clark sighed in relief. "Thank you so much. And I'm with you forever, too."

It would become their favorite recording of *Bolero* because it would always remind them of that Tuesday on the 17th of January when Clark had told Ethan about his eyes.

Ethan's words of support made all the difference to Clark. He started the shots at the end of the month. By the fall of that year, his macular degeneration was in remission. They were ecstatic. The first thing they did to celebrate was book a room for Winterfest 2024 in Quansettville. Hearing Brandalee and whatever recording of *Bolero* she chose to play again? That'd just be icing on the cake.

———————

Originally published in *Pure Slush Bolero Anthology*

Jenny and the Tracliodytes

Jenny walked into the farmhouse kitchen rubbing sleep from her eyes. Something had prompted her to get up early this morning, but she wasn't sure what. Her mother was at the counter stirring pancake batter in a big mixing bowl.

Elise Blake glanced over her shoulder. "Good morning. Would you be a sweetheart and go check on the dogs? They ran off this morning and I haven't seen them since."

"Aw, Mom. Why?"

Her mother stopped stirring, set the wooden spoon aside, and turned. She had "that look" in her eye; a look Jenny knew only too well. "Because I told you to, that's why." The words were stated quietly but emphatically.

Jenny knew there was no room for discussion. She shrugged to show that it didn't make any difference to her that she was agreeing to what her mother wanted her to do. But it did. In her mind, Jenny was eleven going on eighteen, certainly old enough to think for herself and not get pushed around by her mother. Except maybe now. Pick your battles she'd read somewhere and maybe this was one of those times.

"Can I have breakfast first?"

Her mom smiled, picked up the spoon and dripped some batter onto the hot skillet. "Sure."

The Blake family lived and grew organic soybeans on a farm located on the north side of the Minnesota River in the picturesque rolling hills of Willow County. Jenny was the oldest and today was like every other day that summer; she was up early leaving her two younger brothers and two younger sisters still asleep upstairs in the big two-story farmhouse that had been in Jenny's mother's family for four generations. Elise Blake was a strong-willed but fair woman who had more than risen to the task of caring for

43

Jenny and her brothers and sisters after Roland Blake had been killed in a combine accident just over two years ago.

"We'll get through this if we all pull together," Elise told her children a few days after their father's funeral. "Right now I'm in charge and you'll do as I say."

And they did. Elise divided up the chores and hired Joe Sanderson to help when heavy field work was needed. In the third growing season after Roland's death, all was going well. Except for Jenny. Two years after her father's death she was getting restless. She wondered if maybe there wasn't something more to life than farming and performing the hundreds of little tasks that went along with keeping a self-sufficient farm running. Of course, she didn't tell her mother what she was thinking. No, she kept it to herself and only thought about a different future for herself during long walks in the fields when she could be by herself. Like today. Going to look for the dogs was an activity she was very much looking forward to doing in spite of pretending to her mother that it was a pain in the you-know-what.

With her pancakes finished, Jenny washed her dishes and made ready to leave the kitchen through the back door just as her four siblings stumbled in. Aged ten to four, they were a loud handful and Jenny was happy to make a hasty retreat. It'd be nice to be outdoors looking for the two dogs, Beemer and Billy. Besides, it was summertime, late August, the fields were lush and the air was still cool just after sunrise. It'd get hot later.

"Bye, Mom," she said rushing out the door.

"Don't be gone long. I need you to help with laundry."

Good grief. "Okay, Mom. I'll hurry."

Jenny stepped onto the wide back porch with its sheltered roof and took a moment to breathe deeply. At times like these, she loved living on the farm. The early morning sun just peeking over the windbreak. The air was fragrant with the aroma of rich topsoil mixed with the horse manure they spread on the nearby fields. She stood on the top of the steps and smiled. She had an affinity for nature and all things in the natural world and felt right at home being outside. She especially loved wandering through the nearby fields listening to birds, watching out for interesting animals and identifying wildflowers. If people thought she was a bit odd because she wasn't up on the latest video game or pop song, that was fine with her. She loved books and reading. She defied the expectations of kids her age by telling them that she even enjoyed going to school and learning.

Like last year when her science teacher Mr. Benton had told the class about a species of insects that were thought to exist in the upper reaches of the earth's atmosphere, the exosphere, located over a thousand miles above the surface of the earth. Jenny was fascinated by the possibility of new life up there and began a study all on her own. There wasn't much information, but she was able to use the internet to find out the name given to the speculative insects was Tracliodytes, meaning big, hard, shell. They were like nothing she'd ever heard of and the more she learned about them the more intrigued she became. They were rumored to look like big cockroaches, they could fly, and were the size of dinner plates. The new species was thought to have formed out of the recombination of the DNA of certain molecules high above the earth. Those molecules combined to form compounds which formed more complex compounds and so on until a new species was formed: the Tracliodytes.

Only a small percentage of scientists believed they existed; they could count Jenny as not only a fan but also as a believer. She and her active imagination did not doubt that whatsoever. As far as she could tell, their existence had to do with pollution and global warming. The thing about air pollution was that no one really understood how those hydrocarbons would react as global warming got worse. Sure, it was bad, everyone said so, especially the scientists, but most everyone figured that eventually a solution would be found. *Well, they thought wrong* was what Jenny believed.

As she stepped off the porch, she caught a movement in the sky and glanced up. Way up high were cloud-like shapes moving across the sun, throwing flickering shadows on the ground. *Hm*, she thought to herself, *it must be going to rain. Oh, well...*

She put it out of her mind and concentrated on finding the two dogs. "Here you go, Beemer. Come on now, Billy," Jenny called as she walked across the backyard past the barn, and toward the edge of the windbreak. She hardly noticed the breeze picking up. Jenny's great-grandfather had planted nearly one hundred evergreen trees around the property when he had first settled the land in the late 1880s. The trees had grown to an immense size, over sixty feet tall, and so thick it was hard to walk through them. In anticipation of just such an occurrence, Oscar Johnson had built a gate for people to pass through, not needing one for the long driveway between the farmhouse and the county road half a mile away.

"Come on, Beemer. Let's go, Billy," Jenny called again as she headed for the backyard gate, but her mind wasn't really on the dogs. She had a feeling that something wasn't right and turned and looked back at the farmhouse. Her mother was standing on the porch shaking out a rug. She looked up when Jenny turned and waved a friendly hand. Jenny waved back, suddenly overcome with a feeling she couldn't quite put her finger on. Something to do with death. What would she ever do if her mom died? The thought was too much to bear.

She watched her mother go inside and said a slight prayer that her mom would live forever, even though she knew that was impossible. It didn't hurt to dream, though. She walked a little further until she got to the gate that would let her through the windbreak. Once more she called for the dogs, "Here you go, Beemer. Come on, Billy." Then she stopped and listened and looked around. Something was going on. Something weird. Normally there were hundreds of birds singing in the evergreen trees, especially in the morning like now, an hour after sunrise. She listened carefully but could hear no bird songs at all, not even a twitter. It was dead silent, eerily quiet. Jenny felt a sudden clutch in her stomach. Her worry meter shot up and she frantically looked around. Where were the dogs? Where were Beemer and Billy? Normally they would have come to her by now.

"Beemer. Billy," she called. Again, no response.

Movement caused her to look up again. The sky was turning brown and it wasn't from storm clouds. Then she heard something. Once her ears adjusted to the silence, she heard a noise. A sound. It sounded like a low-pitched humming, a sound Jenny was unfamiliar with. She listened carefully as the humming changed to buzzing then to a clacking. It was coming from the other side of the evergreens. Curious as to what it was, she went through the gates and inched forward step by step wondering all the while. *What could be making that noise*? It seemed to be coming from the soybeans. The humming, buzzing, and clacking became louder and louder the closer she came to the field. The wind suddenly gusted and blew through the trees, carrying with it a pungent odor like the smell of rotten eggs. Jenny wrinkled her nose. It smelled like something had died. She made herself hurry the last few steps down the path, now worrying more than ever about the dogs. Something was going on and it wasn't right. As she burst through the trees, she got a clear view of the field and the tree line and hills beyond it and she couldn't help herself. She started screaming.

There, covering the ground and flying through the air were winged insects the likes of which she'd never seen. She made herself quit screaming and tried to collect herself. Tried to think. The air stunk with the aroma of something dead. It made her eyes water. She wiped them dry and looked with a mixture of terror and awe. The day was losing light as more and more insects funneled through the air, blocking the sun. *That's what's turning the sky brown*, she thought to herself. *All those bugs.* Speechless she watched the scene before her: millions of huge insects, flying and landing and feeding on whatever food source they could find.

It was like a scene out of a horror movie. The insects were big, the size of dinner plates and she watched, stunned, as they completed consumed the forty acres field of soybeans that Jenny and her mom and siblings had planted that spring. It took less than a minute. As the insects finished eating, they rose in a pulsating mass and flew off presumably in search of more food.

Jenny stood watching protected by the evergreen forest. Or so she thought. As the insects lifted into the air, they seemed to sense she was nearby and started toward her. Jenny's heart leaped into her throat. They were coming after her! As she turned to run her eyes fell upon the skeletons of what she could only guess at as being Beemer and Billy.

My, God, she thought to herself. *They'll eat anything.* She ran along the evergreen path realizing that the insects were not just your ordinary bugs gone crazy. No. They were those Tracliodytes that she'd been researching, and they were coming to get her. They started landing in the evergreen trees and it was only a matter of time before they began attacking her. As she got to the edge of the windbreak, she saw they were landing in the yard, crawling all over every bit of the lawn eating it as well as the vegetable garden. They were even in the crabapple trees. Their family farm was being invaded and the invasion had just begun.

As Jenny stood at the edge of the windbreak, she saw her mother run from the house and onto the porch. She waved her arms and yelled, "Jenny. Jenny. Hurry. Try and get back here."

The Tracliodytes were not only crawling all over the yard, they were flying everywhere. Jenny knew she had little choice. She had to get to the safely of the farmhouse. "I will, Mom," she yelled back. The problem was that it was about a fifty-yard run from the gate to the back porch. She wasn't sure she could make it. She yelled, "I'm going to the barn first."

Her mom yelled back, but the Tracliodytes were making too much noise with their winging beating while they were flying and their horrible jaws clacking and chewing as the ate. Jenny couldn't hear a word she said. No matter. She knew what she had to do.

After watching the devastation taking place for only a moment, Jenny gathered her courage. With the ground covered in Tracliodytes and more falling from the sky every second, she counted, "One, two, three. Go." Then she ran screaming for the barn, the closest shelter. Tracliodytes rained down from the sky and smashed off her back as she bent to escape their blows. She stumbled once, then again, but kept her balance. The wind blew hard and the sky was nearly blackened by the hordes of insects. The air stank unmercifully, but Jenny was resolute, if not urged on by her fear of being eaten alive by the invading Tracliodytes. Her feet crunched over their bodies as she slipped and slid on her way across the yard. On the porch she saw her mother yelling something but couldn't make out her words. The cacophony of Tracliodytes drowned out all sound but their relentless "clacking, clacking, clacking".

Jenny made it to the barn in about ten seconds and took a moment to catch her breath. The Tracliodytes were literally raining down from the sky and she was thankful for the shelter of the barn. It was small and housed Bossy, their milk cow, and Eddie their old plow horse, along with a smattering of chickens. The animals were all safe, but the cow and horse both looked at her wild-eyed from their respective stalls. Jenny went to them, petted each of them, and tried to soothe them saying, "It's okay, guys, just stay calm." If only she believed it herself.

The door to the far side was open and she ran to close it. Some of the huge insects were trying to crawl in and Jenny kicked them back out into the yard and closed the door. They were fierce-looking creatures, like large cockroaches, with claw-shaped appendages and waving, probing antennae. A few grabbed for her bare legs, leaving tracks of blood. Jenny shivered as she rolled the door shut. Then she ran to the other door and looked out.

It was about fifty feet from where she stood to get to the house. Her mother stood on the porch yelling and waving at her to hurry up. She could just make out her words, "It's getting worse. Run for it."

Jenny didn't have to think. She turned and bid a silent farewell to Bossy and Eddie and then pulled the barn door closed before she stepped into the yard, her fear momentarily overcome by anger. She was getting mad that the giant bugs were ruining the farm that her great grandparents had carved out of the woods with their bare hands. In anger, she kicked more of the huge insects out of the way and sustained more cuts on her already bleeding legs for her effort. She didn't care. Just then three Tracliodytes grabbed her legs and started chewing. Her fear returned. She had to make a run for it. Could she make it to the safety of her home? Her mother kept yelling, "Come on. Hurry up."

Jenny kicked the huge bugs out of the way, called up all of her courage, and counted out, "One, two, three. Go!" Then she sprinted across the yard, yelling and screaming at the top of her lungs, crushing dozens of the Tracliodytes as she ran, not to mention ducking out of the way of those raining down on her from the sky. By the time she made it to the safety of the front porch, she was bruised and battered on her back and bleeding from her legs. But she was home. She was safe.

Elise enveloped her brave daughter in her arms and held her tight. "Thank goodness you're safe." Then she broke down in tears as she rocked her daughter back and forth on the porch, for a minute not paying attention to the horror only a few feet from them beyond the safety of the roof's overhang. Jenny couldn't help herself. Her relief at being home was overwhelming. Back out in the yard, she thought she was going to die, but now she was safe. After a moment of lying securely enfolded in her mother's arms, Jenny started crying too.

After a minute Elise released her grip on her daughter and said, "All right, let's get ourselves together." She wiped tears from her eyes as did Jenny. We've got to do something to protect the home."

Jenny looked at her mother. "Mom, I found Beemer and Billy on the edge of the field. The bugs ate them."

"Oh, my god." Elise stood up and looked out from the safety of the porch. The Tracliodytes were raining down in ever-increasing numbers. They were scurrying round the ground feeding on everything in sight. The green grass was gone. The apple trees near the house had disappeared. The vegetable garden was nothing but a seething mass of hungry giant insects. Even the wooden swing set their father had built years ago was gone. The Tracliodytes were eating everything.

Jenny suddenly pointed. "Mom, look!"

Out along the windbreak the Tracliodytes had taken up residence in the huge evergreens and were destroying them. Jenny and her mother watched in horror as in a matter of minutes the majestic trees disappeared right before their eyes, consumed by hungry bugs. Just like that the protection the trees had offered was gone and replaced with a view of the rolling hills along the Minnesota River valley now stretching all the way to the horizon. What mother and daughter saw was devastation unlike anything they'd ever seen, worse than any tornado could ever have done. The formerly lush farm fields were denuded. Not a living thing was left standing. The landscape was lifeless. The wind kicked up dust. There was no green anywhere. And still, the Tracliodytes flew across the sky and scurried along the ground, looking for food to eat. The sun was blocked by the hordes of insects, leaving the day in twilight, giving the impression the world was going to end.

"Mom, what are we going to do?" Jenny asked, trying to be strong and keep the tremor of fear out of her voice. She wasn't sure she was all that successful.

Elise took her phone from her pocket and held up a hand. "Hold on. I'm calling Joe."

"Good." Joe Sanderson, their hired hand, lived in town. "I'll go inside and turn on the news."

Elise gave Jenny the thumbs-up sign and began speaking to Joe. Jenny went into the kitchen and hurried through it into the living room where she turned on the television. Her siblings, who had been hiding in the basement, ran up the stairs and gathered around her. She comforted them while the local announcer spoke solemnly. "It seems a plague of huge insects has descended on our area…" and she went on to tell Jenny what she already knew. *Yeah,* she thought to herself, *no lie. Descending on the area was putting it mildly.*

She turned on a few lights. It was quite dark in the room due to the millions of Tracliodytes outside flying all over the place.

Local wasn't telling what she already didn't know so she switched to national news. The anchor was saying, trying to act calm, but Jenny knew he wasn't, "…and the infestation seems to be worldwide. Measures are being taken at this very moment…"

But he never got any further because the power went out.

Jenny turned to her mom who had just come into the room. She was staring at her phone with a perplexed look. "What?" Jenny asked.

"The phone quit working."

"Must be the power. The television's off, too."

Her mom grimaced, shook her head, and put her phone in her pocket. "Damn."

Which was an amazing comment coming from Jenny's church-going mother. It was the only swear word her mother ever used. *Wow*, thought Jenny, *Mom must really be worried.* "What'd Joe have to say?"

"He can't get out. There are too many bugs." She let the words hang and then continued. "Looks like we're trapped here. What'd the news have to say?"

"Nothing we don't already know. I guess the main thing is they think it's worldwide."

"Good Lord," Elise said and then she was quiet. So was everyone else, each contemplating their seemingly insurmountable predicament. Silence filled the room.

Then the two younger kids, four-year-old Stevie and five-year-old Emma started crying. Elise and Jenny went to comfort them while the two older ones, seven-year-old Ernie and eight-year-old Susie, stood by trying to be brave. Elise and Jenny made eye contact over the whimpering youngest ones. *What are we going to do?* They were both thinking at the same time. There was one other thought they shared and didn't have to say out loud: If they didn't figure something out and fast, they might get overrun by the horde of Tracliodytes and be eaten alive. They might never make it out of this alive.

Their morbid thoughts were interrupted when Ernie pointed out the front window and cried out, "Mom, they're crawling onto the porch."

Jenny ran with her mother to look. "They're all over the place."

Elise took over. "Susie, you and Ernie take your brother and sister upstairs. You'll be safe there. Jenny, come with me."

While her four siblings hurried upstairs, Jenny asked, "What are we going to do?"

Elise was looking out the window. The Tracliodytes were crawling up the wooden stairs and eating the potted flowers she had planted in the spring. "Grab those brooms from the closet. Let's sweep them off. We can't let them get inside."

It took all of Jenny's courage to step out the front door with only a broom, but she did. With her mom at her side, they swept the bugs off the porch and stood guard over the steps to keep them away. It seemed to be working. The huge bugs were hungry but slow, and against all logic the Tracliodytes were no match for Jenny and her mom armed with just a broom.

After keeping them at bay for a few minutes Elise said, "Jenny, you wait for them here. I'll go check the back porch."

Jenny kept watch while her mom hurried through the house to the back. In a few minutes, she returned. "There's fewer of them back there. None on the porch."

For the next hour, they stood guard, Jenny running upstairs every few minutes to check on her brothers and sisters. Although frightened, they were made of strong stock, with generations of hard work bred into them. After a while, all four of the younger kids came downstairs.

"We can help," Susie said. "Yeah," added Ernie, grabbing a baseball bat. "Let me at 'em."

Jenny and her mom grinned at each other. "Sure," Elise said. "That'd be great."

In the end, the entire family stood guard on the porch with brooms and a baseball bat, protecting their home. It worked.

The Tracliodytes stayed around for most of the morning, feeding on every living thing they could find. They never got into the house, but a few did get into the barn where they feasted on a few of the older, slower chickens. The others escaped to hay bales stacked along one wall. Bossy and Billy valiantly fought the huge bugs off, their hooves being more than enough to kill the ones that were dumb enough to get close, which a lot of them were. Those two old farm animals were strong, though, and had a strong will to live. In the end, they both survived.

By mid-morning the sky became lighter, and it was apparent that the Tracliodytes were beginning to leave the area. The stink wasn't as bad either. The Blake family kept watch on both the front and back porches, sweeping any stragglers away as necessary. By noon the Tracliodytes had fled completely. They left in huge groups, rising in huge spiraling funnels as they circled up, up, up into the sky. Jenny, Elise, and the kids watched in awe as cloud after cloud of spiraling insects eventually vanished from view. When they were gone, Elise broke the tension of the morning by saying, "Okay, let's get this place cleaned up."

Jenny laughed and so did the other kids, relief flooding through the family. Then Elise said, "I'm serious. Let's get started."

Jenny will always remember that moment, with

fondness. It was a farm family motto from way back: "No Rest Until the Chores are Done".

"Okay," she said, picking up a broom. "Where do we begin?"

The destruction left behind was incredible. All living vegetation had been destroyed. The apple orchard was gone, the vegetable garden had disappeared, and, most prominently, the evergreen windbreak was gone, leaving a view of rolling hills that stretched into the distance as far as the eye could see. Which wasn't much. The Tracliodytes had destroyed everything in the area. More than once, as they cleaned up, Jenny saw her mom fight back tears. This was their home, after all.

"Mom, are we going to stay here?" Jenny asked at one point, pausing in her shoveling. A number of the Tracliodytes had died in the feeding frenzy and was up to Jenny, Susie, and Elise to shovel the dead ones into the back of the pickup truck. They'd already taken two loads down the far corner of their property where the plan was to burn them.

Elise stopped and leaned on her shovel. "Of course, we are, young lady." She gave Jenny the same pointed look she'd given her that morning. "This is our home."

Jenny smiled and ran to her mother and held her tight. "I'm glad," was all she could say before tears of joy started flowing.

And they did stay. They stayed and replanted their field the next year and restocked the chickens. Two years after the invasion all was getting back to normal.

One summer night, Jenny, her mom, and the four kids were sitting on the front porch overlooking their land. They'd planted trees where the windbreak used to be but could still see beyond it to the fields rolling into the distance. It's been years before they'd offer any kind of protection.

Jenny had spent two intervening years studying as much as she could about the Tracliodytes and the "Infestation" as it was called, and her mother often asked her about it.

"Did you find out if they might ever come back?" Elise asked her on that night.

"No one knows, Mom," Jenny told her. "Most insects go through periods where very little happens in their lives, and then suddenly something will trigger them to swarm together. Like the Tracliodytes did."

"Why is that?"

"They feed and then breed and then lay eggs and die. It's all part of their life cycle."

"Did those insects, those Tracliodytes you call them, do they do that?"

"No one knows, Mom. No one knows."

"But we're safe, though, right? For a while anyway?"

"Yeah, Mom. We are."

Elise smiled and stood up. "Well, that's good." Then she turned to the children. "Okay, kids, how about we get some ice cream? The freezer's full."

Jenny watched her mom and her four siblings go inside. "I'll be right in," she called out, not knowing if they heard her. That was okay. She was thirteen now, growing up and starting to make her own plans for the future. She didn't want to ever leave the farm but she knew she had to. At least for a little while. Her plan was to go to the University and study insects, specifically Tracliodytes. She wanted to learn as much as she could about them and become as much of an expert as she could. Because she hadn't been completely truthful when she'd been talking to her mother.

The fact of the matter was that no one knew if the Tracliodytes would ever come back. Of course, everyone *hoped* that they wouldn't, but that was just the way humans were: "Learn from yesterday, live for today, and hope for the future". Which did make sense to part of Jenny, the idealist part of her anyway.

However, she was becoming more and more interested in science, and what the science had to say was that the Tracliodytes were some kind of mutant insect, and being insects, they were entirely capable of swarming just like the Tracliodytes had done. That was a fact. So in Jenny's young mind, it was not a question of if they'd return, but when. If she could figure out when they'd come back, then she and others could be ready and save not only lives, but some of their land and crops too.

The Tracliodytes invasion had devastated food production worldwide. Next time they could cripple it irrevocably. Jenny wanted to help ensure that never happened. A big burden for a thirteen-year-old girl, but a burden she was eager to shoulder. After all it was her family's farm that was at stake. Four generations of memories.

Jenny stretched her arms above her head. *Enough thinking*. She stood up, and smiled, calling out, "Here Clyde, here Clem." The two dogs they'd found wandering a few days after the Tracliodytes invasion came bounding up from the far side of the barn. She bent down and petted each of them. "Shall we go inside and get a treat?" The dogs barked their affirmation in unison. "Let's go, then."

She turned and took one last long look at the land; land she had grown to love and wanted to protect at all costs. She tried to put the Tracliodytes out of her mind but was only mildly successful. She shivered a little at the memory of that day when they had invaded Earth and turned to go inside. Yeah, some ice cream sounded really good. Maybe a lot of it.

Originally published in *World of Myth Magazine*

Nitrogen

Twenty years ago, during the spring of the 2020 lockdown, Mom announced, "We are planting a garden."

I was thirteen and my brother Jay was nine so, of course, we complained, me being the loudest, "Aw, Mom. No!"

"What, you'd rather play video games?"

Well, yeah, of course, but I couldn't say that. Instead, I just moped until she said, "And no moping either." She gave me a look like only she could give, one that implied a lot of time *not* playing my precious video games if I didn't shape up. That would not be good. *Fortnite* was helping to get me through the pandemic. I looked at Jay and we silently agreed on the garden idea, but only for the greater good.

The next day we marked off a ten by twenty-foot square on the sunny south side of the house. Dad had left us for good a few years earlier and Mom and Jay and I had developed an easy comradery in his absence, which was fortunate because, for starters, there was a lot of sod. It took us almost a week to dig it all out.

"We can store it behind the garage," Mom said. "It'll rot and turn to compost."

Whatever compost was. But I didn't argue. I must have wheel barreled a hundred loads back there that week, sweating rivers the entire time. You know what? A few years later it had turned to compost. It wasn't the first time Mom had been right, nor the last.

We added manure to the fresh bed we'd dug, and that stuff stank to high heaven, much to the delight of me and my brother.

"It's just horse manure," Mom said. We giggled, our imaginations running wild at how the stuff was collected.

59

We were boys, remember, and easily entertained. When the soil was all prepared, Mom said, "Now the fun begins."

Our ears perked up. "Are we going for ice cream?" I asked.

"How about burgers?" Jay added.

Mom laughed. "You boys should go on the comedy circuit when this pandemic is over." She grabbed her purse and her car keys. "But no such luck. Come on, let's go."

"Where to?" I asked.

"Plant shopping."

Oh.

You could have cut the disappointment with a garden trowel, but what did we know? It turned out to be fun.

Mom pulled our old Toyota into the parking lot and the car shuddered to a halt. We put on our masks and got out. Mom was excited. "You boys pick out what you want," she told us and turned us loose.

Well, all right then.

I walked up and down the aisles making it a point to stay socially distant. It wasn't hard in a place the size of a basketball court with maybe five other people wandering around poking at plants.

I had no idea what I was looking at so instead of going for pretty, I went for strange. I picked out a big, prickly-looking thing with purple flowers. The girl at the checkout told me it was an Echinops. "Another name for it is a globe thistle," she added with a smile.

"Cool," I said, grinning and trying to appear knowledgeable. "Is it one of those meat eaters?" I asked. "Like a Venus fly trap?"

The nice thing about the pandemic was it gave me and Jay a lot of time to watch television when Mom had banned us from video games. I think it was on the Nature Channel or something that we came across plants that ate flies and stuff. Which we thought was pretty amazing.

"No," she said, sadly shaking her head." She was about ten years older than me, and I had the sudden thought that maybe she liked me. "It's just a regular plant."

"Oh," I said, my disappointment palpable.

"It's a good pollinator, though," she remarked, enthusiastically, as if that meant anything to me. I had no idea what a pollinator was. She held the plant up for us both to admire.

"It's very nice, isn't it?" I said, trying to prove I had something on the ball. I'm not sure she bought into it, so I looked around for Mom. I was ready to go.

Jay walked up and stood next to me with his plant. "Look," he said. It was white and yellow and looked like a regular flower. Kind of boring.

"That's a daisy," the girl behind the counter commented.

Jay smiled. "I like it. It's pretty." He could be kind of a nob sometimes.

Mom came up pulling a wagon loaded with a variety of plants. "I'm getting these vegetables."

"What kind did you get?" All I could think of was how long it was going to take to plant all of it.

She proudly stated, "I've got tomato plants, some zucchini, green peppers, and a bunch of beans."

"Cool," I said. I was getting into this pretending that I knew what I was talking about thing.

She gave me her patented look that told me she knew better, and said, "Yes. It's very cool."

Then we checked out.

Back home we spent the afternoon giving, as Mom said, "our new friends a home." It was when we were putting in the beans that I noticed the tag said it was a legume. "What's a legume?" I asked Mom and immediately regretted it.

"I have no idea," she said. "Let's look it up."

I sighed. Why was everything a *learning experience* with her? Why couldn't we just sort of, you know, go with the flow? But she was committed to pounding some knowledge into us one way or the other. And she was persistent, too, I have to give her that.

We took a break, got some lemonade, and sat in the shade while mom took out her phone and looked up legumes. "It says here that beans are members of the legume family."

Hmm. No clue what that meant.

She went on to say that legumes provided a home for a kind of soil bacteria that took nitrogen out of the air in the soil. That was good for the plants because nitrogen helped them grow, and it was good for the bacteria because the plants provided them with food.

I joked with her. "Well, who knew?" I said, and laughed, looking at my brother and winking. Following my lead, he laughed, too.

Mom shook her head. "You boys..." she said, half joking, half exasperated. "I'll be glad when this pandemic is over. Maybe back in school, you'll actually appreciate learning something."

Smart ass that I was, I said, "You can but hope, Mom."

She just grinned and said, "Let's get back to work."

I have to say, looking back, Mom put up with a lot. I give her tons of credit for that.

Eventually, we did go back to face-to-face classes, and four years later I graduated from high school, much to my mom's pride and amazement. My favorite subject had been eleventh-grade ecology. I learned that plants like beans and other legumes were essential to the ecosystem because of their nitrogen-fixing properties. The land was important. Soil, too.

I've been a teacher for seven years now and here's what I tell my tenth-grade biology class: "If you ever get a chance to plant a garden, do it. You'll learn a lot." Most of them laugh. Fresh vegetables are in rare supply these days in 2041. But legumes still are flourishing and that's good. The way things are going, we're going to keep needing them.

Mom still has that garden on the south side of the house, and me and Jay go over and help her plant it every spring. You know what? I wouldn't miss it for the world, because there's no doubt in my mind at all that it was one of the best summers me and Jay and Mom ever had. And that was in spite of the pandemic.

Originally published in *Periodic Stories* Volume One

On the Shore of Walden Pond

The Boss droned on. "Yes, and next quarter we project earnings of..."

Stifling a yawn, he adjusted his tie and feigned attention, nodding occasionally like a good employee should. In his mind, though, it was different. In his mind, he journeyed back across time and space to Walden Pond and the home of Henry David Thoreau.

"Hi. Welcome." Thoreau greeted him, smiling through his bushy beard. He adjusted his straw hat and patted the log he was sitting on. "Come over here. Sit down and join me."

The request seemed perfectly natural, so the employee did. "Thank you," he said. "My name's Alex. Alex Jensen."

"Nice to meet you, Alex. I'm Henry. Henry David Thoreau."

They shook hands.

"Nice to meet you too."

Alex was immediately put at ease by the outdoorsy-looking man. *This is lots better than sitting in a boring meeting*, he thought to himself.

They sat quietly together and gazed out over the sparkling waters of a pond that lay about a hundred feet in front of them. A small flock of purple finches flittered around, popping into and out of nearby bushes. A pair of energetic squirrels played in a maple tree next to them, and a woodpecker drummed on nearby oak. Behind them stood a roughly hewn but solidly built small cabin.

Henry took out his battered briar pipe and lit it. He took a minute to get it going and then blew a stream of aromatic tobacco away from where the two men were sitting. "Nice day," he said.

"It is." Alex nodded. He sat back and sighed a contented

sigh, happy beyond words to be free from the meeting and the office. It felt good to be outdoors. "Now, anyway."

Henry looked at him perplexed. "What do you mean?"

Alex shook his head. "Nothing." He wasn't sure he could explain it. All he knew was that it felt good to be here. Good to be outside in the fresh air. Good to be with this tranquil man.

Henry shrugged his shoulders. "Suit yourself."

Feeling remarkably at ease, Alex asked, "Henry, I have a question for you."

"Ask away."

"Do you mind if I stay here a while?"

The peaceful man puffed his pipe and looked at Alex with eyes as clear as the blue sky above them. "Not at all," he said. "Stay as long as you like."

"Thanks," Alex said, greatly relieved. "I think I will."

Henry nodded. "Good," he said. He watched as Alex stretched his legs and made himself comfortable. Then he added with a twinkle in his eye. "Go ahead and take your tie off, too, if you want." He grinned. "I would."

Alex laughed. He took off his tie, rolled it up, and put it in his pocket. He undid the top two buttons of his dress shirt and then closed his eyes. He tilted his head back feeling the warmth of the sun's rays on his face. Nearby more birds twittered in the bushes and more squirrels chattered from high in a tree. Out on the lake, a loon called.

Alex hadn't felt this relaxed in... well, he couldn't remember.

Next to him, Henry David Thoreau said, "I was thinking about going back to the cabin and making my noon meal. Would you like to join me?"

Alex didn't have to think. "I'd love to," he said.

"Good." Henry got to his feet. "Here, let me help you up."

Alex extended his hand. "Thank you."

Henry pulled him to his feet and Alex followed his new friend toward his cabin. He was kind of hungry and was looking forward to having something to eat. Plus, he was actually pretty good in the kitchen and could help out. And he was in no hurry to go back to work either. Especially if he had to leave the peaceful setting and the quiet companionship of his new friend.

The more he thought about it, the more he thought that going back to work just might have to wait for a while. In fact, he might never go back. He might just stay here and learn to live a different kind of life, one simpler and more fulfilling. Yeah, that seemed like a good idea. A really good idea.

"Henry," he called out.

"What?" Thoreau stopped at the door to his cabin and turned.

"I have a question for you."

"Sure." Henry smiled. "Ask away."

_____

Originally published in *Dancing With Butterflies*

The Painting

The day Ms. Langerford's fourth-grade class went on a field trip to the Minneapolis Institute of Art and Cole saw the painting, little did he know that it would change his life.

"These are works by the Impressionists," she told the class as they strolled through one of the huge exhibition rooms. "They look at the world, interpret it through their own eyes, and paint what they see."

"Like make-believe?" Sara Runkles asked.

Ms. Langerford smiled. "Well, I guess you could say that." Then, seeing she had the fidgety class's attention, she pointed. "Look over there. There's one by Claude Monet called 'Waterlilies'. Let's go and take a look."

The class dutifully followed. All but Cole. He'd seen a painting on the far wall and was drawn to it. A quiet, shy boy, he wasn't missed by the rest of the class as he stood in front of the small painting and read the index card next to it. It was painted in England in the mid-1800s, and it depicted a scene of a man and a woman having a meal together in a large room. They were being served by a young woman wearing a black and white uniform. The man was setting a newspaper to one side in a manner that, to Cole, suggested he was done reading and about to start eating. Across the table, the woman was holding a white kitten in her lap and petting it. A floral-patterned cup and saucer were in front of her. She was smiling.

Outside a large window next to the couple was a rolling countryside with green hills stretching to a misty distance. Near the home there were three horses grazing in a fenced area, a brown one, a black one, and one dappled grey.

The painting was called *Breakfast,* and it stuck in his mind long after the class had been herded to the bus and driven back to school. So much so, in fact, he was eager to tell his mother about it when he got home later that afternoon. He never got the chance.

"Hurry up and get to your room," she whispered, urgently pulling him aside when he walked in the front door. She pointed to the kitchen. His father's swearing was easily heard through the closed doors from where they stood in the tiny living room. "He's in a foul mood."

No doubt about that, thought Cole.

They lived in a small one-story house in a poor section of east Minneapolis. His father drove a city bus and his mom worked as a cashier at a nearby grocery store. Cole was the youngest of five children and his two brothers and two sisters had long since moved away, leaving him home alone with his parents. He was sometimes referred to as "the mistake" especially if his father was drunk. Like now.

Cole didn't want to do anything to provoke the man, which in the past was usually never much, so he didn't hesitate as he hurried to his bedroom at the back of the house, the escalating volume of his father's yelling and cursing following him like a bad dream.

Once safely in his room, Cole quietly shut the door, hoping it would bring a measure of peace. But not today. Today he could hear his mother join in the battle, not only yelling but physically fighting. He could hear punches being thrown and broken glass smashing and furniture flying, all of it filling his young ears with anxiety and dread. Would his father come after him next? He had in the past.

Shivering, not with cold but fear, Cole climbed onto his bed and pulled the covers over his head. The security of his little cave enveloped him like a warm, wool mitten, and a sense of quiet serenity filtered peacefully into his body. His eyelids became heavy and fluttered shut. In a magical moment, he drifted away, floating on a soft, cotton cloud as he left behind the cold, terrifying world of his home with his parents fighting and went to the first place he thought of, the safest place he could imagine, the painting he'd seen earlier that day on the field trip.

It was just like he remembered.

"Hi there," he said to the couple at the table.

They each turned to him. The man spoke first. "Good morning, young man. How are you this fine day?"

Cole hadn't realized until just now that it was not only a different world, but a different time, and was indeed a fine morning. He could hear the horses whinnying through the open window, its curtains billowing with a soft, fragrant breeze that filled the room with the sweet scent of lilacs and lilies of the valley.

"I'm fine, sir," Cole responded, adding the "sir" because it seemed like the right thing to do. "How are you?"

The man smiled and said, "I'm wonderful." He took a bit of something that looked like toast. "By the way, breakfast is very good this morning." He turned to the servant girl. "Katie, could you please set a spot for this fine young man and bring him some of your delicious sausage and eggs?"

"Yes, sir." Kathie curtsied and hurried through a swinging set of doors.

A demure cough to his right drew Cole's attention. The lady was speaking to him. She had long, wavy auburn hair and a voice as smooth as golden honey. "My dear, would you like to come and pet Snowflake? She's such a good little kitty." She bent down and nuzzled the furry, white kitten with her nose. "Aren't you sweetheart?"

Cole loved cats, kittens in particular, and didn't have to think. "Sure." He walked over to the lady and began petting Snowflake like it was the most natural thing in the world to do. "She sure is soft," he remarked. The lady smiled at him. Her eyes were bright and blue, the corneas white, not yellow and red like his father's.

A ruffling of newsprint caused Cole to look toward the man, who now was gazing at his newspaper with a relaxed smile on his lips, drinking his tea. He must have felt Cole's eyes on him because he looked up and said, "How about if you and I go riding after breakfast? Take the horses for some exercise. Would you like that?"

Next to him, the lady exclaimed, "Oh, that's a marvelous idea. Perhaps I could also come along?"

The man smiled. "That'd be lovely. We'll make it a family outing."

Cole listened to the exchange as he absentmindedly petted the kitten. *Wow*, he was thinking. *Is this for real? Horseback riding? Me? This is awesome.*

Then...

"Cole!!" A screaming voice cut into his thoughts. "Cole!! Where the hell are you?"

It was his father. Cole huddled down under his blankets trying to hide but it did no good. "Ah, there you are you little shit." The covers were ripped off and his father stood next to the bed, swaying back and forth with bloodshot eyes, two-days growth of beard, and stinking of old sweat and vomit. He grabbed Cole by the arm. "I'll teach you to hide from me, you little jerk."

He dragged Cole from the room and down the hallway. As they entered the kitchen his mother ran at them with a bottle. She swung it with all her might at her husband's head and connected. Glass shattered and booze flew as he fell to the ground. Dazed, he let go of Cole who scrambled to his feet, ran back to his bedroom, and slammed the door. Panting with fear, he sat on the floor with his back against the door to prevent his father from trying to get back in, knowing it wouldn't do any good. When his father was as drunk as he was, he had almost superhuman strength and was a force to be reckoned with.

Out in the kitchen, the yelling and screaming were escalating rapidly. Cole had heard it all before and knew it could come to no good end. He used all of his strength to pull and shove his dresser in front of the door and made sure it was securely jammed up against it. Then he added his small desk and a chair to the blockade for good measure. Knowing he'd done all he could to keep his drunken father away from him, Cole got back into bed and pulled the blankets over his head. He needed to get away. He closed his eyes. Please…

In a few moments, the room appeared. The couple was at the table just like before. So was Katie. And the kitten.

The man smiled when he saw Cole. "Hi, there," he said. "We wondered where you'd gone."

The lady smiled and said, "So did kitty."

Katie said, "Look. I brought your breakfast."

Cole looked. There, at a place setting just for him, was a steaming plate of food, sausages, eggs and toast. When was the last time he'd had a hot meal? He couldn't remember.

The man spoke. "After you eat, we can go horseback riding like we talked about. Would you like that?"

Cole nodded as he took a mouthful of his breakfast and chewed. It was scrumptious. "Yes, I would," he said groaning with pleasure. He didn't know when he'd ever tasted anything better. He swallowed, looked at the lady, and asked, "Are you coming, too?"

She smiled at him and said, "Whatever you'd like dear. Would you like me to come along?"

He used a linen napkin to wipe his lips. "I'd like that a lot," he grinned at her.

Then, suddenly, in the background, the peaceful scene was shattered by frantic pounding and a drunken voice yelling, "Open up you little shit. You're in for it now."

Frightened, Cole turned to the man. "Can you help me?"

The man glanced behind Cole as he put down the newspaper, his brow furrowed with concern. A determined look darkened his face, though his kindly eyes twinkled, when he said, "Of course, I can help. But first, it appears, young man, that the time is neigh for us to get going." He looked to the lady. "What do you think, dear."

She stood up and set the kitten down. "The sooner the better," she said, and went quickly to Cole, took him firmly by the hand, and pulled him along. "Let's get going, my boy." Then she pointed behind Cole and said to the man, "Take care of the racket, too, will you, dear? Cole and I will meet you at the stables."

The man nodded and stood up, ready for action. "It will be my pleasure."

Cole noticed how fit and strong and capable the man looked. His father wouldn't stand a chance.

He smiled as he hurried out of the room with the lady leading and down a long, wide hallway with walls covered in artwork. As they burst through the front door and ran toward the stable, she asked, "Which color horse would you prefer to ride? The brown or the black or the dappled grey?"

Cole smiled at her and said, "It really doesn't matter."

And he was being honest. It really didn't. Somehow, he knew without a doubt that this was all going to work out just fine.

Originally published in *Short Story Magazine* by Clarendon House

My Brother's Adage

After my pet hamster Squiggles died, we buried him in the vegetable garden in the backyard. It was summertime in 1935, and Mom said that Squiggles would like it there among the vegetables because he loved lettuce. What did I know? I was five years old.

"Okay, Mom," I total her wiping away my tears. "Whatever you say."

My ten-year-old brother Eddie had a different take on what was going on. He smirked, punched me in the arm, and said, "Don't be such a crybaby."

Even though Mom admonished him, I couldn't help it, I started crying some more. Eddie just shook his head as he walked toward the backdoor to go outside and play baseball. I'm positive I heard him mumble "Looser" on his way out the door.

Later that night I crawled out of bed and knelt by my window. My bedroom faced the backyard, and I propped my elbows on the sill and watched the vegetable garden and the spot where we'd buried Squiggles. I was waiting to see him rise from the ground and go to heaven like they said in church would happen. I had my fingers crossed hoping I'd see my beloved pet one more time. Unfortunately, I fell asleep with my head on the windowsill and missed him. For at least a week I kept watch every night but never saw him go up into the sky. Probably because I fell asleep each night. Anyway, at least that's what I told myself at the time.

But the death of Squiggles had a profound impact on my young psyche. I realized something monumental during those nighttime vigils at the window watching the vegetable garden in the backyard. It was this: I was going to die someday. Just like Squiggles. One day I was going to be gone from the world. Dead and buried and no more than a memory. Like Squiggles was to me.

The day after the realization hit me and still reeling at the sudden knowledge of my immortality, I went to Mom. "Am I going to die?" I asked her.

She looked at me, a sense of sadness in her eyes, and said, "Oh, honey, don't worry your little head about things like that."

Eddie was walking by at the time and didn't pause except to say, "Of course, jerk face. We all die someday. You get old, then you die. Everyone knows that."

The door slammed as he continued on his way outside to play. I looked at Mom. She didn't say anything, she just hugged me some more. It was then I knew for a fact – what my brother had said was true. *You get old, then you die.* Geez. Heavy-duty stuff. I thought right then and there that I was glad I was only five. I had a lot of years left to live.

But then Dad died. He was only thirty-three. Not that old in my book. Or my brother's for that matter. I was eleven at the time, Eddie sixteen. At the funeral I reminded my brother about his adage – you get old then you die.

"Dad was only thirty-three," I told him.

He looked at me without a trace of irony and said, "Like I told you after that stupid hamster. You get old then you die." He shrugged his shoulders.

"He was only thirty-three!"

He shrugged his shoulders again. "See, what'd I say? He was old, older than us anyway."

I was no dummy, I knew there was more to it than that, but I couldn't shake the notion of equating getting old with dying.

I turned twenty and congratulated myself on making that milestone. Me and my friends partied and had a good time. I didn't think about dying once.

I turned thirty, just a few years younger than Dad was went he passed away, and only thought about it a little.

I turned forty, then fifty, then sixty. I turned seventy and I then turned eighty. Four years ago, I turned ninety.

I'm still alive. Eddie died a few years ago when he was eighty-seven. I was eighty-two at the time. Mom died when she was seventy-eight. I was fifty-six.

So, yeah, I'm still alive. I'm ninety-four right now. For the last five years, I've lived in Orchard Lake Senior Living. It's clean and tidy and I like it. I worked as a product engineer for a large manufacturing company for many years until I retired at the age of sixty-seven. Ruth, my wife of fifty-five years passed away when I was eighty-one. We had a good marriage, and I've had a good life. I see my kids and my grandkids regularly and I have wonderful memories of my life with Ruth. My days are spent watching birds, reading, talking on the phone with my kids and the few friends I still have, and even taking classes on the Internet. It's been a full life. Still is.

The point is this: for me, ever since that day so many years ago when Eddie told me, "Hey jerk face, you get old then you die," I've continued living. I've looked at life and made the most of it. I'm still kicking. I may be old but that doesn't matter. I'm not done yet. My brother's adage may be true, but not for me. Not yet anyway.

Originally published in *Pure Slush Older Anthology*

Bathtub Gin

Big Ben Barker ran the bootleg arm of Mickey Finn's operation on the south side. He ran it like clockwork and with precision. Mickey called him Ben. Ben Barker's boys called him Boss. And the ladies all called him Mr. Big because he was, well, he was rumored to be well endowed if you know what I mean.

Yeah, it was a fact that the ladies liked Mr. Big and he liked them. Especially Laura Lane. Man, she was something else. A dancer at Club Go Go, she could shake it like no one he'd ever seen. She wore a black cloche hat decorated with gold sequins, and silver silk flapper dresses that shimmered under the spotlights, showing off every curve of her body. Wow! The first time he'd seen her he wanted her like nobody's business. And the first time she'd slid out of that dress in his bedroom… Well, when they said that the sky was the limit, they didn't even come close. There was no limit as far as Laura was concerned. She'd do anything he asked her to do and leave him begging for more. His desire for her knew no bounds.

No bounds that was until Doris Dalrymple came along. Jeez. She was really the cat's meow. Better built than Laura, Doris knew her way to a man's heart that was for sure, and it wasn't through his stomach. Whew! If Laura wore him out, Doris did it in spades.

But Big Ben wasn't getting any younger. After a few weeks of trying to manage it with both ladies, he decided one of them had to go. He flipped a coin and was only sad for a moment. Sorry, Laura. It'd been nice to know ya'.

He knew Laura wouldn't go quietly. Plus, she knew too much about his organization and his business. Enough, anyway, to get nasty if she wanted to, which he figured she would after he gave the news that he was dumping her. So he came up with a fool proof plan.

He booked the presidential suite on the top floor of the Ritz for that Saturday night. He had his boys fill the gold-plated bathtub with gin, knowing that gin-loving Laura would appreciate the gesture. Then, after he'd gotten her good and drunk, he'd drown her in the tub and claim it was an accident. Easy.

That night he took her to dinner and dancing at the 21 Club. Around midnight they left and went to Ben's favorite speakeasy for drinks. After they'd had a few he leaned in close enough to get a good whiff of her Channel not to mention an eye full of her cleavage and said, "Hey there gorgeous, how about you and I blow this place and head for the Ritz. I've got a room for us."

"Oh, honey," Laura said, slurring ever so slightly, "you've got a treat for little old me?" She rubbed her hand against his crotch. "Well, I've got one for you, too." She giggled as she stood up and sauntered off, swinging her hips, driving him and his own personal Mr. Big crazy.

He hurried to catch up and took her by the arm, drooling in anticipation. "I'll have one of the boys drive us," he panted.

Half an hour later they were in the huge bathroom.

Laura purred like a kitten. "Oh, honey, look at all the gin for little old me." She dipped a finger in and licked it.

"All for you, sweetheart." Ben watched her slide her finger around in her mouth and could barely contain himself. *Maybe just once more for old time's sake*, is what he was thinking as Laura sashayed up to him.

"Aw, honey, give me a little kiss," she said wrapping her arms around his neck. "Umm. You feel good."

Ben couldn't help himself. In a moment captured by his uncontrollable lust, he grabbed her in a tight embrace and ran his hand up and down her firm behind.

Laura ignored his hand as she felt him grow hard against

her thigh. That's all she needed. She slowly turned him until the backs of his knees were propped against the rim of the tub. Then she nibbled on his ear lobe whispering, "Oh, my, baby. You feel so good." She rubbed against him sensuously. "Who do you love, honey?" She rubbed some more and took hold of his belt buckle. "Hmm? Do you love little old me?"

She felt Ben's hot breath in her ear. He murmured, "Oh, baby you know how much..." He never finished his thought.

Laura put her hands on his chest and pushed. Backwards he tumbled, splashing into the gin. "What the..." he was starting to say when Laura reached over to the vanity, turned on the electric radio, and dropped it into the tub. Still plugged in. He shook and jiggled and jumped, splashing gin over the sides of the tub and onto the floor.

Laura laughed at Ben's shocked expression. "Do away with me, baby? Not on your life. Oh, wait. I guess I was wrong. On your life, sucker!"

It took less than a minute, and then he was dead.

Half an hour later she emerged from the elevator of the ritzy hotel looking every bit the beautiful woman she was. She stopped by the front desk and said, "I think there's a problem up in the presidential suite. Something's clogging the drain on the tub."

Then she sauntered across the lobby and out the front door never to be seen or heard from again. In her purse was twenty thousand dollars taken from Ben's wallet. Or Little Ben as she now thought of him, because in truth that's what he really was. Tiny, even.

She smiled, as she waved for a cab. One pulled up right away. "Airport, ma'am?" the cabby asked.

"Yes, thank you. And please make it fast. I'm in a hurry."

He saluted and grinned. "You bet, beautiful."

She sat down in the back and breathed a sigh of relief

as the cab peeled away from the curb. Life was good. She was a beautiful woman and she had money, more than enough for airfare to the Bahamas. More than enough to start a new life. No one would ever find her. She stared out the window and watched the lights of the city stream past. She'd never see those lights again and she smiled. That was just fine with her.

Orange Juice

"Damn you, Eric!" I yelled. "Quit being such a jerk!"

I knew I shouldn't swear but, hell (sorry), he had pushed it too far. All morning long my older brother had been teasing me, calling names like "elephant ears" and "dog breath", giving me wedgies, and, in general, making my life miserable. But when he puckered up his fat lips at breakfast and made wet, drippy, kissy sounds, it was just too much. I picked up my full glass of orange juice and without thinking threw it at him.

Time shifted to slow motion as I watched the glass arc through the air toward his grinning freckled head. Orange juice was streaming out in a long yellow ribbon of liquid disaster. *I'll show him!* I could picture the glass smashing into his face and… and…

Oh, oh.

Suddenly, my mind shifted from anger at my brother to *What have I just done?*

Reality reared its head and it wasn't pretty. Eric easily ducked out of the way and leaped to his feet. The glass smashed into the wall behind him, scattering juice and shards all over Mom's impeccable linoleum floor. Eric and I both looked at the mess, orange juice running down the wall and glass everywhere. He was eight years old, three years older than me, and not only quicker to react but smarter too. Wiser to the ways of the world than I'd ever be, he knew there would be "consequences", the term my parents often called the punishment Dad meted out on a regular basis, mostly to me.

Eric gave me the finger, and then, because he knew there was going to be hell (sorry, again) to pay, he sprinted across the kitchen, out the back door, and hightailed it for the safety of the backyard even though it was still winter and really cold outside. I was left alone.

Mom was at the counter, a horrified look on her face. I looked at her and she looked at me. Then she burst into tears.

Dad must have heard the commotion because he hurried into the kitchen where he stopped and took in the whole scene: the shattered glass, the orange juice on the wall, and, most of all, Mom crying hysterically. He turned to me with a look I'd seen all too often; anger mixed with a liberal amount of disgust. In an instant, he immediately assessed blame, sadly shaking his head to emphasize his disappointment in me.

He set his newspaper aside and walked toward me, unbuckling his belt as he slowly crossed the kitchen, avoiding the juice and glass as he did so. I was conscious of Mom weeping by the sink but even more conscious of my dad, the person who was the ongoing terror of my young life.

He stopped in front of me. His thick, worn leather belt was off and folded in half. He slapped it methodically against the palm of his hand, whap, whap, whap, as he stared at me. Time stood still. I could smell his sickly-sweet aftershave; it made me want to puke. Panic set in and I began to gasp for air. I tried not to cry. I also tried not to pee in my pants but failed as warm urine began flowing freely. I sat there watching him, festering in my wet jeans, the embarrassment mixed in with an all too well-known feeling of terror. His eyes were relentlessly unblinking, boring into mine like burning lasers. There was stubble on his chin and a cruel look on his lips. He was sneering at me.

Then he motioned with his head toward the basement door. "Let's go," he said.

His voice was soft yet menacing. I knew what was coming. I glanced at my mom, who had her face buried in a Kleenex. No help there, not that I expected any. Dad was a force to be reckoned with for all of us, Mom included.

I got to my feet. He shoved me a little from behind and made me walk in front of him to the door leading downstairs. "Open it," he said. I did as he instructed and started the long descent down the wooden steps to our musty-smelling cellar. He was right behind me and I had to listen to his menacing footsteps all the way down. Thirteen of them. Each one was filled with horror.

When I reached the bottom, I slowed my pace to a crawl, wanting to delay the inevitable as long as I could. He'd have no part of it and pushed me again. Harder this time. "Move!"

"Okay." I squeezed out a response, trying not to whimper.

He pointed. "Now!"

I shuffled across the cement floor to the workbench, my wet jeans chaffing my thighs. I stopped when I got there and stood facing the workbench and the wall behind it. "Take down your pants," he commanded.

"Yes, sir," I said like I'd been taught to say. I unbuckled my belt and let my wet jeans drop to the floor. *Yes, sir!* I thought to myself. *Anything you say, you big bully!*

"And your underwear, too," he whispered.

"Okay. Yes, sir." I pushed them down below my knees. I couldn't help myself. I started to lose it and began whimpering.

"Bend over," he said.

I did, tears flowing freely now.

He could have cared less.

Ten times with the belt. That was the rule. Ten times. Man, did it hurt.

I found out later that the reason Mom was crying was not for the punishment I was about to receive. Goodness no. Mom and I were close back then and still are even now so many years later. But I deserved to be punished. She knew it and I knew it. For three reasons: two I knew about, one I didn't. I was punished for throwing the glass at Eric and making such a mess. That was reason number one. And for swearing. Swearing was a big "no, no" in our house. That was reason number two.

But I was also being punished for something I found out later, and it was this: I'd made Mom cry.

I didn't realize it, but Dad was incensed. It was Valentine's Day and I guess he'd planned a special day for Mom. He was going to have my aunt come over and stay with me and Eric and he was going to take Mom out to brunch and then the two of them were going to go for a long drive down the Mississippi River where they were going to have a nice dinner and spend the night at a fancy Bed and Breakfast in Red Wing. I guess I'd wrecked the mood or something with my behavior. Their whole day was shot, at least in Dad's eyes. He was going to make me pay and boy did he ever. My butt was red and sore for the next couple of days.

So, yeah, I'd made mom cry and ruined my dad's romantic plans. That was the main reason for my beating. Well, in my defense, how was I to know? Valentine's Day? No clue. Remember, I was five years old.

Eric explained it to me this way later that day after he and I had made up. And after I'd cleaned up the mess I'd made. And changed my pants, too, of course.

We were at the park a couple of blocks down the street from our house where we'd gone to get away from the tension at home. We were ice skating.

"You big bozo," he said to me, by way of explanation. "Are you completely clueless?"

Apparently, I was. I had no idea what he was talking about. "What do you mean?" I asked.

"It's Valentine's Day today," he said. He turned to skate backward so he could face me. I was doing my best to keep up because my big brother was way more coordinated than me, and a pretty skater to boot. "Valentine's Day is a big romantic holiday," he added to make his point perfectly clear to his clueless younger brother. "It's a big deal for Mom and Dad."

"Why?"

He shrugged his shoulders. "I don't know. It just is."

That didn't help.

Nor did it help three years later when I tried to get an answer from Mom. "Why is Valentine's Day such a big deal?" I asked her.

Mom hugged me. I was helping her fold laundry. "Oh, honey," she said. "It just is."

Which didn't help much, either. Nor did it when my friend Andy filled me in a few days after Mom and I had talked in the laundry room. "It's all about romance," he said, grinning. "It's a time when parents make babies."

"Really?"

He nodded wisely. "Yep."

Amazing. I had no idea. I guess I had a lot to learn. But, at the time, for eight-year-old me, that was good enough.

However, the older I got, the more the real reason became clear. At least in our family. Back then, Mom was what you would call a little sensitive to things. Seeing new babies or puppies or kittens made her tear up. Same with certain television shows. Holidays, too.

She loved to get gifts, and it's my belief that she knew Dad had planned on doing something special for her on that day, the day I spoiled so momentously when I'd heaved the orange juice at Eric. She just didn't know what he had planned, but my behavior had spoiled the surprise. In her mind, she saw a nice, mellow, trouble-free day (mostly with my dad) and I'd ruined the mellowness part of it. Who knew? It was my first exposure to how complicated life really was.

But on the day of the orange juice incident, I had no idea about any of that stuff. All I knew was that I'd made Mom sad, and I wanted to do something about it. So, I did.

After Eric and I got back from skating, I went to our bedroom, got out some colored construction paper, sat at our desk (on a pillow for my sore butt), and went to work. Eric didn't even bother me. He must have known I was serious because I was. I made Mom a Valentine's Day card. It was the first one I'd ever made, but once I knew it was Valentine's Day, I remembered seeing pictures of them.

The card I made was on white paper that I folded in half. On the front, I glued concentric construction paper hearts I'd cut out, starting with a big red one and then filling it in with smaller and smaller cut-out hearts colored, green, yellow, and blue. Inside I used a red crayon and printed, Happy Valentine's Day, Mom! I love you!! I signed it with my name, Ben.

I gave it to her later that afternoon when Dad went to get Aunt Bea. Despite my behavior, Dad was intent on salvaging the day. I guess they were going to go out to eat at some fancy hotel in Minneapolis.

"Here, Mom," I said, handing her my card. I'd even found an envelope for it. Mom was sitting at the kitchen table drinking coffee and smoking one of her ever-present Kools.

She set her cup down and looked at me. "What's this?" she asked, surprised. She snubbed out her cigarette and took my card in her hands. She smiled when she realized what it was and held it carefully like she was holding a valuable gemstone. She grinned. "Oh, Ben. Whatever have you done?"

"It's for you, Mom," I said. "Happy Valentine's Day." Then I shuffled my feet, hung my head, and added, "And I'm sorry about the orange juice."

"Oh, sweetie," she said. Her face broke into a huge smile, and she gave me a big hug. "Thank you so much."

It made me happy to see her happy. Which was a valuable lesson I learned that day: That I should always try to do what I could to make people feel good. I didn't always remember that as I got older, but I tried.

"Open it," I said.

And she did. She read the words and she cried, but they were tears of joy this time, not sadness. I sat with her while she read and re-read my little card.

I gave her a handmade card every year after that. Even last year. And you know what? It always makes her happy. I know because she always cries. Tears of joy.

Sometimes I do too.

Originally published in *Holiday Stories*

Pete the Penguin

On his way to Larry's birthday party, Tim stopped at a Quick-Trip for a twelve-pack of Miller. On his way to pay for it, he passed a toy section and that's when he first heard Pete. Of course, he didn't know it was Pete at the time. What he heard was a faint "squeak, squeak". He looked. There in a toy bin was a four-inch-tall, black and white soft rubber penguin with a yellow beak and yellow feet. It's dark, shiny eyes seemed to plead, "Please take me home." He picked it up and squeezed it and the little penguin squeaked. Too cute! How could Tim resist? He felt a connection right away and thought Larry would as well. So he paid for his purchases and continued on his way, happily squeezing the little penguin, squeaking it the rest of the way to St. Paul.

The party, Larry's thirtieth, was in full swing by the time Tim arrived.

"Hey, man," Larry slurred coming up and hugging his friend. "Thought you'd never get here."

Behind him, Tim saw Karen shaking her head. She looked pissed. She didn't like it when her husband drank to excess.

Tim understood, he had a little trouble overindulging himself sometimes. But today was special, he reasoned, you were only thirty once. Plus, he and Ann were on the outs, so it was a night he was especially looking forward to, unwinding with his best friend. He handed over the gas station plastic bag. "Here you go, buddy. Happy birthday."

"Hey, pal, I'm touched," Larry joked. Then he opened the bag and took out the penguin. He squeaked it once. Then again. Then again and again and again, "squeak, squeak, squeak!"

For many it was annoying but not for Larry. His eyes lit

up. "I love him," he said, immediately assigning the penguin a male gender. He pulled Tim to him and hugged him tight. "Best present ever." And this was coming from a guy who'd just opened a new CD player from his brother. He turned and yelled, "Hey, everyone, look what Tim gave me." He held the penguin high in the air and started squeezing it. There was something about the little penguin's squeaky voice that was endearing to both Larry and Tim. Even Karen smiled. "His name's going to be Pete," Larry announced, squeaking the penguin some more. "Pete the penguin."

And that's how it started.

Nearly every Saturday night for the next couple of years Larry, Karen, and Tim would get together. They'd have a few beers and talk over their work week at their respective jobs. Tim worked at a hardware store, Larry was an assistant professor of history at the University of Minnesota and Karen was a secretary for an insurance company. Pete was always with them. "He's part of the group," Larry said early on, giving him a squeak. Pete had a stately yet easy going demeanor. He was non-judgmental and easy to care for, only requiring the occasional bit of fish for food. Most importantly, he had a calming effect and always put folks in a good mood.

Karen grew to love Pete and made little outfits for him to wear: A cowboy hat and chaps for Cowboy Pete. A red cape and black mask for Superhero Pete. A surfboard and knee length trunks for Surfer Dude Pete. And many others. Pete came to occupy a place of honor near wherever they sat, being squeaked whenever someone was in the mood, which was usually quite often, especially after a few beers.

Larry created a narrative he called, *The Story of Pete.* "Pete was born in the Arctic and fell in love with Paula, the most beautiful penguin within a thousand miles of the Arctic Circle. During a violent storm, she got lost at sea and Pete

began searching the world high and low for her. His search was thwarted, however, when a huge wave smashed him upon the rocky shoreline of Lake Superior during a winter blizzard. He was airlifted to recovery at the University of Minnesota Avian Recovery Center where he was to be destined for the local zoo. But he escaped and ended up in a toy bin in a gas station in western St. Paul. That's when Tim found him, rescued him, and gave him to Larry." (This got Tim to think the "squeak, squeak" he heard that day might have actually been "Please. Help me".)

Tim loved listening to *The Story of Pete*, and over that first year Pete's life became real to them all, right down to Pete developing a craving for Swenson's Gourmet canned sardines. By the time Larry's thirty-first birthday rolled around, he had adopted the little penguin, becoming his father. Karen became his mother and Tim, of course, became Pete's uncle.

For seven years all was well with the four of them until Life intervened. Larry was offered a teaching job at the University of Madison. Karen's mother was in poor health and lived nearby in the town of Pardyville, so after very little deliberation the couple decided to move to Wisconsin.

"We'll stay in touch, buddy," Larry told Tim, giving him a farewell hug just after his thirty-seventh birthday. "That's what email and Facebook are for."

"Sounds good," Tim said. He and Larry had been friends since grade school and he was confident their friendship would survive.

So was Pete. "Squeak, squeak!" said the little penguin.

But, over time, they drifted apart. Larry became head of the history department and he and Karen adopted a child from Korea. Then another one. Karen's mom moved in with them, and their lives became increasingly busy and complex. Tim's wife divorced him. They shared custody with their two kids and Tim devoted his time to being a better father. He quit drinking and became the manager of the hardware store. A few more years went by and eventually, the friends lost touch.

So, imagine Tim's surprise when out of the blue he got a friend request on Facebook. It was from Pete the Penguin. Tim had to laugh because it was accompanied by a picture of Pete wearing a tie-dye tee shirt and red headband. "Hippy-Dippy Pete wants to become your friend," the caption read.

In an instant, all the memories of his friendship with Larry and Karen came flooding back, warm memories of nights spent together hanging out and talking, times of companionship and goodwill with Pete calmly standing nearby keeping them company. It'd been too long. Tim immediately confirmed the request. Within minutes Pete sent a message: "My mom is giving a fiftieth birthday party next month for my dad. It's going to be a surprise, and she would very much like it if you would attend. It would mean the world to all of us."

Tim didn't have to think. He replied right back, "I'll be there."

And that's what put him on the road that day, driving to Madison to see his friends, friends he hadn't seen for over ten years. What would their reunion be like? He didn't party anymore. He'd never met their kids. Larry and Karen and he were different people than they'd been when they were thirty and Pete the penguin had first entered their lives. It could be a disaster.

Or could it?

The more he thought about it, the more he thought, naw, no way. As friends went the three of them had something special, and Tim's overwhelming feeling was that their friendship could withstand the test of time. It had to. They had Pete the penguin as their glue. And if that sounded like a weird thing to say, and if other people didn't get it, well, too bad. As far as Nate was concerned it only meant those people had never met a penguin quite like Pete, because if they had he was convinced they'd be singing a different tune. Or squeaking one, for that matter.

Speaking of Pete, Tim almost forgot. Outside of Madison he pulled into a grocery store and roamed the isles until he found what he was looking for: a can of sardines, Swenson's Gourmet, of course. They were a gift for Pete. It was the least he could do for the little guy for bringing the friends back together. Then he remembered to pick up another can. He'd almost forgotten. He'd heard a rumor that Pete had found his old girlfriend, Paula, and she might be at the party. It wouldn't hurt to have some extra food on hand for the happy couple, just to be on the safe side. When it came to penguins Tim knew one thing for sure, you could never have too many sardines.

He paid his bill, got in his car, and continued to Larry and Karen's home. He couldn't wait to get there. He could already hear Pete's enthusiastic voice, greeting him, "squeak, squeak, squeak!"

And that's all it took to make him smile.

_____

This story is dedicated to my friend Johnny.

Platinum

I had been doing research on an article I was writing when I came across a story in one of those online blogs that were so popular in the first part of the twenty-first century. This one was written in 2022. The blogger's name is Jared. I think it's his first post. It certainly is his last. It's pretty self-explanatory.

Hi. My name's Jared. I'm addicted to my credit card – my treasured platinum one. Or was. I don't know, maybe I still am. Addicted, I mean. Anyway, the point is I'm trying to break my habit. My counselor suggested I share my story, so I thought I'd give it a try.

I'll never forget how it all started. My wife Brittany and I had just returned home from a long weekend up north on Lake Superior. It had been nice to get away, but we were already bemoaning the amount of money we'd spent for two nights at the swanky hotel, The Inn On The Lake, not to mention the four-star meals we'd eaten and the souvenirs we'd purchased. Plus, I'd secretly bought Brit a Lake Superior agate pendant for her birthday the following month. My credit card was maxed out.

We were sorting through the mail when Brit took one look at the envelope addressed to Mr. and Mrs. Jenkins and screamed. "Yea! I'll bet this is it!"

I dropped the stack of bills I was dutifully sifting through and hurried to her side. "Is it…?" I peered eagerly over her shoulder. "Is it what I think it is?"

Brit ripped open the envelope, her big blue eyes wide with excitement. She pulled out the letter and quickly scanned it. "It is!" she grinned, nodding at me. An excited sheen of perspiration appeared on her forehead. "Look." She held up a sheet of paper. "It's an application."

"Oh. My. God," I said. A grin exploded on my face from ear to ear. "I can't believe it." I'm not a demonstrative man by nature, but I couldn't help myself. I started dancing around the room waving the letter above my head. "Yahoo!!"

Brit grabbed me by the shoulders and turned me so I was facing her. "Believe it, honey-bun." She leaped into my arms and wrapped her long legs around my waist. "We've finally made it."

"Our own platinum credit cards!" I gushed.

"One for each of us!" she added. Her eyes were sparkling with unbridled excitement. "I'm so happy!"

I began kissing her passionately. She returned my kisses just as enthusiastically if not even more so. Wow! So, this is what it's like to be among the financial elites! Access to all the money we want and a rockin' sex life to boot. Wow and WOW! Who said dreams don't come true? Ours just had. Big time! No more gold cards for us. No sirree. It was platinum all the way, baby. One for each of us. Could life get any better? No way.

We wasted zero time. We filled out the application online and sent it in. We were approved immediately. It was so easy!

Within six months our lives had changed dramatically. Gone was the tiny two-thousand-square-foot condo in the high-rise in downtown Minneapolis overlooking the Mississippi River. In its place was a steel and glass, two-story, five thousand square foot mansion in a gated community in Lakeview, a suburb south of Minneapolis.

We purchased his and her Teslas – red for Brit and platinum (of course) for me.

Then there were the new clothes to reflect our new status and new "accessories" (as Brit called them) for our new home: a cook, a maid, and a gardener. To top it all off we hired a butler for when we entertained, which was a lot. After all, if you can't flaunt it what's the point?

No doubt about it, life was good. We were young, both being twenty-eight. We had good jobs: I worked at a prestigious law firm that specialized in personal injury and was on the fast track to becoming a partner in a few years. Brit was a buyer for a chic department store. She had such an eye for fashion and what would be trendy not just three months in the future, but six months or even a year out, that she was paid a handsome salary. There was talk of her becoming part owner. So, yeah, life was good.

Having that platinum card made it even better. Why pay cash when you could charge? And charge we did.

And there the blog had ended. I'd read it, taking notes as I went along. The article I was writing was for the online magazine *Pandemonium*. The editor had asked me to come up with something on spending habits now in 2070 and compare them to how it was back in Jared's time, nearly fifty years ago.

It was an interesting assignment because it was on a subject I'd never really thought about. Nowadays, of course, we are all given a stipend to live on. There are no rich people anymore like there were back in Jared's time. Or poor people, either, for that matter but, that's a story for another time. Nowadays, of course, all of us live on the same income.

So, I wrote my article, being careful not to ruffle any feathers of the powers that be, and gave it to my editor. Then I went home to my wife Jackie.

"How'd it go?" she asked when I walked into our living space, a one-bedroom apartment in the Citi Center complex. She meant the story.

"Fine," I told her. Shakira already read it. She told me that she liked it. It'll run a few months from now in the August edition.

"That's good." Jackie mused my hair. Then she turned and stepped to the kitchen on the other side of the room. You hardly noticed her limp.

We sat down for a meal of what we called Muck, a mixture of soy paste and vitamins. It's pretty tasteless, but, you know, healthy. We ate in silence, not talking much. When we were done, I cleared the table and washed the dishes. I made us some herbal tea and joined Jackie at the table. I set the cups down with a soy cookie for each of us.

Jackie had been scanning her phone. She looked up when I set down the tea. "Thanks," she said and took a tiny sip. "You know, I've been thinking about that story you wrote."

"Oh, yeah? What?" I asked. I was looking through my phone. Nothing interesting was going on. I sighed. Watching programs on our phones was our only form of entertainment. In the last few years, the air outside had become too polluted for us to go for a walk. Plus, there was talk of another pandemic surfacing its ugly head, so going outside was risky. But we'd been forced to be inside most of our entire marriage and were used to it.

"I wonder what ever happened to Jared."

"Really?" I set down my phone and turned to her.

Jackie was thirty-five, the same age as me. We'd been married for fifteen years to take advantage of the extra

95

money we received for a "marriage stipend" to encourage monogamy. We had no children. Again, our choice. We were given extra money not to have kids. You know, overpopulation, lack of food. That kind of thing.

"Yeah, really," Jackie said, reaching across the table and taking my hand. "I'm curious."

I smiled. Jackie had always been curious. It was one of the things I liked about her. She was a research scientist, looking into ways to produce new food. The way we thought about it, and just about every other sane person you talked to, anything would be an improvement on Muck.

"Well, in that case, you're in for a surprise."

"Why?"

"I happen to know exactly what happened to him."

"Really?"

"Yeah." I took a sip of tea. "I interviewed him for the article."

"No kidding?"

"Yeah. I tracked him down."

Jackie sipped her tea. "Cool. How'd that go?"

"Good." I smiled. "He was quite talkative. I think he was lonely."

"Lonely?"

"Yeah. He's still here in Minnesota. Apparently, he never left. He's living up north in Duluth in a retirement home."

"Still alive. Hm," she mused. "Imagine that." She took a bite of her cookie. "How old is he?"

"Nearly eighty."

She chewed slowly, thinking, I'm sure, about her own situation. The doctors had given her less than two years to live. "What'd you talk about?"

"I read you that blog entry of his, right?"

"Yeah. It was interesting."

"Well, I asked him whatever happened to him and his wife."

"His wife, Brit?"

"Yeah."

"So what happened?"

"Guess," I said, joking with her. It was nice to chat like this. We didn't do it much anymore.

Jackie grinned, reached across the table, and slugged me in the arm. "Mark! Tell me."

"Okay, okay," I said, rubbing my arm and pretending she'd hurt me. She didn't. She didn't have much strength anymore. "I'll tell you."

I took another sip of tea and said, "It was a sad story, but I suppose one all too common back then. They bought lots of stuff, accumulated lots of possessions, and bought and bought and kept getting further and further into debt. Creditors started sending them notices which they ignored. Then their bank wouldn't honor their card."

"They each had one, right? Platinum?"

"Right." I sighed and sipped my tea. "They were able to get more cards and it just got out of hand. Their spending, I mean."

Jackie nodded. "Sounds like it." But I could see she was drifting and having a tough time focusing.

I hurried along. "So, to put it in a nutshell, they lost everything and had to go through what they called bankruptcy. Their credit was shot, and their reputations were ruined. It affected their work and their relationship. They lost their jobs and got divorced."

At the word "divorce" Jackie lifted her eyes to mine. "They got divorced?"

"Yeah. It was bad."

"So, what eventually happened?"

Jackie was getting tired, I could tell. Time to wrap it up.

"I guess Brit married some clothes buyer she met in New York City." I shrugged my shoulders. "Jared lost touch with her."

"What happened to him?"

I smiled. "Well, that's kind of interesting."

"How so?" Jackie leaned forward on the table. She'd perked up. It was good to see her so engaged.

"He became a teacher."

"Really?"

"Yeah. He told me that during the time they were going through bankruptcy, he'd gone into counseling and tried to turn his life around. He'd always been interested in science, so he became a science teacher."

Jackie nodded thoughtfully. "Cool. Good for him. Did he enjoy it?"

"Yes. Very much. He said that one of the first things he did was to learn about platinum."

Jackie laughed. "Seriously? That's ironic."

"Yeah. He found out about how rare it was. Still is, of course." She nodded pensively but didn't say anything. "He learned how it was used in catalytic convertors back then because they were impervious to corrosion." More nodding from Jackie. "How, because of its rarity, it was associated with prestige; like in the record industry back then how one-million albums sold was considered platinum and how it was considered prestigious to own a platinum credit card."

Jackie looked at me. "Even though it was made of plastic."

I nodded. "Exactly. Like the one that got him and his wife into so much trouble." I was silent for a moment. Then I said, "They used it in watches and things like that because it was so durable."

"But rare," Jackie said.

"Yeah. Rare."

We were both quiet then, thinking. Jackie's illness was rare, too. The doctors couldn't do anything for her. Our decision was to live our lives together the best way we knew how. There was talk of using valves made of platinum as part of her treatment. However, the doctors cautioned us that such thinking could be dangerous. "We're still many years away," one of them had said.

Jackie took my hand and squeezed it. "So, Jared ended up doing okay?"

"Yeah, he did. He taught science at the high school in Agate Bay up north of Duluth. He taught biology, chemistry, and physics. I guess he liked chemistry the best."

Jackie nodded. "That's good to hear."

Chemistry was what Jackie had been trained in when she was in school. She had an aptitude for it, hence her ability as a research scientist. But I could see she was getting tired. "Do you want to lie down?" I asked.

She smiled at me. "Sure. That'd be nice."

I folded out the couch and made our bed. We stretched out on top of the covers. I put my arm around her and she lay her head on my chest. After a few minutes, I could feel her breathing slow down. Outside, through our one window, the light faded from the sky. Next to me, I could feel Jackie's heart beating. The doctors had said that her heart valves were wearing out. Platinum valves were thought to be a possible solution, but they were still many years in the future from being made viable. Plus, how'd we pay for them? We didn't have all that much money, and, you know, credit cards like the one that got Jared and his wife into so much trouble years ago were things of the past.

As if she could read my mind, Jackie stirred and said, "You know, Mark, I was wondering."

It was nice to be talking. I'm glad she still wanted to. "About what, sweetheart?"

"Do you think it would be possible for me to meet Jared?"

"I suppose so. Why?"

"He sounds kind of intriguing," she said. "He went through a lot and made something of his life. It'd be interesting to talk to him." She was silent for a few moments and then said. "Plus, you know, he likes science. Like me."

I grinned and held her tight. "Sure," I said. "I'm sure he'd love to talk to you. As I understand it, he doesn't have many friends up there. I'll send him a message. We can set up a video chat. Would you like that?"

"Yeah, I would." Jackie nestled closer and kissed my cheek. "I'd like that a lot."

We fell asleep.

The next day I arranged for a video chat with Jared. It went well. Jackie and he got along great, so much so that they now chat on a weekly basis. The staff at the nursing home tell me they haven't seen him doing so well in years.

Jackie's doctors say the same thing.

Me? I'm holding out hope that they'll be able to find a cure for Jackie with those platinum valves. Do I find it ironic that Jared's problem with a platinum credit card led to him becoming part of the article I wrote that eventually resulted in him and Jackie becoming friends? Yes, I do. Do I care? Not at all. All I care about is Jackie's happiness. Whether or not platinum plays a role in our future, only time will tell. Until then, I'll keep my fingers crossed that it does. Like Jared told me once, "Those platinum cards ruined my life. And they were just plastic. It'd be wonderful if real platinum could be used to help Jackie."

He couldn't have said it any better.

———————————

Originally published in *Periodic Stories* Volume IV

Red Sky

Suki lay on the couch with her eyes closed listening to her daughter April and her sister's boy chattering away a mile a minute about some game they'd made up. The aroma of pancakes made her stomach growl. Kyla was humming a tune, her pretty voice a sharp contrast to the mood Suki was in. She rolled over and faced the back of the couch, not ready to face the world yet. God, just let me have a few more minutes of peace and quiet. But no.

"Mommy, Mommy." April tickled her arm. "Mommy, time to get up. Auntie says so."

Oh, God.

"Come on, Mommy."

"Go away, April. Just let Mommy sleep a little more."

Violent shaking. Kyla yelling, "No, damn it! No more lazing around, Suki. Time to get up. We've got a lot to do. Lots of cleanup after the riots last night." Kyla, thin of build but strong of purpose, pulled on her older sister's arm. "Let's go." With one final tug, Suki tumbled off the couch and onto the floor. Laughing, April fell on her mother and started wrestling with her. Evan joined in. Suki let them crawl all over, thinking, what a way to start the first day of the rest of my life.

She'd arrived late last night in the midst of the downtown riots, having finally had it with that idiot boyfriend of hers. His street name was Zeke, but his real name was Benjamin. He was the father of April, and an all-around bad seed. Why she'd put up with him all those years she'd never know. But he'd come home last night drunk and high and waving a gun talking nonsense about shooting some protesters and Suki didn't hesitate.

"I'm out of here, Zeke. Don't bother looking for me. I'm going to Seattle to live with my brother."

So, she lied. She doubted Zeke even remembered she had a sister, let alone one who lived in Minneapolis.

After she'd called her younger sister and told her the situation, Kyla had demanded that Suki and April come live with her.

"That guy's a piece of crap. I've never liked him," were some of the kinder words she spoke during their short conversation. "Get your ass down here."

"I'm on my way."

It was early evening and she'd taken the bus in from Circle Pines right into downtown and the middle of the protests over the killing of George Floyd. They were peaceful protests and Suki was all for them, even marched along with April as she made her way to Kyla's home, getting there around ten that night. They'd sat on the porch of the duplex Kyla rented and talked until midnight.

Around midnight the sky over downtown started turning red. Kyla flipped on the television and they watched in horror.

"Rioters are setting fires along Lake Street. The National Guard is being deployed. The governor is declaring a state of emergency."

"Good lord," Kyla said.

"What?"

"I was wondering why the sky was red. It's the glow from those fires." She got up. "You stay here with the kids." Evan and April were asleep in Evan's room. "I'm going to check it out." Kyla lived on Pleasant Avenue, one block off Lake Street and about six blocks from the fires.

"Be careful."

They hugged. "I will."

She was gone for an hour. Suki watched the news coverage and was fascinated by the contrast between the peaceful protesters, quietly walking down Lakestreet and the violent few rioters who were indiscriminately setting fires to buildings, cars, even trash cans. By the time her sister returned she was beside herself.

When she saw Kyla coming down the block she ran to meet her. "Are you okay?"

They hugged again. "Yeah, but it's a real mess over there."

"I know. I've been watching the news."

The rest of the night was spent sitting on the front porch and watching the red sky west of them and talking. Finally, Suki went in and crashed on the couch. Kyla had stayed on the porch. "We've got to do something," she told her sister when they said goodnight.

Suki yawned. "What?"

"I've got a plan. I'll tell you in the morning."

Now it was morning. The kids were fed and the two sisters were sitting on the porch. It was just after sunrise, and the city was starting to awaken.

"What's the plan, sister?" Suki asked, lighting up a cigarette. Kyla took it from her and crushed it out.

"No smoking around here," she pointed. "Especially with the kids."

"Fine." Suki watched a couple of people walk by. They were carrying buckets and a mop. "What's up with them?"

Kyla smiled. "You'll see. We're joining them."

"What! Are you nuts? For what?"

"We're going to clean up."

"Clean up what."

"From last night. From those damn rioters." She stood up and pulled her reluctant sister to her feet. "Come on. It'll be fun." She grinned. "You'll meet some good people. Better than that creep, Zeke, that's for sure."

They went inside and gathered some buckets and cleaning supplies, grabbed the kids, went back outside, and joined more of their neighbors heading for Lake Street to clean up after the riots. Suki met a guy named Ronny who worked in a bookstore and was in charge of a crew that was painting over graffiti.

By the time the two sisters and the kids returned home, their efforts and that of about one hundred others had helped clean most of the debris from the night before giving the smoke-damaged building a fresh look.

After dinner, they sat on the porch and watched the news and learned that the peaceful protests had moved to a different part of the city.

Suki turned to Kyla. "Thanks for today. And thanks for letting me and April stay with you."

"I just want you to take care of yourself. You and your daughter. You are both important to me."

"I really appreciate it." Then she changed the subject. "It was good working with you today. I enjoyed it."

Kyla reached over and squeezed her sister's arm. "I liked it, too."

They sat back and looked out onto the street. Off in the distance, they heard police and fire sirens. A little later, after the sun went down, the sky over downtown started to turn red. The two sisters looked at each other.

Kyla said, "Looks like we're going to have our work cut out for us tomorrow."

Suki watched, thinking how much better her life was now that she was away from Zeke. It was a good feeling. "Well, we should probably turn in. It's going to be a long day."

"Yeah, but probably a good day," Kyla said, standing and turning off the porch light.

"I'm looking forward to it," Suki said.

Kyla smiled and hugged her sister. "Me, too."

Senior Life Saving

Mr. Downy clapped his hands to get our attention. "Class! I'm going to have some help with the rescue portion of the test." He pointed. "My friend Alex is going to assist."

I watched as a muscle-bound man sauntered into the pool area. Lordy. Where Mr. Downy was tall and thin, Alex was short and squat like a bowling ball. He had buzz-cut hair and small piercing eyes that looked like those of a rapid guard dog. He cast those eyes over the group of us skinny seniors and smirked. "I can't wait."

Can't wait for what I had no idea, but I was soon to find out.

Mr. Downy had us count off, "One, two, one, two."

"Okay," he said. "The ones will rescue me. The twos," he pointed, "will rescue Alex."

Of course, I was a two. I looked at Alex. He looked at me and pointed a finger like a pistol. He pulled the trigger and mouthed, *Gotch ya, bro.*

Geez.

I come from a family of achievers. Mom was a well-respected author of children's books. Dad was a decorated pilot in the war and for a while was in the running to become an astronaut on the Gemini Mission until a car accident shattered not only his leg but his chances of going to space. Still, he became a long-time pilot for a major airline. My grandfather was the treasurer for a county in the southern part of the state, and my grandmother ran a successful dry goods store.

It was a distinguished group that I came from and, unfortunately, it was a group I was not destined to join.

You see, I was one of those people who from an early age was distinguished by not being anything special. In grade school I could draw and read and write but so could everyone else. My pictures were a step above stick figures and my reading and writing skills were squarely in the middle of the pack.

I remember my fifth-grade teacher telling my mom and dad during Parent/Teacher night, "Alan is a good student. He's solidly average."

Which was fine with me. It took the pressure off of having to live up to my family's lofty standards. Sort of. But in the back of my mind, I always wondered what it would it be like to accomplish something. To do something truly special.

Unexpectedly, a chance came when I was a senior in high school.

I had always liked to swim. There was a lake near where I grew up and I went down there as often as I could. There was always a lifeguard on duty. He or she would sit high up on a viewing stand, nose covered in white lotion, whistle hanging around their neck, tanned, and in charge. Boy, to a kid growing up, the lifeguard was something special. So, in the winter of my senior year when an after-school class was offered to become a lifeguard, I seized upon the opportunity. *Maybe I can amount to something*, I told myself. *Maybe I can finally accomplish something special.*

The class ran for eight weeks in February and March. It was taught by the swimming coach, Mr. Downy, a nice, soft-spoken man who was eminently likable. On the last day, we had to do a series of tests, culminating with saving our instructor. I felt I had a good chance to pass.

But then Alex showed up.

My group was five guys. We did rock paper scissors to see who went first. I lost.

Alex swam out to the middle of the pool, treaded water, and then motioned. "Come get me," he yelled.

I took a deep breath, dove in, and started swimming the breaststroke, keeping my eyes glued to him the entire time. He attacked me before I even got close. He lunged and wrapped his arms around me and held on tight. I had been trained to fight off just such an attack by forcing my hand up along the side of the person's face. That's what I did with Alex. I got my hand in there as we went underwater and pushed against his scratchy beaded chin with all my strength. I broke his grip and forced him back. I had been taught to swim away and rescue myself before attempting to rescue the victim again. Which I did.

I got myself ready and swam carefully toward him once more. But before he could attack, I dove and swam up to him underwater. I was able to get him turned and my arm around him into an over-the-shoulder carry. He fought hard but I held firm and eventually got him close to the side of the pool. He tried to turn on me one more time, but I wouldn't let him. Still holding him tight, I got an arm over the side of the pool. We were safe. I'd rescued Alex.

The rest of the class were standing there and they cheered.

Mr. Downy leaned down and said to me, "Good job Alan." To Alex, he said, "Let me talk to you for a minute."

I never thought I'd pass that final test. I thought for sure I'd screwed up the rescue. But I was wrong. Of the class of ten, only two kids made it and I was one of them. Mr. Downy gave me my certificate that spring and shook my hand.

"Good job, Alan," he said. "You did real good."

I was surprised. "Thank you," was all I could think of to say.

Later that day I showed Mom my certificate. She smiled. "Good job. I knew you could do it."

Dad said pretty much the same thing.

It felt good to set out to accomplish something and to

succeed. As I said, it hadn't happened growing up. It didn't happen afterward either. But that was okay. That one time? Well, that was good enough for me.

―――――――――

Originally published in *Pure Slush Lifetime Series – Achievement*

Silver

The Riverview Restaurant was on the first floor of an 1880s Victorian House that was the cornerstone of the town of Wild Rose, Wisconsin. The upper two floors had six quaint rooms designed for guests who wanted the peace and quiet of a time and era long past: no televisions, phones, or Wi-Fi Conversation and board games were strongly encouraged. So was reading.

The house was painted soft yellow, had coral trim, and sat on a hill across the street from the Mississippi River. For fifty years it had drawn dinner guests and couples on getaways from all over the upper Midwest. Its motto "Come for the food, stay for the beauty" was its hallmark catch phase.

It was a quiet Thursday in early October when Marge Lange, the longtime hostess at the restaurant, glanced up when a couple came in through the front door. The lady hung up her jacket while Marge smiled a distracted smile and went back to her dinner reservation list. *Wait a minute.* She looked again and unconsciously brought her hand to her throat. *Oh, my, God,* she thought to herself. *Those poor people.*

She'd seen a lot in her thirty-five years in the hospitality business, but never anything like what just walked in. He was nicely dressed in a dark brown suit which was fine. Most guests did dress up. But his body, his poor body, was twisted like a corkscrew. It was so bad that he used two canes to walk, if that's what you could call his shambling gait, tossing one leg and then the other forward. It was a marvel he didn't kick anything over. His face had ragged scars that his sparse beard couldn't hide. *Yuck.* Then she noticed his eyes. His eyes, though, were clear and lively, intelligent looking, almost gleaming, like he knew what she was thinking. She blinked and tried to put neutral thoughts into her mind. And failed.

Embarrassed by her response to the man, Marge quickly looked at his companion and immediately wished she hadn't. *Oh, lord*! She had to stop herself from gagging. Where he was obviously some sort of a cripple, the lady with him was just plain ugly. A rail-thin, skinny woman, a head taller than him, she was completely devoid of any shape or figure at all. She wore an obvious wig, cut short and the color of a sun-faded pumpkin, and a shimmering dark blue dress that hung limp on her featureless body. The definition of a broomstick came to mind, and Marge almost laughed out loud. But she didn't because her eyes were locked on a hideous purple birthmark that covered the entire left side of the woman's face extending down from her hairline and encompassing her nose and mouth all the way to her neck before disappearing beneath the collar of her dress.

Marge coughed into her fist to cover her discomfort. She had never seen people like them before in her life, let alone two of them together. *I wonder if they're from a circus freak show*? she thought to herself. But as far as she knew, most of the traveling circuses in the region had headed south after Labor Day which had been a month ago.

No matter how disturbing they looked, though, a paying customer was a paying customer. She mentally pinched herself to get focused and pasted on a smile. "Hi. Welcome to The Riverview. How may I help you?"

The man smiled a ghastly (in Marge's mind) smile and said, "Good evening. I believe you have reservations for my wife and I." He set his canes aside and took his companion's hand. "Dinner at 5:30 if I'm not mistaken," he added, glancing at an expensive-looking wristwatch. "I'm Bryce by the way, and this lovely lady is Abigail. I call her Abby."

Abby extended her hand. "Pleased to meet you."

Not one to enjoy touching people, let alone freaks, Marge made herself briefly shake hands. Nice to meet you, too." She checked her sheet. Yep. There they were. Mr. and Mrs. Mason. "I've got you right here," Marge added, nodding to Bryce and Abby. "Right this way. I've got you at our best table. It's overlooking the river, just like you requested."

"Great," Bryce said, picking up his canes and indicating with one of them. Lead the way."

Once at their table, Bryce held the chair for Abby. Then he sat down himself, leaning his canes against the wall. Both of them looked out the large window. "This is wonderful," Abby exclaimed to Marge. "Thank you."

Somewhat surprised by the woman's comment, Marge responded, "Well, that's quite all right. I'm glad you like it." She looked out the window. Not fifty yards away, a pair of bald eagles were soaring over the river. Trees on both the near and far shore were turning red, yellow, and orange with their fall colors, and the setting sun was casting long shadows across the water. Marge had to admit it really was quite lovely.

"Your waitperson will be with you shortly," she told them, turning to leave.

"Thank you," Bryce said, pulling his gaze away from the view of the river and smiling at her. "We'll be right here," he joked.

Marge nodded in acknowledgment, then left them to themselves, thinking *what a strange-looking but surprisingly nice couple.*

A minute later, their waitperson, who introduced himself as Ronny, came by and filled their water glasses, recited the evening specials, and gave them each a menu. He was a stocky man in his mid-twenties who had short-cropped hair, a trimmed beard, and an engaging smile. "I'll

111

be back shortly for your order," he said with a grin, not put off at all by their appearance. "Or would you rather take your time?"

"I'm in no hurry," Bryce said.

"Me neither," added Abby.

"Sounds good." Ronny looked around the empty dining room. Just give me a wave when you're ready, okay?"

"Will do. Bryce grinned.

As Ronny walked away, Abby took Bryce's gnarled hand. The car accident that had killed his parents when he was only three years old had crushed his back and left him badly crippled. His hands had been badly broken as well, but a lifetime of operations and therapy had brought them back so they were nearly one hundred percent useful. She looked him in the eyes. "This is just perfect. I've always wanted to take a getaway like this and you're making it happen."

Bryce smiled. "It's my pleasure, sweetheart. But we deserve it. It's our twenty-fifth anniversary, our silver anniversary, and we owe ourselves something special."

She leaned across the table and kissed him longingly on the lips, then sat back. "I actually am pretty hungry." She smiled coyly at him. "In more ways than one."

Bryce laughed and stroked her face, the left side where the birthmark was. "Me, too."

They ordered dinner and ate slowly, savoring every bite. Bryce had grilled salmon glazed with mustard sauce, and Abby opted for broiled rainbow trout garnished with a tasty dill sauce. While they ate, a few more guests entered the dining room. Marge sat them away from *The Freaks* as she thought of Bryce and Abby. They both noticed her reticence toward them, but it was no big deal. They were used to it. Besides, they were here for each other, not for other people.

"So," Bryce said, smiling and savoring his salmon. "Twenty-five years for us. Quite the ride. Here we are forty-seven years old."

Abby set down her fork, took a sip of water, dapped her lips with her napkin, and reached for his hand. "I've loved every minute of it."

"Me too." He paused. "Are you still okay not ever having any kids?"

"I'm fine. Especially now."

"Yeah." A cloud passed over his eyes, remembering the real reason they had come to Wisconsin that night. He put his hand in his suit jacket pocket to check on the bottle of pills. It was still there. "I hear you."

"There, there, dear. Don't worry about it."

Bryce squeezed Abby's hand. "I'll try not to." He knew she needed him to be strong for both of them. For what lay ahead.

"Do you remember when we first met?" she asked, changing the subject.

He brightened and grinned. "Back at the University of Minnesota. Yah, you bettcha," he said, joking to relieve the tension with a mock Norwegian accent that made her laugh. "I'll never forget it. How about you?"

"Absolutely. I was just starting as a librarian. It was my first job. And you came in…"

"Gimped in…" he laughed.

"Yeah, you gimped in, and I thought it'd take you forever to get to the desk."

"Slow and steady wins the race, I always say."

Abby grinned. "You've got that right."

Since he'd lost his parents at an early age, Bryce became interested in genealogy as he got older. He'd been brought up by his maternal grandparents and was able to use them and some of their records and memories to trace

113

his lineage back to Sheffield, England, in the 1660s where one of his ancestors had been a tinsmith. Armed with that new knowledge, he was hooked. Instead of going to college, he started doing independent research and then enrolled in an online course that gave him accreditation. Soon after, he started his own business, "Your Family Tree", and by the time he was twenty-two when he and Abby met, he'd been living alone for two years in a small apartment near the campus.

"How about you?" Bryce asked, taking a sip of water. "All things considered, have you been happy?"

She leaned over and brushed a lock of hair off his forehead. "Absolutely." She pointed to her face. "Most people just couldn't get beyond this. By the time I met you, I was resigned to being by myself."

"People can be real jerks and idiots."

"Well, whatever… You, though… You didn't see that, did you? You saw beyond it."

Bryce laughed. "I saw the real you!" He caressed her hand. "I still do."

Abby grinned. "See. You always make me smile."

And it was true. Growing up was hard on her. Kids in school were mean. She withdrew and by the time she was in seventh grade, she had been marked as an anti-social wallflower. In truth, though, by then she didn't mind. She'd discovered books at an early age, became an avid reader, and even had written some poetry. Not very good, she'd be quick to admit, but it was a start. Growing up, her books and her writing kept her busy and kept her from thinking too much about how lonely she was.

She went to college at the University of Minnesota and got a degree in library science and interned at the Wilson Library on campus. The head librarian liked her and offered her a job. A year later she met Bryce. Two years later she had her first book of poetry, *The Secret Smile*, published, and, over the years, nine more were to follow.

Yes, she would have to say, it had been a good life. All the way up until earlier in the year when she'd been diagnosed with cancer. Ovarian. Inoperable. Deadly.

Bryce took both of her hands in his. "Penny for your thoughts?"

She brought his hands to her lips and kissed them, not wanting to lose the wonderful feeling of this, their last meal together. She put on a bright smile. "I was just thinking about how nice some dessert would taste."

Bryce grinned and signaled for Ronny. "I thought you'd never ask."

They shared a delightful crème brûlée.' They didn't say much, just gazed affectionately at one another enjoying the moment and occasionally caressing each other's hand. Watching them, Marge said to Ronny, "God, why don't they just get a room?"

Ronny laughed. "What's your problem? They're nice people. Friendly. They told me she's a librarian and he does family history research. I like them."

Marge knew she was not being what folks called *politically correct*, but she couldn't help herself. The two freaky-looking people crawling all over each other made her uncomfortable. "I just don't like looking at them."

Ronny shook his head. "God, Marge. Get over yourself. They're people. They can't help how they look. They're living a good life. Cut them some slack."

Marge glanced at Abby's birthmark and quickly looked away. Nope. Hard to ignore. It was not going to work.

Ronny watched her and shook his head. "Well, you should get your act together." Then he left to check on the couple. Marge watched, wishing they'd just hurry up and leave.

Later, Bryce paid for their meal with a credit card and left a generous tip for Ronny. On their way out he made it a point to speak to Marge. "I just wanted to say thank you for such a lovely evening. We don't get out much and this getaway has been wonderful for us."

Abby smiled and added, "You've got a lovely restaurant. The food was delightful."

Ronny was standing next to Marge. He smiled and said, "It was great serving you." Then he nudged the hostess.

"Yes," Marge said, as if it pained her to do so. "Thank you for your business."

Ronny rolled his eyes, and stepped forward. "Here, I'll get Abby's jacket and the door for you."

"Thank you," Bryce said. He used his canes to follow, Abby keeping pace next to him. As they left the restaurant, he winked at Ronny and glanced over his shoulder. "Good luck with her."

"Thanks. "Ronnie grinned.

Outside in the parking lot, Abby walked slowly next to her husband. The air was crisp and cool, almost cold. Bryce's canes and his shuffling feet moving across the gravel were the only sounds. She looked up at the sky. High clouds were drifting past the moon and a slight breeze was blowing. A few bright stars were visible. There was the aroma of burning leaves in the air. An unexpected tear formed in the corner of her eye that she furiously wiped away. *This was no good.*

Abby stepped in front of Bryce, suddenly, causing him to pull up short.

"What's going on?"

She blurted out, "I just wanted you to know that I had a wonderful time tonight."

Bryce watched her, unsure of where she was coming from. The breeze ruffled the hair on her wig and she pulled her jacket tightly against her thin body. His love for her was as strong as it had ever been. Maybe stronger. All he could say in response was what was in his heart, "I did, too, my dear. It was unforgettable. Just like you are."

Abby stepped to him and wrapped her arms around him, holding him close. "I'm not sure I'm ready to go through with this."

"Our plan?"

"Yes."

Bryce expected her to let him go, but she didn't. Instead, she squeezed him tighter. He dropped his canes and held her. "Are you okay?"

"No." Tears suddenly began streaming down her cheeks. He could feel them wet against his face. "I'm not ready to give up. Not yet. I'm not ready to leave you."

Bryce's heart raced with joy. "Are you saying what I think you're saying?"

"Yes. Let's keep those pills for another time. We can use them whenever we want. Right?"

"Of course."

Bryce had been saving his pain medication for years. He knew he had enough for both him and Abby when the time came. It was supposed to have been tonight. He had the pills in his jacket pocket. Tonight, they were going to have a nice meal, drive to a spot high above town overlooking the Mississippi River, take the pills, and go to sleep. And that would be that. Since Abby had cancer and was going to die anyway, Bryce wanted to go with her. Now with her change of mind, they had a reprieve. He'd never been so happy. They would stay together. At least for a little while longer. At least for tonight.

Abby released Bryce from her embrace and looked him in the eyes. "Are you sure you're okay with that?"

"What a thing to ask!! Of course, I am."

To prove it, he hugged her tightly, and she hugged him in return. For a long, long time. Both secure in the knowledge that for now, for at least a little while longer, they would stay together, almost like this night would never end, and go on and on and on. And that was all they needed to know.

Later, back in the restaurant, the door opened. Marge looked up and gasped. "Bryce and Abigail!" she exclaimed. "Back so soon?"

Bryce smiled. "Yes we are. We had such a nice time this evening that we decided we wanted to book a room for the night. Do you have one available?"

Marge knew the place was empty and momentarily thought about lying and saying it was full. But then Ronny's words came back to her, *Get your act together.* She cleared her throat and said, "We do. We've got a nice room overlooking the river. How'd you like that one?"

Bryce and Abby spoke in unison, "We'd like it just fine." Then they both laughed.

Marge couldn't help it. She laughed with them.

_____

Originally published in *Periodic Stories* Volume Two

Simon Hope

My assistant, Jan Walkin, knocked once on the door jam, took three steps across the floor, and dropped a sheet of paper on my desk. "Here's the report, Simon." She shrugged her thin shoulders. "Such as it is."

I turned to her from staring out the second-floor window of the office I rented. "Such as it is?" I asked. "That's a helluva thing to say."

Jan puffed up to the full height of her four-foot-ten-inch frame and said, "It's a helluva business you've got going here, Simon." She pointed to the one book on the bookshelf behind my desk. "Pretending to be like your hero." It was my treasured collection of Sherlock Holmes.

"So… What's your point?" I asked.

"What's your favorite story?"

"The Lady In Red."

"Conan Doyle's first full-length novel. Right?"

"Exactly. I love that one."

"What else?"

"Well, there's The Hound of the Baskervilles."

"Another novel."

"Correct. And The Adventure of the Dancing Men and A Scandal in Bohemia and…"

"Right. Short Stories. And if I stood here all day I'm sure you'd name them all."

"Well…"

I turned red. She was right. I have loved Sherlock Holmes since I was twelve years old. Ever since my aunt had given me the *Complete Sherlock Holmes* shortly after I'd come to live with her after my parents had been killed in a car accident. My older brother and sister had died too. I had been in the same accident and was in bad shape physically and emotionally, but I eventually recovered.

119

Physically anyway. It's been a long time emotionally, twenty-five years, but who's counting? Ha, ha. Escaping with Sherlock has helped immensely.

"So what?" I said, somewhat defensively.

"I know you want to be a detective like him. I respect that."

"Your point being?"

She indicated the photos on the wall. Scotty, the Tennessee Walker, who I'd found in a stud farm in Iowa. Hector, the German Shepard guide dog I rescued from a breeding kennel north of Minneapolis in Chisago Country. Snowflake, a terminally ill boy's treasured kitten who had wandered off and been locked in a storage shed for a week. I'd found them all. It's what I did. I found lost pets.

"My point is that Sherlock used his smarts and intuition to solve crimes, find jewels, and stop wars from happening. You…" She pointed at my photos on the wall. In addition to the three I'd mentioned there were over a dozen more. "You just…" She slammed her hand on my desk making me jump. "Oh, I don't know. It just seems like you aren't trying hard enough." She shook her head. "Like you're just pretending to play detective rather than truly being one." She pointed to my framed photo of Jeremy Brett as Sherlock on the corner of my desk. "Mark my words, your hero Sherlock would just laugh his ass off."

With that scathing comment, she turned on her heel and left. *Oh, yeah*, I said to myself. *Well, we'll see about that!* Not the pithiest retort, I'll grant you, but hell, I didn't want to piss her off any more than she already was. Once we'd been lovers. Now? Now I was lucky she was still with me.

Her words were harsh, and, compared to Sherlock Holmes and his abilities, probably true. But I couldn't help it. I liked my job. I liked animals. My best friend for years was my aunt's big tabby cat named Rusty.

I looked around my office. I liked my Persian rug and the false fireplace. I liked my microscope on the rolltop desk in the corner and the hat rack with the black top hat I wore occasionally. So what if I tried to replicate Sherlock Holmes' living room? It worked for me.

Jan's concern was that there wasn't much money searching for lost pets and my time would be better spent at a "Real Job" like being a mailman or working for a big box store, two occupations I'd tried but found deeply unsatisfying. Nowadays my part-time gig as a voice actor in commercials helped cover expenses if work in the pet rescue world was slow. Producers loved my English accent. I was considered the go-to guy for Mrs. Compton's Magnificent Marmalade.

I sat back and glanced at the report Jan had left. I'd tracked down a poodle named Lulu who'd taken up with a bloodhound named Rex in southwest Minneapolis and all was well. I was contemplating what the resulting puppies would look like when Jan stepped into my office.

"Phone call," she said, pointing to the light blinking on my desk phone. We still had a landline. "A Mrs. Jorgenson. Something about a missing dog." She raised her eyebrows and mouthed, *Again*. But she smiled as she went back to her desk. I did too. Arguing with her made me realize how much I liked my job. And Jan. Not everyone was so fortunate.

I picked up the receiver. "Simon Hope here," I said. "How can I help?"

I listened, interjecting occasionally, taking notes all the while. When she was done speaking, I summarized our conversation: "So, your Pomeranian doggy Snuffy ran off last night and you're worried. You live west of Minneapolis near Lake Minnetonka. Is that correct?"

"Yes. I'm incredibly concerned. Coyotes have been sighted in our area."

I said soothingly. "Please don't worry, Mrs. Jorgenson. I'll be out there within the hour and start the search. I'm sure I can find Snuffy."

"Oh, thank you!"

I went to my coat rack and put on my tweet jacket and my Sherlock Holmes deerstalker cap. I was all set. I headed out the door. The game was afoot. Snuffy was loose and needed to be found before something horrible happened to her. I was just the man for it.

I adjusted my cap and waved to Jan as I went out the door. If she rolled her eyes, I didn't notice. I was already on the hunt.

———————————

Originally published in *Pure Slush Books Anthology*

Super Sensitive to Sound

"Alan, help me," Jeremy panicked, pleading with his eyes, beseeching. "I'm scared."

I reached for my lover and held him before turning to Janet, our hospice caregiver. "Could you please give us a moment."

She, like me, knew the end was near. She nodded and quietly left the room, the bedroom Jeremy and I had shared for over thirty years. Even though he couldn't hear me, I whispered in his ear, "I've got you, my love. You're not alone."

He squeezed me tightly, kissed my cheek, and then closed his eyes, body relaxing. I could barely feel his faint heartbeat, but it was there. He was still with me.

Jeremy used to be, in his words, "super sensitive to sound". When I first met him, he was wearing headphones and my immediate thought was that he was just some weirdo living in his own world, listening to baroque music or something. I was wrong.

"Here's your package," I said, handing him the large envelope, ready to run off to my next delivery. He removed the headphones and said, "What?"

I repeated myself, starting to get irritated. The courier service paid me to make deliveries, not waste my time trying to explain the obvious. "Your package?" I stated.

"Oh, yes, thank you. Thank you very much," he said, politely. "I really appreciate it." He smiled at me with bright white teeth. He had a thin build, close-cropped beard and hair, piercing blue eyes. Physically, I was attracted to him right away. "I've been waiting for this."

I was suddenly curious. "What is it?" It felt like a manuscript of some sort.

"It's a rough draft of a novel." He smiled shyly. "I'm an editor."

I was intrigued. I loved books and reading. I was still in college, working on my PhD in literature and writing my thesis. We got to talking (courier quota be damned) and immediately hit it off. Six months later I moved in and we've been together ever since, nearly thirty years.

Now this.

I must have held him for an hour. Janet stopped in often to check on us. "Just stay with him, Alan. He needs you." She didn't have to ask twice.

The room was peaceful and quiet, far different from the world Jeremy was accustomed to living in. He heard everything exponentially: the noises I took for granted drove him up the wall. He heard the refrigerator running at night even though it was in the kitchen and we were in bed upstairs. He heard normal sounds like traffic in the street or an airplane flying overhead ten times louder than normal people, and the noise gave him headaches. Bad ones. Nowadays he might have been called autistic. I don't know about that, but I've always felt he was unique and quirky and I loved him all the more for it.

He wore the headphones to dampen noise, and they worked well, but a few years ago we went on a picnic in the park near our home and I convinced him to take them off. "Just try it, Jeremy," I said. "Give yourself a break. Listen to the world the way it really is."

He cautiously removed them and listened. Birds were singing and children playing on a swing set were laughing. A boisterous pickup game of basketball was going on nearby. Even though I knew the noise was painful for him, I could tell he was entranced, and mesmerized. After a few moments, he grinned and spread his arms wide. "It all sounds beautiful."

He started wearing his headphones less and less after that. Even though he still got headaches, he was determined to live life to the fullest. "To listen to the sounds of life," was how he put it. By the time the tumor had riddled his brain, he'd ditched them completely and was learning to live with his painful headaches. He never complained. He was incredibly brave. Now the tumor had robbed him of the ability to hear anything. The irony was almost too much to bear.

I felt him stir in my arms. I sat up and looked. His eyes were open so I massaged his shoulders. "How are you doing?"

He smiled. Now completely deaf, I could tell he was reading my lips. "I can't hear you, but I'm doing all right. Hold me some more."

I did.

Maybe we both drifted, lost in old memories, but suddenly he was gripping me tight. "Alan. Alan!" he called out. He had tears in his eyes.

I held on. Tight. "I love you," I told him.

"What?" he asked, holding me close.

I yelled in his ear, "I. Love. You."

"I love you, too," he whispered.

We embraced with all the passion of our lifelong love for each other. In a little while his breathing slowed and his heartbeat faded. Then, with one final exhale, he passed on.

When I felt him slip away I screamed, "No!" Then, again, "No!"

Thankfully, Janet gave me a few minutes before she came in and together we took care of what needed to be taken care of.

An hour later she left me alone one last time and I sat on the bed with Jeremy. Outside, in spite of my sorrow, I could hear the laughter of children playing and the melodic songs of birds singing, sounds in the last few years Jeremy had been listening to and learning to appreciate for their own beauty.

Those sounds suddenly gave me an idea, one last joy we could share. I went to the window, opened it wide, and let the noisy world drift in, filling the room and overflowing. I went to the bed, sat down, and took Jeremy's hand, leaned in close, and whispered, "How about if we listen to those sounds of life one more time? Just like we used to?"

And together we did. They sounded beautiful.

Moshi

Before he died, Moshi and I became quite close. In fact, to be honest, I have to say that he was the best friend I ever had.

I met him when I took a break from my work as a biologist researching mermaids for the Woods Hole Institute out of Massachusetts. I'd been intrigued with those marvelous creatures as far back as I could remember and certainly throughout my career, participating in several research expeditions as well as writing the definitive paper, "Mermaids: Myths Debunked".

But the field had become severely overcrowded with hoards of scientists jumping onto the mermaid bandwagon and it all got to be a little too much. Don't get me wrong, I could understand the allure. After all, the study of mermaids was a very sexy subject not to mention a wonderful topic of conversation at any dinner party or crowded sports bar. But, geez, you'd think we'd discovered a space alien or something every time we captured a new and previously unidentified mermaid in one of our nets. Personally, the hype of it all got to be a little too much so ten years ago I took a step back to re-evaluate my life.

With re-charging my emotional batteries in mind, I decided to do something I'd wanted to do ever since I'd been a kid growing up on the south shore of Long Island; sail along the eastern seaboard from Miami to Nova Scotia. It was on that fateful trip that I met Moshi, as charming a merman as there ever was. In fact, it turned out he was the only one. I never found another merman and to this day no one else ever has either. Even Moshi figured he was the last of his kind. He told me once that he'd not seen another merman for over one hundred and fifty years so who was I to doubt him?

We met when I saved his life. I was making good time on a southwest wind sailing my thirty-two-foot boat The Wanderer along the coast of North Carolina. The two-foot-high swells were gently breaking and a deep blue sky foretold of a high-pressure system that would make for fantastic sailing for at least three days. Above me herring gulls circled and called, keeping me company and occasionally diving down to pick up a floating fish.

I was in good spirits wearing my Oakley wraparounds, faded cutoff jeans, and worn flip-flops, sporting what I called my Robinson Crusoe beard and shoulder-length hair held in place by my sun visor. I was scanning the horizon and keeping a lookout for those huge cargo ships that frequent the shipping lanes off the east coast when I caught a glint of something about one hundred yards off the starboard bow. It was shiny and reflected the sunlight. Metal of some sort?

Curious as to what it might be, I sailed over to check it out. As I approached, the mystery made itself clear. What I thought might have been a solitary floating aluminum can turned out to be worse. Much worse. It was part of an immense flotilla of plastic.

I was furious. For years I'd been fighting a battle for stricter measures regarding the disposal of plastic in landfills along the east coast. The brutal fact that the oceans were becoming the world's dumping ground for garbage was a cause near and dear to my heart. But my anger turned to horror when I saw something living was struggling in the toxic debris.

Thinking it might be a dolphin, I dropped the mainsail, fired up the auxiliary motor, and moved in for a closer look. When I realized the trapped creature was not a dolphin but a merman I almost fainted. I'd heard rumors that mermen existed but had always ignored them as only so much gossipy

128

baloney. I'd been wrong. Here one was right before my eyes entangled in a festering plastic mess, nearly choking to death on the yellow tie string of a garbage bag wrapped tightly around his throat.

As I was wondering what to do, he coughed politely and asked, "Um… can you please help me? I seem to be stuck."

Talk about an understatement. Not only was the garbage bag string nearly choking him, but countless other strands of plastic were also wrapped so tightly around his body that he could barely move. "I'll see what I can do," I said, not wanting him to drown and feeling an overwhelming desire to save him.

I spent the next ten minutes using my knife to cut away what seemed like half a ton of plastic. When he was free, he smiled and swam around my boat and even leaped out of the water a few times. I'd saved his life, and he was thrilled to be alive. It was the beginning of our friendship.

I should probably say that we didn't really "talk" in the strictest sense of the word. His language was impossible for me to understand let alone speak, but I have to say he was more than patient when he tried to help me learn; I just could never get the hang of it. Moshi, the name I gave him, was a version of Xmykkezm, his name in the language of mermen. Mermaids, too, for that matter. You can see why I gave up. Instead, we communicated telepathically, which seemed to come naturally between us and was much easier than learning Yylaczackim, the language of both mermaids and mermen. No wonder we never figured out how to communicate with our captured mermaids! Their language was beyond the skill of us humans to figure out, not to mention the fact that unlike Moshi and me, the mermaids had no desire to communicate with their captors. In a way, I suppose, I couldn't blame them.

But Moshi and I got along great from the very beginning. He started traveling with me as my summer vacation morphed into me living full-time on The Wanderer while I traveled up and down the East Coast. I quit my job at the institute and concentrated on writing articles about ocean pollution to make money. I hung out with Moshi, too, of course; we had a lot in common, our love for the sea being first and foremost.

And he saved my life. A few years after we met, I was anchored off the coast of northern Florida. It was a hot day, and I had decided to go for a swim to cool off, completely unaware there was a hammerhead shark in the vicinity until he swam close enough to try to nibble at my toes. It scared the crap out of me. Fortunately, Moshi was floating nearby, resting, and noticed what was going on. He immediately swam to my side and frightened the hammerhead away. As kind-natured as he was, he could be really aggressive if he needed to be.

After he saved my life, our relationship moved to a deeper level. I found that I enjoyed being with him more than I did with my friends, and took extra precautions to keep the two worlds separate. The thought of Moshi being "discovered" made me physically ill. Whoever did would turn the event into a media circus for sure; something I wasn't going to let happen. Not to my friend.

So I kept him to myself and we had some wonderful years together. I even cared for him in those last agonizing months before he passed away due to old age; he was two hundred and thirty-five years old according to my calculations. The fact that he'd been around since just after the Revolutionary War was pretty incredible to think about. When he finally did die, I buried him in a favorite spot off the coast of Maine near Boothbay Harbor, weighted down with rocks of course.

After his passing, I was going to write a scientific paper about Moshi. Lord knows I'd accumulated pages and pages of notes and observations throughout those years we were together. But in the end, I burned them in a bonfire on the coast near where I'd buried my friend. It seemed at the time like the right thing to do. It still does.

Nowadays I sail up and down the eastern seaboard, writing about ocean pollution and thinking of Moshi, wondering if there might be the possibility of another merman out there someplace. I doubt it, but even if there is who am I kidding? There could never be anyone like him ever again. At least not for me. He was one of a kind.

Originally published in *Journeys III* edited by Elaine Carnegie

Bismuth

I was in my room studying for a chemistry test and had my favorite CD on and *Welcome to the Jungle* was blasting through my headphones. Mom had to knock extra loud to get my attention.

I took my headphones off, got up, and turned off my boombox. I opened the door. "What's up, Mom?"

"Mrs. Callahan at the grocery store needs a sitter tonight. I thought you could use the money so..."

"Oh, no, Mom!! Not Mrs. Callahan. Those kids are horrors."

Mom smiled indulgently. "Oh, they aren't so bad. Just high-spirited."

The Callahan twins. Now, I was brought up in Christian Science and was taught to love thy neighbor as thyself, but let me tell you, those seven-year-old twin girls were monsters from Hell like you could never imagine. Oh, they could be sweet, that's for sure. Both blue-eyed and blond, they could be the epitome of politeness. But I knew it was just a game. Their true nature had to do with making my life difficult at every turn.

They lived nearly a mile away, but they were still able to find ways to torment me. They let the air out of the tires of my bike. They put gum in my baseball mitt. They stole the lace out of my shoes when my friend Tim and I were swimming at the town swimming pool. They even made up stories that I had a crush on Peggy Swanson, the most popular girl in high school.

Where they came up with that stuff, I'll never know. But they did.

So, why did I agree to take the job? Well, like Mom said. I needed the money. I really wanted to buy a new microscope and I had one all picked out. A nice one.

So, at seven o'clock that Saturday night, I knocked at the door of the Callahans. Mr. Callahan answered.

"Lee, my boy," he said, shaking my hand. "How the heck are you?"

Mom and Dad have been friends with Ben and Beverly Callahan ever since I can remember. And ever since I can remember, I've been "Lee, my boy" to Mr. Callahan.

"I'm fine, sir," I said, shaking his meaty hand. Mr. Callahan was a butcher and the grocery store he owned with his wife. His hands always reminded me of something he might have cut up earlier in the day.

"Girls!" he yelled. "Your sitter is here!"

I could feel the red blush rising up my neck. Sitter. Right. I knew for a fact that their normal "sitter" was Mrs. Fredrickson, a no-nonsense lady who I swear must have at one time been a prison guard at the maximum-security prison the next town over. She was a big, dark-skinned woman who took no guff from anyone. She was perfect for the girls. Too bad that night she was on the East Coast on her honeymoon. My mind reeled at what her poor husband must be going through.

Anyway, at the beckoning call from their father, the twins Alicia (Ally) and Ann (Annie) came bounding down the stairs. They had bandanas around their foreheads and were banishing plastic swords. They had on red and blue striped tee shirts, cut-off blue jeans, and pink tennis shoes. They each wore an eye patch.

"Ahoy, matey!" One of them (Ally?) said.

"Prepare to die!" the other one (Ann?) said.

Mr. Callahan laughed. "Girls, girls. Calm down. Let's let Mr. Brown get settled."

Mr. Brown? No. That wasn't going to fly. Mr. Brown was my dad. I stepped forward. "Hi, girls," I said. "You can call me Lee."

"Okay, Lee," Ally (we're going with Ally) said. Then she pulled out a squirt gun and squirted me with it. Right in the face. Then the two of them took off through the front door and ran outside.

I took off my glasses and dried them on my shirt tail.

Mr. Callahan just laughed. Mrs. Callahan floated into the room from somewhere smelling of wine and said, "Hi. Lee." Then she turned to her husband. "Shall we go, dear?"

And they left, driving off in their baby blue Eldorado Cadillac leaving me with the two pirates.

I'd seen them tear across the nicely manicured front lawn and around the corner. They must be in the backyard, I thought to myself. I decided to investigate.

"Hi, Mr. Brown!" Two voices came at me from up in the branches of a huge oak tree situated right in the middle of the yard. I looked up. The two girls with their pirate bandanas and eye patches were smiling at me. They were on a ten-foot by ten-foot platform nestled about twenty feet above me. Like a tree house without the sides. Cool, I thought to myself. "Come up and join us!" They called out.

So I did. I climbed up the side of the tree using wooden slates, which I found out later their handyman had put in for them along with building the treehouse. It was becoming apparent to me that the Callahans had a lot of money. He never put up the sides. The girls didn't want it. I guess they liked to look out on their world. They called it their "tree fort".

I climbed up and sat down.

"Here," Ally said. She handed me a red bandana. "Put this on."

So, I did.

"Here's your eye patch, matey," Annie said.

So, I put it on.

I have to admit that my initial trepidation with the girls

was quickly vanishing. I was an only child, so I didn't have a lot of experience being around kids. Ally and Annie didn't seem to be half bad.

"Want to play cards?" Ally asked.

"Sure!"

Annie took a deck out of her pocket and started shuffling. "We can play rummy, okay?"

"Sure!"

While Annie shuffled, Ally opened a wooden box and took out a bag of red licorice. "Want some?" she handed it to me. "It's strawberry."

"Sure!" I took a strand and held it in my hand. I really shouldn't, I thought to myself. Mom didn't allow candy in the house. Don't ask me why, she was just funny that way. But I'd also wondered about candy and stuff that most kids ate but I'd never had the chance to try. Now was my chance. It was great. "Can I have another one?" I asked. Ally happily handed me the bag.

Long story short, we ate the whole thing.

After playing rummy, the girls wanted to go to the park. It was just down the street and over a couple of blocks. The girls rode their bikes and I jogged along with them. I was actually having fun with them. They weren't the terrors I'd psyched myself up into believing. It was a beautiful Saturday night, the last week in May. Lilacs were in bloom and there was a scent of spring in the air. It was like living in a dream.

At the park the girls wanted to play on everything, so we did. I remember sliding a lot, using the swings and, especially, the merry-go-round. Around and around and around!

Finally, we took a break. Well, I did. I had to catch my breath. Those girls had a lot of energy! As I rested the girls ran up to me. "Mr. Brown! Can we have some ice cream?"

There was a vendor selling snacks and drinks.

"Sure," I said.

"They each grabbed a hand and pulled me along. "Come with!"

So, I did. I bought us all ice cream and fizzy drinks. I had an ice cream sandwich and a root beer float, two things I'd never had before.

It was about this time, my stomach started rumbling. The girls could hear it. They giggled. "Mr. Brown is hungry!"

Was I? Maybe I was.

Allie said, "Let's go home and order pizza!"

"Yeah!" Annie said.

It seemed like a good idea to me. I'd never had one before. This whole evening was turning into one big food experiment for me!

Back home we ordered sausage and pepperoni with cheese and mushroom. Mr. Callahan had left money so we ordered bread sticks and dipping sauce, too.

We ate it all up in the treehouse. I have to say, it tasted awfully good.

We also played rummy and it was about the time the sun was starting to go down that all of the food, the pizza, the breadsticks, the ice cream sandwich, the root beer, and the licorice started to hit. I'm not kidding you, the cramping was unlike anything I'd ever experienced before. I bent over. "Ow!" I moaned. "Ow, ow, ow!"

The girls giggled at first. "Are you joking with us, Mr. Brown?"

"No!" I said, writhing on the platform trying not to fall off. "My stomach is killing me!"

Ally looked at Annie. Then they both looked at me.

"Come with us," they said.

We climbed down and as soon as I hit the ground, the cramping became so bad, I thought my guts were going to spill out.

Ally looked at me. "Mr. Brown, you don't look so good."

Really? I wanted to say. But I could talk. I was afraid if I opened my mouth… Well, you know.

Annie grabbed my hand. "Come on. Let's go inside."

Ally said. "We've got just the thing for you." She grabbed my other hand and pulled me along. "Daddy uses it."

Then led me into their home, up a wide flight of stairs, and down a long hallway to their parents' bedroom. "Come on," Ally said, pulling on my arm. I was a little hesitant. "It's okay."

"Come on, Mr. Brown," Annie said. Letting go of my hand and pushing me toward the bathroom. "Hurry."

She must have surmised something bad was about to happen. I took her advice and let them pull and push me into the spacious bathroom of Mr. and Mrs. Callahan.

I quickly sat on the edge of the tub, put my head in my hands, and tried to stop the world from spinning. "Now what?" I mumbled. I thought that at any moment I was going projectile vomit everything I'd eaten in the three hours I'd been with the girls. It was not a pretty thought.

Ally went to the cupboard and opened it. While she did, I closed my eyes and tried to stop the world from spinning. It didn't work.

Annie rubbed my back. "It'll be okay, Mr. Brown."

Easy for you to say, I thought to myself. I felt like an earthquake was tearing my guts apart.

Ally poked me in the arm. "Here," she said. "This'll help."

I opened my eyes and looked. "What's this?"

She handed me a pink bottle. "It's what daddy calls his 'magic drink'."

I read the label. It was Pepto-Bismol. I'd heard of this stuff. I looked at Ally. Then Annie. "Your daddy uses this?"

The girls nodded.

"Yep," Ally said.

"A lot," Annie added.

"And it works?" I asked. I was holding the bottle, but it was slippery. Along with my forehead, my hands were sweating.

They both nodded some more.

"Try it," they said.

Now, like I said earlier. I'd been raised in the Christian Science church. We followed the teaching of Mary Baker Eddy. If you got sick, we prayed. If we were really sick, we prayed a lot. I'd never had any medicine in my life. Not even an aspirin. So when Ally offered me that pink bottle I have to admit that I had a moment's hesitation. A "should I or shouldn't I" kind of moment. But, let me tell you, it didn't take but a moment for me to put all thoughts of hell and the devil aside. I reached for that bottle with the speed of a cobra striking. And I took a drink right out of the bottle. Which the girls loved by the way.

"Thank you," I said, wiping my lips.

The girls were great. "You're welcome," they said.

Then they took me downstairs and we watched cartoons. I have to say, it was a pretty fun evening.

Later that night I looked up Pepto-Bismol. Bismuth is a metal that has been around since ancient times. The Incas used it as knives. It's considered one of the first ten metals discovered. It's nowadays used in the pharmaceutical industry. Its active ingredient is Bismuth subsalicylate, and is sold generically as pink bismuth and under the brand names Pepto-Bismol and BisBacter It's an antacid elixir medication used to treat temporary discomforts of the stomach and gastrointestinal tract, such as nausea, heartburn, indigestion, upset stomach, and diarrhea.

All I know is that it worked.

I became the Callahans' regular sitter after that. It was fun hanging out with the girls and I made some good money, enough to buy that new guitar. I almost chose a pink one, but no. I went with fire engine red, instead. Just like that strawberry licorice, we ate up in the tree fort.

_____

Originally published in *Periodic Stories* Volume IV

Crispy

Joel noticed, or felt, rather, a movement to his right. He moved his eyes in that direction and recognized Darnell, the nurse he liked the most, as he entered the room.

"How's it going today?" the big man asked, their little joke.

If Joel could have laughed, he would have. *How's it going, indeed? You try laying here in the burn unit after your wife torches the house with you in it, and then ask. "How's it going?" It's going like shit, that's how it's going.*

Darnell busied himself checking Joel's vital signs, talking all the time. "It's a real nice day out there today. Tomorrow's the Fourth of July and I'm taking my wife and kids to the fireworks. Of course, we have to stay in the car because of the Covid thing, but that's okay. It'll be good to be together."

Joel had heard all about Darnell and his family. And, truth be told, he was envious. His wife Sally and he had started drifting apart ten years into their twenty-five-year marriage. By the final year, he'd had a casual fling or two, or three, and Sally had taken to drinking more and more wine. What Joel didn't know was that Sally's depression had been slowly worsening over the years, especially after their only child, Allison, or Allie, as everyone called her, had left home. That had been five years ago, and Sally's mental health had only gone downhill from there. He'd been so blind to his wife's needs that he'd hadn't even noticed.

Sally had taken a load of sleeping pills six weeks ago, disconnected the gas line in the basement, and then gone to sleep.

Joel had already passed out from his nightly tumbler of Jack Daniels and hadn't a clue what was going on until he woke up in the burn unit at Hennepin County Medical, and they told him about the fire. And the explosion. And that Sally was dead.

According to tests like the Baux Score he shouldn't even be alive. Right. Lucky him.

Back in the present, Darnell had quit talking about the upcoming holiday and was chatting aimlessly. Joel had almost drifted off to sleep when something the nurse said caught his attention. He focused his eyes on Darnell and frantically blinked.

"Oh, hi there," Darnell said, his eyes crinkling into a smile above his protective mask. "So you're still with us?" Joel blinked again. He appreciated the nurses' attempt at humor; it helped him feel less like a victim and a little more human, if being burnt to a crisp and looking like a grilled bratwurst could be described as human. He couldn't talk. A morphine drip kept the pain at bay, but just barely. In Joel's opinion, it was not a life worth living. He could check out anytime, as far as he was concerned, and damn the hospital for keeping him alive.

He stared at Darnell, trying to communicate. *What were you saying? Something about a visitor?*

"Yeah, I hear you've got a visitor coming today. He looked at the clock on the wall. "Should be here any minute."

Who, God damn it! The few friends and co-workers that had bothered to visit in the first weeks after the fire had dwindled off to nothing. Who could it be?

"Well, since you asked," Darnell said, eyes crinkling at his joke. "I'll tell you. It's your daughter. Allie, I think they told me her name was."

Oh, my, God. Allie! He hadn't seen her since a rather stilted luncheon they'd had a couple of years ago. He remembered it well. She'd screamed at him for how poorly he'd treated Sally over all those years. It ended badly when she stormed out, saying, "I never want to see you again."

Now she was coming to see him! He was beside himself with joy.

But he was also tired and drifted off. When he awoke, he sensed a presence in the room. He shifted his eyes to the right toward the door and looked. *Oh, my god. There she was! Allie.*

She moved until she was standing beside the bed. "Hello, Daddy," she said.

He wanted to say *"Hi"* back to her. He wanted to hold her and tell her he loved her and missed her. He wanted to reminisce with her about going for walks when she was a little girl and he, her daddy, told her about the natural world and nature and the life cycle of butterflies. He wanted to talk with her about how much fun they'd had planting vegetables in the little garden plot they'd dug together. He just wanted to be with her.

"I've missed you so much," she said.

I've missed you, too, honey. I've missed not talking to you about your job at the coffee shop and your friends, and who your current boyfriend is, and what your plans are for the future.

"I brought a book to read to you, Daddy. Would you like that?"

Would I? Of course, I would. What's the title? Oh, I don't care. Please, sit with me and read.

"Okay. I've brought one of your favorites."

She started reading and at the first words, Joel thought his heart would burst with joy. *Oh, thank you, sweetheart. I love this one. Thank you so much.*

An hour later, Allie stopped reading. Her father's eyes were closed. *He's probably sleeping*, she thought. Darnell came in as she was preparing to leave.

"How's he doing?" she asked.

"Oh, you know. Has his good days, but mostly they're bad. He's in lots of pain. On a heavy dose of morphine."

A thick silence developed between them. Both of them knew the big question that lay unspoken. Finally, Allie asked, "So what are his chances. Will he make it?"

Darnell was a compassionate man. But he was also a nurse and realistic. "The chances? Based on his age and the amount of skin burned, not good, I'm afraid." He watched tears form in Allie's eyes and hurried to add, "You being here will help, though. In fact, it might help a lot."

"You think?"

"I do."

"Thank you," she said. "Thanks for caring."

"And remember," Darnell added looking at Joel with fondness and then back to Allie, "miracles can occur."

"You're very kind."

"You coming back tomorrow?"

"Yes. Definitely. My father and I were close, especially when I was young. We just drifted apart. I want to spend as much time with him now as I can."

"That's good," Darnell said. "That's really good."

"See you tomorrow."

"I'll walk you out."

Joel watched the two of them leave and blinked back a tear. He'd heard every word they'd said, and the only thing he remembered, the only words of any significance to him were the ones Allie had spoken at the end, "I want to spend as much time with him as I can."

He might be dying and that couldn't be helped. But for now, there was tomorrow. And as far as Joel was concerned, tomorrow couldn't come soon enough.

Storytime

Some might call it "serendipity", others might term it "pure hell". Whatever the case, the situation was not a pleasant one.

The job I'd worked at my entire life had been demanding but I was okay with that. It was the price I paid for earning the money I did to have the things I wanted: a beautiful house in a gated community, a lovely trophy wife, Erin, and all the money I could ever want. The plan was to travel and see the world, something I looked forward to doing.

Then, BAM! A massive stroke hit me. It was a week after a lavish retirement party where I officially resigned from my job as CEO at *Upper Mississippi Solutions,* the three-hundred-employee consulting firm I'd built from the ground up. Instead of traveling with Erin, I ended up in the hospital. After three months of around-the-clock care, I was sent home for further recovery under the watchful eyes of healthcare professionals. I was told it was going to be a long process. It has been. I'll tell you this: retirement is not like I expected it was going to be.

Erin is certainly drifting away. Sure, she stops in for a few minutes in the morning, and then in the afternoon, but that's about it. I really can't blame her. I'm certainly not the man I used to be.

My home healthcare workers are attentive but that's not surprising. I pay them well. However, they are mainly just so many faces. There's Sidney who is remarkable because of all the women he's the only guy in the bunch. Then there's Ramona who wears beads in her dreadlocks. But all the others? Unremarkable.

If this all sounds depressing, let me tell you, it certainly could be, "could" being the operative word here. But it's not. Why? Because of my grandson, Simon.

In fact, he's just arrived! I smile to myself as he comes into my room.

"Grandpa!" he grins and raises his hand in greeting. Even though it's nearly impossible for me to move or talk, I make the effort.

"Simon," I mumble. It sounds like I have marbles in my mouth. For a former CEO, it's extremely embarrassing.

My seventeen-year-old grandson doesn't mind. He hurries to my bedside. "Good to see you again Grandpa." He hugs me. I can't do much of anything except lie there and imagine hugging him back. Which I do. An imaginary hug. It's better than nothing and the feeling it gives me is wonderful.

"How are you doing, Grandpa?"

Simon asks the same rhetorical question he always asks, and I give him the same response I always give. I flick my right index finger. It's the only thing I can do to acknowledge him.

"Gool," he says. "That's really good."

How he knows what that flick of the finger means I have no idea. But then, there is a lot I'm learning about as I lie in bed mulling over my life – a life that I now believe was wasted in the pursuit of so many materialistic goals.

Simon pulls up a chair. "I brought our book," he says, sitting down and making himself comfortable. He holds up *Walden* by Thoreau. "Would you like me to read to you?"

I'll tell you right off the bat that for my entire life I was never a reader. Too busy, right? Too busy wasting my life is what I'd now say if I could. Thank goodness for Simon. And my son, too. Jack. I definitely need to mention him. Somehow, Jack turned out okay. In fact, really good. Even though I didn't talk to him much after I moved out, divorced his mother, and got on with my life with Erin, Jack had made it a point to try to stay in touch.

145

"You're my dad," he'd always say. "I'll always love you."

Thank goodness for my son and his persistence.

And thank goodness for his son Simon. My unselfish and loving grandson.

"Grandpa," Simon says, opening the book, "do you want me to read or are you too tired?"

Too tired? Man, all I do is lie here twenty-four-seven trying to come to grips with my wasted life. I cherish these times with Simon.

I flick my finger. "Read," I mumble. "Please."

Simon smiles. "Okay."

He starts reading. His voice is soft and soothing. Why has it taken a stroke for me to realize the importance of him? And of my son, too, for that matter?

Both good questions.

I must have dozed off. In the instant when my eyes shoot open, I wonder if Simon is still there. Thankfully, he is, right next to my bed.

"Hi Grandpa," he says, patting my arm.

I try to smile but can't. Damn! I flick my finger instead. "I love you," I mumble.

"I love you, too," Simon says. He kisses my forehead, then glances at his watch and frowns. "I've got to go." He looks at me. "My job." He teaches swimming to five-year-olds at the YMCA. "See you tomorrow?" For the last three months, ever since I've been home, he's come over every day to see me. He's got more compassion in his little finger than I ever had. I could learn a lot from him. I'm trying to. A tear leaks out of my eye and runs down my cheek. Simon reaches over and wipes it away. He looks at his watch and then says, "How about if I stay a few more minutes? Would you like that?"

I don't want him to be late for work. As if reading my

mind, he says, "Don't worry. I won't be late for my job." He grabs the book. "I'll just read another page."

I flick my finger and try to smile. Simon smiles at me and starts reading. I close my eyes and listen, thinking to myself that I'm the luckiest man in the world. Because I am.

———————

Originally published in *Pure Slush Retirement Anthology*

Barium

On my younger brother's seventieth birthday, I grilled him a steak, filled a pipe with Minnesota Nice, and asked him, "If you could do anything you wanted, Owen, what would it be?"

I gave him the pipe and he lit it with a beat-up zippo. Then he took a hit, held it in, exhaled, and said, "Easy, Frankie. I'd go back to the Stillwater Canyon and climb that rock again."

I took the steak off the grill, cut it in half, and put it on his plate along with some roasted red potatoes and steamed green beans from my garden. "Here you go," I told him. "Happy birthday."

"He grinned, took another hit from the pipe, set it aside, and dug in. "Thanks. For a big brother, you're okay."

I fixed my own plate and sat down next to him. We were on a little brick patio in his backyard. He'd lived in the well-kept bungalow for the last forty years, most of that time with his wife, but the last two years by himself ever since she'd passed away from ovarian cancer.

"So, getting back to my question, you really want to go back there?"

"Yeah, I do." He paused, then burped. He slammed his knife and fork down, brought his napkin to his mouth, and burped again. "Damn it all anyway." He pushed his plate away. "I hate this." He lit the pipe again.

My brother had gotten the test results eight weeks earlier. They'd shot some barium into him and the findings were everything we hoped they wouldn't be: he had cancer of the large intestine. He was given less than a year to live.

I looked at him. Once tall and handsome, over the past months he'd shrunk about an inch and lost maybe fifty pounds. His face was sunken, exposing cheekbones I'd never seen before, and his skin, once perpetually tanned from being outside working in his yard, had turned a sickly, sallow grey. But not all was bad. He still had the same green eyes that had sparkled looking out at his students as a high school music teacher, or when he'd told me about a marathon he was training for. And he still had his sense of humor, telling me the same lame jokes that always made me laugh.

And he still had his spirit of adventure.

"Yeah," he said, burping into his napkin again. "Yeah, I'd love to go back to Montana."

"Okay," I said, stepping over to shake his hand, our long-time brotherly way of sealing any deal we agreed upon. "Let's do it."

Three days later, just after sunrise, I stood at the front door and kissed my wife goodbye. We lived twenty miles west of my brother in the little town of Orchard Lake, and I wanted to get a move on, but Faith took my arm and stopped me.

"You sure this is a good idea?" she asked, giving me one of her patented critical looks, a look I was used to receiving. "He's not well, you know."

Talk about an understatement. "Yeah, I know," I said. "He's dying. But I think this trip is important to him. He seemed, I don't know, more enthusiastic about things the more we talked about it."

"What things?"

"It's hard to explain," I said. "He just seems a little happier. Less depressed. I don't know." I looked her in the eyes, searching but coming up with nothing more concrete than, "It's complicated."

She sighed a long-suffering sigh and said, with barely a hint of irony, "I hear you. Look, I know you've got your mind made up. I understand." She hugged me. "Your brother and you have something special. You're not just related by blood, but you're also friends. I get it. Just be careful."

I smiled. We'd been married nearly fifty years. It was nice to know she still cared. I hugged her back. "I love you."

"Love you, too."

The drive to Owen's took half an hour. I was dressed for comfort, planning to put some long hours in behind the wheel, and was wearing tan cargo pants, a black tee shirt, and a Nature Conservancy baseball cap. Along with tennis shoes for driving.

I parked in the driveway and went around the back and into the kitchen. My brother was hunched over, cradling a cup of tea.

"Good morning!" I greeted him. "Ready to go?"

He was wearing cut-off jeans and a faded Minnesota Wild tee shirt. He had on sandals and a floppy straw hat. Along with his beard and hat, he kind of looked like Claude Monet.

He looked up from his cup with a forlorn expression. "I've had better days."

"Want me to help you pack?"

"Yeah, I'd appreciate it."

So, I did. It was obvious he'd been having what he called "a slow morning" which meant he was too tired to do anything other than climb out of bed, drag himself to the kitchen, make a cup of tea, and sit at the table.

But he could direct me. He was always good at that, and today was no exception. "I want another pair of cut-off jeans and a pair of long jeans, some tee-shirts, toiletries, my meds, stuff like that."

"Okay," I said, hurrying to toss everything he listed in a backpack. It took about ten minutes. When I was done, I asked, "Okay, I think that's it. You ready?"

He stood up and immediately sat down. "Oh, man…"

I could see he was having trouble with his balance. It was one of the side effects of the medication he was taking.

"You alright?" I reached for him.

Stoically, he steeled himself and took my hand. I helped him to his feet. "Yeah." He grimaced. "Thanks."

I rinsed his teacup. "You good to go for this?" I asked, setting it on the drying rack and starting to get a twinge of worry. Maybe we should have talked to his doctor about our plan. But if we had, and she had told us that it wasn't a good idea, then what? Sit around in Owen's backyard, grilling steaks he couldn't eat and waiting for him to die? We both agreed, without saying it out loud, that anything was better than that.

He smiled, picked up his pipe and tin can full of weed, added it to the backpack, and said, "Don't worry about me Frankie. I'm good to go."

In the back of my mind, I could see Faith shaking her head with a bemused smile on her face. She was probably right; this wasn't my best idea, not by far. But it was a good idea, nevertheless. Of that, I was sure. A point reinforced when Owen smiled, clapped me on the shoulder, and said, "Come on, Bro. Let's get this show on the road." He started for the door. "Grab my walker, will you? I'm going to try it with just my cane for a while."

"All right," I told him, picking up his backpack and his walker and following close behind. "Montana, here we come."

We were headed for the Woodbine campground. It was in the southern part of the state in the Beartooth mountain range, home of Grizzly Peak, at over ten thousand feet the highest mountain in Montana. We drove my twelve-year-old Ford Fiesta, a small car, but it got good gas mileage.

151

Once on Interstate 94 heading west, Owen pushed the seat back, took a sip of bottled water, and smiled. "Oh, man, Frankie, this is the life."

I smiled at him. "We should be there tomorrow. Next day at the latest."

"I'm in no rush, Bro. Take your time."

I kept the speedometer at seventy miles an hour and we watched the rural Minnesota landscape roll by all the way to Fargo, where the land flattened out and wheat replaced Minnesota's corn and soybean fields.

The journey was uneventful other than Owen's running commentary describing everything he saw: cows, horses, old barns, farmhouses, hawks, farmers in their fields riding tractors. It was fun to see him engaged and excited. It made me realize that getting away from his home and the constant reminder of not only his wife being gone but of his imminent death, was a good thing. It reinforced how glad I was we had made the trip.

We stopped the first night in Mandan, North Dakota, in the middle of the state on the Missouri River. We got up early the next morning, and, after a quick breakfast at the motel, we were on the road once again. After a few hours, we crossed the border into eastern Montana, Owen commenting on the land changing from flat, cultivated fields to rolling, undulating range land. The further we traveled west, we encountered less water, fewer trees, more sage, and scrub brush. We'd crest a rise, and the land would stretch out before us to the far horizon, the sky above as blue as could be. No wonder Montana was referred to as Big Sky Country.

The second night we stopped in Columbus, in the southcentral part of the state, sixty miles west of Billings.

I pulled off the interstate and drove into town. We found a room for the night at a place called the Creekside Motel which seemed like a logical name to me since there was a tiny stream meandering nearby. Next door was a café called the Buckin' Bronco with a weathered sign of a cowboy riding guess what? Yep, a bucking bronco.

After checking in, we left the car at the motel and walked next door to the café for dinner, taking our time. Owen was using his cane instead of his walker, so the going was slow.

"Damn," he muttered under his breath. Then louder. "Damn this cancer to hell!"

"Can I help?"

"No. Damn it. Thanks anyway," he said, stopping to catch his breath. He pointed west with his cane. "It's beautiful, though, isn't it?"

Less than fifty miles away the Beartooth Mountains, our final destination, rose toward the setting sun. On the tallest peaks, snow glistened bright white against the indigo sky. Closer to us, the heat of the day had unleased the scent of sage which mixed with the hot, dry wind creating an earthy, wild fragrance found only in the West. When we'd come here with our parents during the summer back in 1959, we stopped at a local dry-goods store and bought snap button cowboy shirts and cowboy hats. When I reminded Owen of the experience of wearing our cowboy hats everywhere we went the rest of that trip he said, "People must have thought we were nuts." He chuckled. "It was sure fun, though."

"It was." I laughed. "No one would ever have guessed we were tourists."

Owen laughed with me. It was good to see. He seemed more content right now than I'd seen him since we got the cancer prognosis two months ago. I was happy for him.

We entered the café and made ourselves comfortable at a table for two. It had a red checked tablecloth and was adorned only with a white salt and a black pepper shaker. The aroma of french fries and seared beef filled the air. Old-

153

time country music blared from the sound system, and when our ears picked up Patsy Cline's *I Fall To Pieces*, Owen and I looked at each other and smiled. We both liked old-time music, country or rock and roll, it didn't matter.

We perused the small menu and both of us agreed on dinner, ordering fresh trout with new potatoes and asparagus. Service was quick and efficient and we wolfed down our meal with hardly a word being spoken. I hadn't realized how hungry I was. It was one of the best meals I'd had in a long time.

Owen loved it, too. "I can't believe how tasty that trout was," he said, smacking his lips when he was finished and sitting back with a satisfied sigh.

He looked around the dining area. It was about half full and Mary Robbins was singing *El Paso* in the background. "I could get used to this."

It was good to see him happy. And eating. The colon cancer wasn't doing his appetite any favors and all day yesterday on the drive from Minneapolis to Mandan he'd complained of stomach pains. Today the pain hadn't been as bad. He'd munched on saltines and sipped bottled water across western North Dakota and eastern Montana and seemed to be doing lots better. Seeing him have a nice meal made me feel good for my brother.

I signaled for the bill, but he refused to let me pay and took the slip from the waitress when she arrived. He smiled at her. "Thank you."

She smiled back. "You're welcome."

"Nice place here. Great food."

She grinned. "It's been in my family for three generations. I'll tell my dad what you said. He's the boss."

What the heck? I thought to myself. Are they flirting with each other? Whatever the case, I could see that Owen was relaxing even more and beginning to have some fun.

After he paid the bill and left a nice tip, we got up to

leave. "I've got an idea," I said. "I know we've been in the car a lot, but how about if we go take a little drive around town? Check out the sights?"

"Sure," he said, "that'd be good.

We slowly made our way to the door, the cane tip-tapping on the linoleum floor. "Damn thing," he muttered. Then he smiled. "Hell, it's better than that walker, though, right? I'm glad we left it in the car." He'd been using the walker for the past few months but didn't like it, commenting time and time again that it made him feel too old.

"Take your time," I told him, as we stepped aside to avoid a young couple coming through the front door hand in hand. "No rush."

As we made our way out the door, Owen turned and waved at the waitress. She smiled and waved back. He grinned and winked at me. "She's really pretty."

The thought that ran through my mind was, *geez, cool your jets you old geezer. She's half your age*. But to him, I said, "Cool you bootheels, cowboy. Let's go for a drive."

He laughed. "I'm just joking around. Having fun."

He was, and it was good to see.

It only took a few minutes to check out Columbus. It had a population of about two thousand people and was located on the Yellowstone River, a fast-flowing, picturesque watercourse that ran through the outskirts of town. We found a city park on the south bank where we stopped and watched the sunset while eating ice cream cones from a nearby Dairy Queen.

"This is the life," Owen said, admiring the setting sun turning the foothills to the east a brilliant orange. He turned to me. "I'm glad we did this. Thank you."

"I'm glad we came," I told him. And I was. We watched some mergansers float down the river, and I noticed Owen grinning at the antics of the little family of ducks. Just to see him smile, made the whole trip worth it.

And we'd only just begun. The next day we left our little motel and had breakfast at Buckin' Bronco. "Best oatmeal, I've ever eaten," Owen exclaimed, to the waitress. He didn't seem to mind that it wasn't the lady from last night. He just grinned at her and left another nice tip.

Then we set off for our destination. It took nearly three hours, following a twisting two-lane highway from Columbus, through the small towns of Fishtail and Absorkee, all the while moving deeper into the mountains and the Stillwater River valley.

Owen's commentary mentioned the Yellowstone River and cottonwood trees lining its banks while the foothills of the Rocky's rose behind them; more sage; a few homes and ranches; more land and wide-open spaces. And always, the Beartooth Mountains rose in front of us, getting closer and closer the further we drove until finally, it seemed we could reach out and touch them.

Eventually, the highway turned from pavement to gravel and led us through the middle of a five-mile-long valley transected by the Stillwater River which flowed clean and clear on our left. On either side of it, the land rose gently up rocky slopes dotted here and there with pine trees and aspen clumps all the way to the very top of the majestic mountains.

"Look at that.," Owen said.

I slowed down and glanced out my window as Owen pointed to a big bird soaring high on the thermals above the valley. "I'll bet it's a golden eagle," I guessed.

My brother and I had been lifelong birdwatchers. "I think you're right," he said, staring at the big raptor while I went back to focusing on driving. "How cool is that?"

"It's very cool," I said, grinning.

The Stillwater River was less than a quarter of a mile to our left. The sky was blue and cloudless. The sun was hot and the air smelled sweet with the scent of sage. The wheels of the car crunched over the gravel, kicking up a plume of dust as we made our way further into the valley. Neither of us felt the need to speak, our wide smiles said it all: this was an incredible adventure.

On our right, the land rose sharply with the snow-covered peaks so close it seemed like we could hike to their summit in a matter of minutes, but that wasn't going to happen because they were nearly two miles high. It'd take days to get there. Instead, we just enjoyed their beauty from where we were.

Ahead of us, the gravel road forked. To the left, it crossed a bridge and continued to the campground. We followed the fork to the right and after about half a mile entered a pine forest with a space carved out for parking. It was the end of the road. It was also the trailhead for a hiking trail that followed the river into the mountains and eventually ended in Cooke City, Wyoming, thirty-three miles away.

I parked and we got out. Owen leaned against the car and took a deep breath. The scent of pine released by the blazing sun filled the air. "Man, this smells just like I remember," he said, exhaling and breathing deeply again. "Nothing better."

I agreed. "It's a good day for a hike," I said.

The ground was soft sand mixed with pine needles, and we sat down and put on our hiking boots. Then I reached into the backseat and took out a small day backpack with a few bottles of water and some granola bars.

In the background was the faint sound of the river's rushing rapids echoing off the walls of the canyon. It was hidden by the trees and about a hundred yards from us. Owen used his cane and started walking towards it but faltered when he stumbled on a hidden rock.

"Damn it."

I hurried to his side. "Here, hold on to my arm." Reluctantly, he did.

"I hate that I'm getting to be like this," he murmured.

157

"Don't worry about it. At least we're here," I said, stating the obvious and trying to cheer him up. I pointed to a well-used wooden picnic table. "Let's sit over there and get our bearings."

We made our way to it and sat down. I set the daypack on top and opened up a bottled water and handed it to him. He drank thirstily. There was not a whisper of a breeze; the air was calm and hot, but the pine trees provided some much-appreciated shade. Nearby a couple of red squirrels were chasing each other, and a Whiskey Jack, a western blue jay, was scolding them. I couldn't imagine a more delightful or calming scene.

I glanced at Owen and was happy to see that he was enthralled, looking around and taking it all in. I took out a bottle of water for myself, opened it, and had a sip. I felt myself relaxing. The long drive and the miles began melting away and were replaced by the peace and serenity of the mountains.

Owen turned to me. "Remember coming here with Mom and Dad?"

"Yeah, I remember like it was yesterday. You were nine and I was eleven. We stayed two days." I pointed behind us in the direction of the campground. "Dad wanted to try to fly fish. Mom was writing her poetry and was happy to let us explore." I smiled at him. "It was great."

"We found that rock we climbed. Remember?"

"Of course, I do."

The Stillwater River began its life high in the mountains and was fed by snow melt. On the river's journey through the valley, it passed through a mile-long, steep-sided canyon defined by granite walls and huge boulders. As young boys, we were captivated by the rushing rapids and decided to explore the canyon.

Owen grinned. "I don't know why I ever let you talk me into climbing it."

"Ah, the power of being a big brother," I chided him.

"Yeah. I would have followed you anywhere."

I laughed. "Not my best idea, I'll tell you that."

"Not by a long shot, Bro."

That day, while exploring the canyon, we found a huge boulder on the edge of the river resting against the side of the canyon wall. It gently sloped upward, curving out of sight as it reached the top, thirty feet above the rushing water. "Let's climb it," I had suggested. Owen was all for it.

"I didn't think it'd be all that tricky," I said, taking another sip of water. "There were enough handholds, so climbing wasn't too bad. Plus, I could use the side of the canyon to maintain my balance. It was pretty easy."

"Yeah. I followed right behind like an obedient brother," Owen said. "Or a Billy Goat," he added, laughing.

We had made it to the top of the rock and enjoyed the view up and down the canyon. The river pounded through the narrow gorge and the water cascaded over the huge boulders filling the air with a cooling mist. The rapids had been so loud, that we could barely hear ourselves speak, so we didn't talk and just enjoyed the sights.

After about fifteen minutes I had yelled in Owen's ear. "We should get back to the campsite. Mom and Dad might start to get worried."

We'd been gone most of the afternoon.

"Okay," Owen had said, agreeably.

But going down hadn't been as easy as going up.

"I'll never forget that look on your face," Owen said, opening a granola bar. "You were scared. First time I'd ever seen it."

"I know. It freaked me out."

These days, I'll be the first to admit that I lost my courage when it came to climbing down from the top of that rock. Back then, though, for an overly confident eleven-year-old,

159

it was hard to admit. But I was scared. Really scared. The way the boulder curved, I was afraid if I tried to go down, I'd lose my footing and slip and go crashing into the rocks thirty feet below, breaking who knew how many bones on the way down. I literally froze. "Let's wait," I told Owen.

"Why?" he asked.

I didn't have the heart to tell him I had lost my nerve, so I lied. "Let me catch my breath," I said, even though we'd been there long enough for me to have already caught it many times over.

Ever the amiable brother, he said, "Okay."

"I remember putting my trust in you completely," Owen said, arms folded on the picnic table, munching on his granola bar.

I grinned sheepishly. "Yeah, I know." I took a sip of water. "That only made it worse."

Finally, I talked myself into attempting the climb because the reality was that I had no other choice. I had to get myself down, and I had to get my brother down. So, I turned on my stomach and used my hands to push myself backward. Inch by careful inch, I started a slow slide downward, pulled by gravity. The overriding fear was not knowing if I could grab a handhold as I slipped backward. But I reasoned that if I'd been able to grab something on the way up, I'd be able to on the way down.

Luckily, I did.

After sliding backward for what seemed like twenty feet but was probably only one foot or two at the most, I found a handhold, a small crack in the rock. I held on for a couple of minutes to catch my breath.

From above me Owen, called, "How's it going?"

I looked up but couldn't see him beyond the slope of the rock. "Great!" I yelled, again lying through my teeth. But I didn't want him to get scared, so I tried to sound confident. "Almost at the bottom," I called back to him. Which was another lie. I wasn't even close.

I tried to ignore the pounding of my heart in my chest and steeled my courage. Then, I let myself slip, my fingernails scraping along the rough surface, frantically searching for a crack or a bump on the rock, anything I could hold on to.

I lucked out again. After dropping down another foot or two, I found a handhold. I'd never been so happy in my life. It was then the thought came to me, *Hey, this might work.*

And, it did. By slipping and sliding backward, a little at a time, I was able to work myself all the way down to the bottom of the huge rock. Sweating, scratched up, and shaking with adrenalin and exertion, I finally stood on solid ground. The river was right next to me. I squatted down and cupped my hands, washed my face and drank deeply. Water never tasted so good.

"Then I had to come down," Owen said, taking a sip of water from his bottle.

"Yeah, I remember it taking a long time to talk you down."

"You climbed back up and helped."

"That's right, I did." I looked at him and grinned. If there ever was a time when the unbreakable bond between us was forged, it was that day.

I knew that I had to help Owen get down. He was shorter than me and not as strong, so I climbed most of the way up and called out, "Come on. Get on your stomach like I did. Start sliding and I'll catch you."

I didn't blame him for being hesitant, but finally, he did it. He slid down to me and I grabbed his foot. Then, I slid backward holding his foot, grabbing for handholds, and together we worked our way to the bottom.

Sitting across from me at the picnic table, Owen grinned. "I remember it like it was yesterday, Bro. We got down, looked back up at that rock and both of us just laughed. I think you said, 'Well, that was a piece of cake,' or something like that."

"I was scared out of my mind. But I knew if something happened to you on my watch, Mom would have killed me."

Owen burst out laughing. "You've got that right."

I laughed with him, happy beyond words we'd made the drive to get here.

You know what? We never did get to the rock like we'd planned. Instead, we sat at the picnic table the rest of the day and talked and reminisced and had a wonderful time. Toward sunset, Owen said, "Say, Frankie, I've got a favor to ask."

"Sure, what's up?"

"Could we come back here again sometime? I'd like that."

"Sure, I told him. Anytime."

The unspoken reality of the situation with Owen's cancer was not even mentioned. What good would it have done? We had now. We had this moment in time. We had each other. That's all that mattered.

"That's good, Frankie. That's really good."

We shook on it, making a pact and sealing the deal.

When the sun started setting toward the mountains, I helped him to the car and we sat for a moment with the windows down, listening to the sounds of the forest all around us. In the background, the Stillwater River thundered through the canyon on its way to the Yellowstone River and then out of Montana for good. The air was sweet and the late afternoon light was soft and magical. I couldn't think of a better place for us to be.

"Should we go?" I asked.

"Sure," Owen said, sticking his head out the window and breathing deeply. "But take your time, okay?"

"Okay," I told him.

We drove to Columbus and got there long after sundown. Like Owen had asked, I'd taken my time.

We've been home a month, and, so far, his health is pretty good. We're spending a lot of time together. Owen can even eat a little steak when I grill it for him.

I'm glad we made our pact to come back to Montana again. Even with the odds being against Owen surviving much longer, if there's one thing we'd both learned on our trip to the Stillwater River Valley, it was that if we were able to climb that rock all those years ago and get safely back down, anything was possible. There's no doubt in my mind.

Or Owen's. As he put it recently, "Hell, I'll bet we can even beat this damn cancer."

I like that he said "we".

"No kidding," I told him. "Piece of cake."

And we shook on it.

Originally published in *Periodic Stories* Volume Two

The Magic Wand

Roxy set her purse in the back room and got ready to face the raucous crowd at Yesterday's Gone. She checked her look in the mirror and liked what she saw. She'd dyed her pixy haircut black for Halloween and was wearing black jeans and a black pullover, a gift from her friend. She smiled, reading the lettering on the front. Witches Rule. Monte was a warlock, so he thought it'd be just the thing for her to wear, it being All Hallows' Eve and all. He especially thought it was perfect since he'd given it to her to help cast a spell on that jerk Big Ed who'd been hassling her for the last month.

Even though the bar was packed with people dressed up in costumes and ready to party she'd seen him on the way in. He was trouble with a capital "T". Well, she was ready for him now. She checked her purse to see if the magic wand Monte had given her was still there. It was. To her, it looked like a twig, like something out of Harry Potter, but Monte insisted on calling it a magic wand because that's what it was.

"It came from up on the north shore of Lake Superior," he'd told her earlier that day. "It's made from diamond willow, and it's got a lot of mojo going for it."

So if Monte wanted to call it a magic wand, great. The important thing was that he had taught her how to use it, how to cast a spell, so now she was all set if that big jerk wanted to hassle her. In fact, she felt better than she had in the month since he'd first shown up and started giving her a hard time.

Well, now I'm ready, she thought to herself. *Bring it on.*

Big Ed surveyed the crowd with interest, wondering how many people envied his good looks and his awesome build. Probably a lot. Man, he loved Yesterday's Gone. As far as neighborhood bars went it would rate right up at the top of his book. If he kept a book, that is, which he didn't. But the drinks were cheap and more importantly, they were big, and that's what mattered. The sound system pumped out classic rock with Zeppelin and ZZ Top heavy in the rotation, plus, you could take an occasional hit in the bathroom, and no one minded. So, yeah, what was not to like?

The waitresses weren't bad either. Especially the cute little chick with the pixy haircut. Roxy. Man, what he wouldn't give... Well, she was all right, one of the main reasons he kept talking his buddies into coming back. Tonight, especially. Halloween. He'd dressed up as a professional wrestler in a form-fitting, light blue tank top and a pair of tight, purple shorts. He had the build for it – muscles on top of muscles from working out and a gut that wasn't so bad as long as he remembered to suck it in. It was going to be a good night. As long the beers and the shots of Jack were flowing. Speaking of... She spied Roxy. Time for more drinks.

"Hey there, darling," he yelled, snapping his fingers. "How about another round for your boy over here?" He'd been spending the evening trying to chat her up but she was so busy she wasn't able to spend any time with him. Like now. She just hurried over, dropped off their drinks, and left quickly before he could give her a hug and a little kiss. Man, what he wouldn't give...

Finally, around eleven he'd had enough. She had just dropped off another round when he motioned to her. "Aw, Roxy, come here little girl. Come and sit on Big Ed's lap and let's cuddle a bit."

She scowled at him. "I've told you before. Back off. I've got work to do. Leave me alone."

Big Ed was having none of it. "Come on, girly girl. Just one little kiss for your favorite customer."

165

He grabbed for her, but she slapped his hand away and dodged off to the side. He was able to get a hold of her arm for a moment, but she pulled away. "Stop it! God, you make me sick. Just leave me the hell alone."

He grinned. He could tell she was just flirting with him. Just like every other girl. They all did. He loved it.

"Aw, sweetheart…" he was saying but stopped and watched as she ran off to the back room. Now where's going? Maybe to freshen up a bit for him. He smiled. Good. He took a sip of whiskey and was turning to his buddies when he noticed her coming back. He brightened and a smile formed on his face as she quickly made her way to his table. Changed her mind, I guess, is what he was thinking.

He stood up to greet her, wobbling and weaving to gain his balance as he opened his arms. "Come back for a hug from Big Ed?"

He never got the chance. "Not on your life," Roxy said, stopping in front of him.

He wasn't used to being rejected by any woman, especially a tiny waitress like this one. He started to get angry. "Quit fooling around and come here. Now."

"Never!" Roxy yelled and pulled her magic wand out of her back pocket.

Big Ed was startled for a moment. "What's this, little girl? A toothpick for me. A toothpick for your daddy? He started to reach out but stopped when Roxy began waving the wand slowly, weaving it hypnotically back and forth, back and forth, in front of his eyes. He stopped and stood still, watching. What was going on?

Roxy took a deep breath and let it out watching as Big Ed's eyes turned glassy. Then she began chanting in a soft, sing-songy kind of way, "Hut two three four. Hut two three four. Time for Big Ed to start matching around the floor."

"What the hell…" he started to say but then stopped. As she kept her wand weaving back and forth, back and forth, Roxy watched as a perplexed look came over Big Ed's face. Then his feet start moving, shuffling forward and backward, forward and backward. He tried to stop them but couldn't. Then out of nowhere, words started coming out of his mouth, spilling forth like water from a spigot. He put his hand up and tried to stop them but couldn't. Quietly at first, the words forced their way out from between his fingers. "Hut two three four. Hut two three four." And then louder, "HUT TWO THREE FOUR! HUT TWO THREE FOUR!"

Roxy could barely contain her laughter. It was working! She spoke up, loud and clear, so the entire bar could hear. "START MARCHING!" she commanded. Big Ed stared at her, pleading, but she had no sympathy and gave him a devilish look in return. "NOW!"

So he did. He started marching around the bar in time to his chant, "HUT TWO THREE FOUR! HUT TWO THREE FOUR!" Bumping into patrons and tables and chairs, stumbling and falling on occasion, only to arise and begin marching again, chanting, "HUT TWO THREE FOUR! HUT TWO THREE FOUR!"

Roxy stood back and watched, her eyes wide with wonder. She was ecstatic. Thank goodness for Monte. He'd said, "Let's teach that jerk a lesson, Let's make him pay." He'd given her the wand, told her about it coming from a special place on the north shore and taught her the chant. All of this, however, only after she'd held the wand, and, as Monte had said, bonded with it. She'd felt it's heat emanate into hand and fingers, finally feeling it's power flowing into her entire body, filling her with not only with warmth, but a measure of confidence she'd never felt before. It was a good feeling, kind of like curling up under a warm comforter on a cold night.

Now she watched as that jerk Big Ed marched around the bar in time to "HUT TWO THREE FOUR! HUT TWO THREE FOUR!" while the place erupted with laughter and cat-calls from not only the customers, but Big Ed's friends as well. It was apparent to Roxy: The magic wand had worked.

Later that night on her way home from work she stopped to see Monte and thank him.

"How'd it go?" he asked pouring her a cup of coffee. They were sitting in the small living room of the apartment he lived in.

"Fabulous." Roxy smiled and told him all about all about it; the hut two three fours, and the marching and how everyone laughed at Big Ed. When she was finished, she took a sip from her mug and turned serious. "I have a question, though."

"What's that?" Monte asked. He was in a really good mood. He was happy things had gone well for his friend. Guys like Big Ed needed to be put in their place and he was glad to have played a small part in helping out. But it was really all Roxy's doing. The wand had uncovered something deep inside of her that she didn't know she had – the power of magic. From now on she didn't have to take crap from anyone anymore.

"Toward the end the boss came out and told the jerk and his friend to leave and never come back. On his way out the creep called me a witch. I just grinned and tipped my wand at him and didn't bother telling him the spell would wear off in another hour." She laughed. "Let him think he's going to marching around saying 'Hut two three four' for the rest of his life." Her smiled faded, though, as she took Monte's hand and asked, "But, I'm not really a witch, am I? Just because I could chant the words you told me and make him do weird stuff, that doesn't automatically make me a witch, right?"

168

Monte was quiet, thinking how to answer. "Well, look what happened tonight. What do you think? Do you think you're a witch?"

Roxy thought for a moment, forehead furled. Finally, she said, "No. I doubt it. I'm just a girl who was sick of getting pushed around and you helped me. You and that magic twig, I mean, wand," she corrected herself and smiled. Then she took the wand out of her purse and handed it to him. "Here. I guess you'll want this back."

Monte held up his hands. "No. No way. I want you to have it. You'll never know when you might need it again."

Roxy looked skeptical. Then she grinned. "You sure?"

"I am. In fact, from now on we'll call it your magic twig. It's all yours. You keep your magic twig handy and you'll never be pushed around again. I guarantee it."

"All right!" she said, enthusiastically. Then she paused, thinking, and added, "But will you give me more lessons? You know, teach me how to use it to do more magic stuff?"

Monte was glad Roxy wanted to learn more. Deep down he knew the truth – she really was a witch at heart, she just didn't know it yet. She was going to make a great one.

"Absolutely. If you want to learn I'll be happy to teach you."

Roxy smiled and sipped her coffee. She felt the best she'd felt in a long time and if it had to do with the twig and it's magic, so be it. "Great," she said. "When should we get started?"

He set his mug down, stood up, and took her hand. "How about now?"

———————————

Originally published by *Spillwords*

The Manure Spreader

I watched my cousin with awe along with a little bit of envy.

"Man, you've sure got a way with that shovel."

Stevie grinned and waved the stump on his right shoulder. "Yeah. When you're born with this bad boy, you learn to make the most of things."

I bent towards my task. We were cleaning out my uncle's horse barn, shoveling the manure into the spreader we'd towed into the center between the stalls. Getting the spreader there had itself been an adventure.

Stevie had led me into the shed where they kept an ancient, faded orange, Allis-Chalmer's tractor. "Cool," I said when I saw it.

My cousin grinned at me. "You want to try it?"

Me? Drive a tractor? I was ten years old and only a few days earlier had arrived on my aunt and uncle's farm. I'd been sent there by my mom from our home in the city where I'd been spending the summer at loose ends learning how to become a juvenile delinquent. In short, going nowhere fast. "You serious?"

"I'm serious, cousin." He punched me in the arm with what I could only surmise was his way of showing me we were buddies. "Absolutely. Go for it." When he saw my hesitancy, he added, "It's okay. I'll teach you."

"Okay!"

And he did. He showed me how to get the tractor started by turning the key and pushing a button. He showed me how to put it in gear, back it out of the shed, hook it to the spreader and drive it to the barn where I parked it between the stalls. We each had one side to do, five stalls each, and at our age, Stevie was ten like me, everything was a competition, mostly friendly. In this race, Stevie was kicking my ass.

Eventually, I stopped and wiped my brow. I was exhausted. "Okay, okay, okay," I said, setting my three-pronged pitchfork against the side of the second stall from the end. "I give up."

Stevie was a stall ahead of me. "Just a second," he said, grinning over his shoulder. "I'm almost done."

"Funny," I said, collapsing onto a bale of hay. "Real funny."

Steve whistled as he worked. He used a small, bladed shovel and wielded it with his left arm like a magician with a wand. I hadn't seen him in two years and in that time, he'd grown taller than me by four inches and out-weighed me by easily thirty pounds. All of it muscle.

"It's all in the wrist," he said, finishing up and sitting next to me. "And the arm, too," he added, flexing it. "That helps a lot." He winked at me.

I used to hate him. He used to be a squirrelly little kid who played with his sister's dolls. He liked to read. And he didn't like any of the video games I liked to play. He was just plain weird.

But I hadn't seen him in two years, and I guess in that time he'd changed. I know I sure had.

And not for the best.

Earlier that year my dad left home. Mom was having a rough go of it, and I reacted by doing the only thing I knew how to do that didn't require any skill – be a jerk. I began fighting with my younger brother and younger sister all the time. Davey, my best friend, and I started smoking cigarettes and I began sneaking out at night, running around with Davey, his older brother Frank and Frank's friend Walt. The night we spray painted a smiley face a water tower and got caught was the night Mom said, "That's it, Joe. I've had it with you. I'm sending you to your aunt and uncle's farm. Maybe they can do something with you."

171

"So what?" I yelled. "See if I care!" I added, secretly caring a lot.

I stomped off to my room and slammed the door. Then I burst into tears. Damn. Already I missed her.

Five days later I was shoveling manure from the horse stalls and hanging out with Stevie. I was learning that he was a good guy. Lots better than I was, that was for sure. I was already sorry for being such a jerk back home.

After we'd taken a break, Stevie said, "Let get this stuff spread."

"How do we do that?"

"Come on. I'll show you." He clasped me on the shoulder. "It's fun."

It was. Remember, I was ten, but on a farm, everyone was given a lot of responsibility and spreading the manure was Stevie's job. Now it was mine, too.

I got in the driver's seat and started the engine. Steve stood behind me, resting his hands on my shoulders. I drove us through the doors on the far side of the barn and out to one of the fallow fields where we stopped, letting the tractor idle. Stevie reached back and pulled a lever. He tapped me on the shoulder and pointed to the spreader.

"When we start driving, that spool with those spikes on it spins, catches the manure and flings it out the back."

"Far out."

He grinned. "Yeah, it is. Let's go."

I shifted into gear and we set to work, spreading that manure. I'll tell you, for a ten-year-old, born and raised in the city, being outside on sunny day, driving up and down a farm field in the country with my cousin by my side whistling some obscure rock and roll song, all the while I'm pretending like I know what I was doing, well, it was a pretty good way to go.

I stayed there all summer. We spread manure every week and it was always fun.

I cleaned up my act, too, when I went home and was lots nicer to my mom and brother and sister.

And next summer, when they invited me back, I couldn't say "yes" fast enough.

_____

Originally published in *Pure Slush Lifetime Series – Working*

The Paddlefish

The first time I heard the story was in the early 80s when we were sitting on the back of the houseboat where he lived after he came back from Vietnam. It was in a tiny marina on the Mississippi River just downriver from Wabasha, Minnesota. I was eight years old at the time. Uncle John was writing in his journal and sipping on his ever-present tumbler of Jack Daniels. Mom had dropped me off for the weekend.

"Have a good time," she'd said. Then she winked, lit a Marlboro, and drove off in a cloud of dust to be with her boyfriend.

Uncle John and I had been spending a weekend a month together for as long as I could remember. I loved being with him, and I'm pretty sure he felt the same way.

He looked up as I walked onto the deck. "Hi Sport," he said. "How they hanging?"

I laughed. I liked that my uncle didn't pull a lot of punches around me. However, I did turn red at the comment before answering, "Fine. I guess."

"Good." He patted a deck chair next to him. "Come on. Sit and keep me company."

Uncle John was a fishing guide. After he'd returned from Vietnam in the early 70s, he told people he was looking forward to spending time on The River as we called the Mississippi and that's what he did. He used his savings to buy the houseboat we were now on and spent his time guiding fishermen up and down The River. They fished for largemouth bass mostly, but sometimes bigger fish, like walleyes, northerns, and even the occasional muskie. He was a well-respected guide because he was quiet and competent and knew the ways of the river well.

He pointed to a cooler next to us. "There's a coke in there for you." He grinned. "I know you like it."

"Thanks!"

I took out an ice-cold can, popped the top, and took a long drink. It was late afternoon in August. The temperature was nearly 95 degrees. Even though we were shaded by the tall cottonwood trees on the shoreline, the coke tasted great.

Uncle John sipped his whiskey, made a few notes in this journal, and closed it. He turned to me. "Hot enough for you?"

I took another drink. "Yeah." I wasn't much of a talker.

He nodded and we looked out over the water. We were in a wide part of the river with the other side about half a mile away. Like on our side, the far shore was lined with tall cottonwood trees. Gulls flew back and forth, and eagles' nests were visible in the crowns of some of the trees. Upriver a few hundred yards was the quaint town of Wabasha with a population of around 3,000 people. In front of us, we watched pleasure boats cruising up and down sharing the river with a smattering of fishing boats. I counted two heavily laden barges, one going upstream, one going down.

Uncle John looked at me. "I love it here," he said. "It's so peaceful."

I grinned. "Me, too."

He'd given me a book earlier in the summer called *Life on the Mississip*pi and I was enjoying reading it. It was about Mark Twain (pen name for Samuel Clemens) and growing up on the Mississippi and working on a steamboat. I was fascinated by the history of back then on the river in the 1870s, and I loved being on the houseboat with Uncle John.

He turned to me and asked, "Did I ever tell you about me and the paddlefish?"

I was all ears. "No. Why? What happened?"

He grinned. "I caught one once."

"Really?" Paddlefish along with sturgeon and channel catfish were considered the big three when it came to monster fish in the Mississippi.

"Yeah. I was about your age. My friend Eddie and I were fishing the shoreline a few miles south of here. We were in an old wooden boat and just drifting along using the oars to keep us straight."

"What bait were you using?"

"Balled up dough and corn tied in a sack of cheesecloth."

"Going for catfish?"

"Yep. Big ones."

Channel catfish hid in the muddy banks of the river. They could get big, four feet long, and weigh up to forty pounds.

"Cool!"

"Yeah. We fished for about an hour before we got our first bite." He looked at me. "It was huge."

"Wow!"

"Yeah. It was so big, it started pulling the boat into the main channel of the river."

My eyes went wide. "No kidding!"

"I kid you not. It pulled us downstream and then switched and pulled us upstream."

"That's incredible!"

"Yeah. We fought it for an hour."

"What happened?"

Uncle John sighed. "We lost it. It broke the line."

"No!"

"Yeah. It got caught on a snag or something."

"Oh, geez, that's too bad."

"But we did get a look at it. It was a paddlefish. We saw the paddle. It was a huge sucker. Maybe six feet long. Had to weigh a hundred pounds."

"Oh, man, that's so cool!"

176

Uncle John grinned and took a sip of his whiskey. "It truly was."

How could a young boy not love the Mississippi after a story like that? And I did. I grew up to work for the Department of Natural Resources and was eventually assigned my dream job of patrolling the Mississippi between Wabash and south to Lock and Dam Number Three. It's been a great life.

I've read *Life on the Mississippi* more times than I can count. And I still visit with Uncle John. At eighty he's as spry as ever. He still lives on his houseboat and even does a little guiding. These days I've got stories to tell him, and we talk a lot back and forth. But none of my stories are as good as the paddlefish that got away. Not even close.

—————————

Originally published on *CaféLit*

The Parachute Jump

To this day my brother Will still shakes his head and says that he can't believe my friend Davey and I threw him off a cliff. "My god, Ronnie, what the hell were you thinking?" Or something to that effect is what he generally says whenever the occasion comes up. Which is a lot, believe me, because it's a pretty good story.

We'd been playing in the backyard of a home that was being built across the street, and the landscapers had dumped all the extra dirt and sand over the edge of a precipice that dropped down to Nine Mile Creek fifty feet below. Telling him how much fun it'd be, Davey and talked five-year-old Willy into letting us lift him by the hands and feet and swing him out over the edge. It was easy to do, after all, because he was six years younger than us, not to mention that he weighed only about thirty pounds, so light I'm surprised he didn't float away.

Well, he certainly didn't float. He dropped like a sack of cement after I counted out, "One. Two. Three," and then said to Davey, "Let him go." And we did.

I still can't believe I did that to my brother. Neither can Will, although He's always been a good sport about it. Even that day, after I'd jumped over the edge and slid down the embankment to make sure he was okay, he said, "Wow. I felt like I was flying." He wasn't joking. Or even mad. Or hurt, thank god.

But I'd learned my lesson. I was his older brother and he trusted me. A year or two after the cliff incident our parents got divorced and life for us became complicated. Will and I learned to depend on each other to survive, and we continued to stay close even after he moved to Arizona when he was twenty while I stayed in Minnesota.

So when he called from his home in Lake Havasu City

and said he had a favor to ask, I was more than willing to accommodate him. "Sure. What's up?" I asked.

"Well, you know my fortieth birthday is coming up, right?"

"Yep. Next month on the thirteenth. Why?"

"I want to celebrate it in a special way."

"Cool. What do you have in mind?"

"Well, you know I've been taking sky diving lessons."

"Yeah…?" Hmm, I felt a clutch in my gut. Where was this going?

"I've just passed my test so that I can do tandem jumping. I want to do my first jump without an instructor to be special. I want to do it with you. On my fortieth birthday." There was silence on the line. Then, "Ronnie? You there?"

I'd dropped the phone. Over the years I had developed a nasty fear of heights. I'd kept it to myself so Will had no idea, but the thought of jumping out of an airplane made me nearly sick to my stomach. Add to that, skydiving while being strapped to my brother, well, let me tell you, that's recipe for disaster. I could barely climb up to the roof of my one-story home without getting nauseous. My hands began sweating and my heart started pounding, adrenaline racing through my veins. Jump out of a plane? I couldn't do it. Not on my life, or anybody else's life for that matter.

But then I thought, wait a minute. That was a BS way of looking at things. He was my brother, after all. Maybe I owed him something for throwing him off that cliff so many years ago.

"Yeah, I'm here," I told him, trying (probably unsuccessfully) to keep the resignation in my voice to a minimum. "Parachute together you say?" I heard the words come out of my mouth, quivering with fear, croaking like a frog with laryngitis.

"Yep," Will said, his excitement palpable. "It'll be fun."

Fun? No way, but, as I said, maybe I owed him. "Okay," I told him, trying to catch my breath, calm my rapidly beating heart and keep the rising bile at bay, "I'll be there."

So I flew the redeye to Arizona that next month and on the day of Will's fortieth birthday we went up in a single-engine Cessna out of Havasu Airfield near the Colorado River, about ten miles from his home in the foothills above Lake Havasu City. Will was a jet ski racer. He was also a successful businessman who owned and operated Havasu High-Speed Sports, a small company that specialized in modifying jet skis for competitive racing. Skydiving was one of many of what I'd call his extreme hobbies, mixed in with mountain climbing, white water kayaking, and running triathlons. Jumping out of a plane was kid's stuff to him.

"You'll love it," he told me during takeoff. "It'll be a piece of cake."

A piece of cake? That I didn't know about, but I did know one thing: it'd be something. Turns out I was right. It was something, and it was way more enjoyable than a piece of cake. In three words – I loved it. We went out at thirteen thousand feet and free-fell for about one minute. I thought I was going to die. I'll be honest. I kept my eyes closed the whole time and tried to concentrate on not throwing up into my safety helmet (successfully, I might add.)

But after the chute opened, man, I'll tell you, it was like nothing I'd ever experienced before in my entire life. First off, I opened my eyes. That helped. I could see for miles and miles in every direction. We had radio communication through our helmets and Will talked to me the entire time. I don't remember much of what he said, all I know is that the experience of floating through the air in a harness strapped to Will's chest was unbelievably amazing. I actually felt like I was a bird. Or dreaming. I was neither and I was glad because it was real, and it was incredible.

At one point I wondered if maybe Will was paying me back for that day so long ago when me and Davey threw him off that cliff. If he was, that was just fine with me. I know I deserved it. Besides, who cared, anyway? The entire jump was thrilling.

We drifted through the sky for maybe fifteen minutes before landing. Once on the ground we got out of the harness and were gathering up the parachute when Will turned to me, grinning like there was no tomorrow. "What'd you think, big brother? Pretty awesome, right?"

I didn't have to think. I grabbed him in a bear hug, a hug that was more than for just that moment, but also for that day on the cliff so long ago and for all the years since, and for how much he meant to me.

"It was fantastic," I said, literally fighting back tears. "Unforgettable."

"I glad you feel that way," he said, smiling, hugging me back. "Maybe we could do it again. If you're up for it that is. Believe me, it's way better than getting thrown off a cliff."

Yeah, I'll bet.

I didn't have to think. "You're on," I told him. "I'd jump with you again. Anytime."

"Good," he said, checking his watch. "I've booked us for another jump at noon."

"Great," I managed to say.

I hardly felt queasy at all.

The Outbuilding

Maggie and I were relaxing on the couch watching television. Finally, I couldn't contain myself any longer and made a big point of clearing my throat as a prelude to what I felt I had to say. In response, she casually glanced at me. I took it as my chance.

"You know, Mags," I said, turning to face her. "I noticed you posted some old photos on Facebook today. I can't believe you put up that old building."

"That cool outbuilding on my parent's farm? Why?"

"Well, you know," I stammered.

Now, for some reason, I was suddenly at a loss for words, not to mention embarrassed. It obviously hadn't meant the same thing to her as it did to me.

"No, Matt, I don't know. What is it?" she asked just before she got distracted and started fiddling with her phone. A text had come in.

"Well," I ventured, "don't you remember? That night after we'd gone to the movie? We'd been dating for a couple of months. You suggested we go for a drive and we ended up out there; out on the back forty of your parent's farm." I watched my wife, searching for signs of recognition. There were none. She was concentrating on reading her message. Finally, exasperated, I spit it out, "Geez, Maggie. It's where we first made love."

She set the phone aside and looked up. "Oh yeah, that," she said and grinned. "Don't worry, sweetheart, you weren't so bad." She was joking, I think, as she patted me on the arm before turning back to her phone, completely losing interest in what I was saying. So much so, in fact, she changed the subject. "I just got a text from Mom. She and Dad want us to come visit this weekend. She said that the fall colors are gorgeous." Maggie took my hand. "It'd

182

be fun. We've got nothing pressing planned. It's only a couple of hours drive."

"Still, about that photo…" I wasn't ready to give up on this, what was in my mind anyway, a historic event.

She seemed completely disinterested, but then again maybe not. She snuggled up next to me and toyed with a button and my shirt. "After we chat with my mom and dad for a while and get caught up, maybe you and I could take a little drive. Go and check out that old outbuilding you're so keen on."

Was that a provocative smile she gave me? I think it was. Hmm. My imagination began running wild.

"Really? You sure?" I ventured. I was pretty much ready to go right now.

"Absolutely," she winked, squeezing my arm. "It'll be fun. Take a little drive down memory lane so to speak."

I reached for her and hugged her. "That'd be great," I said, breathing in the scent of her hair, imagining us together out in the country. Alone.

Maggie gave me a quick kiss and stood up, already texting her mom that we were coming. I watched as she headed toward the kitchen, thinking what a great weekend it could be: time alone in the country with its fresh air and wide-open spaces. Checking out that old outbuilding again. Kind of romantic. My heart was already beating rapidly, blood pumping like crazy.

Then Maggie turned her head and smiled at me over her shoulder. "As long as you don't mind if I bring my camera." She winked. "I might get some really good pictures."

Originally published in *Mad Swirl*

The Sweet Stakes Robbery

I knew for a fact that Mr. Zilcher's magic candy would be just the thing to help Mom get better. I just had to steal some first. Tonight was Halloween and it seemed like the perfect time to do it.

They were called Sweet Stakes, and the rumor was they were the best candy in the world. That was good enough for me.

"Jenny," I told my best friend, "you've got to help me."

She grinned and looked me right in the eye, which was daunting because she must have grown three inches this year and was now taller than me by an inch or two. "First, say 'please'." She smiled and popped a huge bubble from her pink bubble gum. "Say, 'pretty please'."

Grrr. This was no time for messing around. "Okay," I groused. I was way more serious than her, and she was always joking and goofing around with me. Still, since I needed her help, I complied. "Pretty please," I said.

"All right, Zak." She grinned and gave me a high-five. "Let do it!"

I had a sudden thought. "Hey, maybe we should dress up. What do you think? It's Halloween you know."

Jenny looked at me like I was nuts. We were in sixth grade, and I'm sure in her mind she was way too old to dress up in a costume. My thinking was right on the money. "What you think we are, ten years old?" She scoffed. "No way, Jose." She rolled her eyes at me. Then she snapped her fingers. "Wait a minute. How about if we dress in black?"

"Cool," I said. "Like secret agents?"

She punched me on the arm. It kind of hurt. "No, goofy." She struck a pose. "Like Ninja Warriors."

The pain in my arm went away and I grinned. "Sounds good to me."

Gran was taking care of Mom and thought I was going trick-or-treating with Jenny, so all she said to me when I left was, "Have fun. Don't do anything I wouldn't do." Ha. If she only knew.

"Don't worry, Gran," I told her, "I won't." I hated to lie, but I was learning that it was sometimes better to ask for forgiveness than to ask for permission. This seemed like one of those times. "See ya!"

I slung my daypack over my shoulder, jumped on my bike and took off, kicking up a plume dust the entire half mile to Jenny's house. I passed bunches of trick-or-treaters on the way. Lots of boys dressed in superman and spiderman costumes and quite a few girls dressed as princesses. There were a few cat women, too. Even some Ninja Turtles. I felt if I had a purple bandana like Donatello, I'd fit right in. I was dressed in black jeans, a black long sleeve pullover and my favorite black trainers. On my head I wore an old, brown stocking hat.

Even though the sun had set, and the temperature was in the low 40s, I was sweating like crazy when I got to Jenny's. But there was a crispness in the air along with an aroma of burning leaves and a hint of frost. It seemed like our little town of Able, Iowa, was all ready for Halloween.

Jenny was waiting in front of her house on the sidewalk watching trick-or-treaters as I slid to a stop. She was dressed in black tights, black trainers (like mine), and a black sweatshirt that said *Unicorns Rule* on the front. "All set?" she asked, pulling a black watch-cap down over her short, auburn hair.

"All set," I said. She looked me over. "What?" I asked.

"We need something else," she said. She reached into her backpack. "I'm glad I brought this."

"What is it," I asked. She took out a small round can the size of a hockey puck.

185

"Black shoe wax," she said. She took the lid off. "I got it from my dad's workroom."

"What's it for?"

"For us, dummy." She stuck two fingers in and pulled out a glob. "To cut the glare." She smeared it on her face and turned to me. "How do I look?"

She looked like a raccoon, but I didn't say that. Instead, I said, "Looks great."

She stepped close to me and pulled out another glob. "Stand still," she said. Then she spread it all over my face. I kind of liked how it smelled.

As she put the can away, she asked, "Are you nervous?"

I was, but tried not to show it. "Naw. Not at all."

She laughed. "You big liar!" Then she punched me in the arm.

"Ow!"

I swear Jenny was more like a guy than any of the guys I knew, but we'd been best friends ever since I could remember. We were both eleven years old, so it went back a while, five years at least. My memory's not the greatest. Just ask my Gran. Or my teacher, Miss Luckenstock. Well, on second thought, maybe not her.

Anyway, we got on our bikes and sped down the street dodging costumed kids and their parents along the way. Fifteen minutes later we'd come to the outskirts of our little town. Mr. Zilcher lived in the last house at the end of a wooded lane called Mulberry Way. We'd passed the last streetlight a few blocks before we'd gotten to it. It was dark, dark, dark out there.

We parked our bikes down the lane and crept through the woods to Mr. Zilcher's house, kept company by the hooting of an owl. I glanced at Jenny. Her eyes were set off by the shoe polish and looked huge. She grinned. "Having fun, yet?"

"Absolutely," I said, and tried to ignore the rapid beating of my heart. And that owl. For some reason, it kind of freaked me out. All of a sudden, I was having second thoughts about what we were doing, but I kept them to myself. Mom was counting on me, I told myself.

At the edge of Mr. Zilcher's property, we hid behind a big evergreen tree and peered through its branches. The sky was full of thick clouds obscuring the moon. I'd never been anywhere so dark in my life. The house was an ancient, two story, dilapidated structure, with a covered front porch that sagged to the right. A couple windows in the second story were busted out. Why, I didn't know, but in my mind, it looked exactly like a house from the Alfred Hitchcock shows my mom wouldn't let me watch, but I did anyway.

Mom. My thoughts went to her. She'd been sick for a week and just had to get better. Dad had left home a few years ago to, as he put it, "Search for the gold at the end of the rainbow." Which I thought was a cool thing to do until Mom told me that he was just making it all up.

"He didn't want to tell you the truth, Zak," she said.

"The truth?"

"Yeah, the truth," Gran spat out. She'd been staying with us since he left. "The big jerk just doesn't want to live with you guys anymore." Gran was always what they called a "straight shooter". Nevertheless, the words stung.

All I could think to ask was, "Why?"

Mom looked at me and shrugged her thin shoulders. Then she gave me a hug and said, "Who knows?"

Gran told me later that he left because he gambled and owed people a bunch of money and was afraid for his life. I'm not sure if she was telling me the truth or not, but it sounded better than him having left because he didn't love us anymore.

So, for the last few years, it's been me and Mom and

187

Gran, and now, with Mom sick, I had to do something to help her get better. The Sweet Stakes were just the thing.

As we watched the house, an outdoor flood light suddenly came on. Jenny tugged on my sleeve, bringing me back to the present. "Look at that," she pointed.

I looked. "Geez, cool!" I whispered.

Mr. Zilcher was the town's undertaker. We didn't see him, but with the yard illuminated we could see parked along the side of the house a long black hearse. Real long. The back door was open and we could see there was casket in it.

"Do you suppose that's old man Jorgenson?" I whispered.

In a small town like ours, everybody pretty much knew everyone else's business. Old man Jorgenson had gotten kicked in the head by a mule last week. "Dropped like a stone," some said. "Deader than a doornail before he hit the ground," others added. I didn't have an opinion, but I had no trouble imagining him being a goner. It made sense the casket was his.

"We need to get inside the house to find the candy," I told Jenny.

"Yeah, I heard he kept it in a safe in his office."

"How are we going to open it?"

I glanced at her. She was watching the side of the house intently, the gears of her brain click-clacking away, picking up and discarding ideas one after another, trying to come up with a perfect plan.

"I'll think of something," she said. "But first things first. First, we need to figure out…"

Just then Mr. Zilcher came striding outside though the side door of his house. He stood in the yard next to the hearse and looked around, twisting the waxed tips of his mustache. He was a tall, thin man, and he was dressed in a black suit, black coat and a black top hat. He looked like a sinister undertaker but more demented, and that made him all the more frightening. In the background, the owl began to hoot again. I shivered.

Jenny looked at me. "What's wrong?" she asked.

"Nothing," I said. "Just kind of cold."

She gave me a look. "Right." Then she leaned close and whispered. "Anyway, if he leaves, maybe we can figure out a way to break it."

I whispered back. "Good idea."

It was a good idea. And it was an idea that worked because the creepy undertaker took out a set of keys, turned off the outdoor floodlight, locked the door to his house, slammed the back of the hearse shut, got in and drove off.

"He's probably going to the funeral home in town," Jenny whispered.

We didn't have to keep our voices down, but it seemed like a smart thing to do. With the dilapidated house and the dark night, it was scary around Zilcher's place. Who knew what kind of weird stuff could happen to us if we were caught?

We watched the hearse disappear down the road, clouds of dust billowing behind it. Then all was quiet except for the hooting of the owl and some crickets chirping. Through the clouds the moon suddenly appeared, casting enough light for us to see pretty well.

Jenny elbowed me in the ribs. "Okay, sport. Showtime. Let's go."

We hurried from our hiding place and across the uncut grass of the yard to the house. I pointed to the broken windows on the second floor. "Let's climb up to them," I said. "We should be able to get in easy."

"Good idea," Jenny agreed. We both looked around until she pointed to a tree next to the front porch. "Let's climb that one."

189

"Right on!"

Jenny went first, grabbed ahold of a low-hanging branch, and quickly worked her way up. I followed close behind, my heart racing. In less than five minutes we were on the overhanging roof above the porch and the front door.

"Let's check the broken windows," I said.

Jenny pointed to one along the front. "How about that one?"

"Looks good."

She took off her black watch cap and wiped some sweat from her forehead smearing shoe polish. She turned to me, smiling, and said, "This is fun."

Well, I was a lot more cautious than her any day, but I had to admit that it was kind of fun. Scary, too. But still... kind of fun. I took off my stocking hat and wiped sweat off my face smearing my own shoe polish. We looked at each other and chuckled. Our faces were a smeary mess, but we didn't care.

"Let's get inside," I said.

Jenny grinned. "Go for it."

I used my shoe to kick away a few shards of glass and then climbed through the window with Jenny close behind. We stood for a moment letting our eyes adjust to the dark. It looked like we were in an old bedroom. The first step I took scared up a bunch of bats that darted around for a minute before flying out the window.

Jenny watched, smiling. "Cool," she said and squeezed my arm. "I like bats." I shooed the last one away thinking, *of course you do.*

I turned to her. "Let's get searching for those Sweet Stakes before Zilcher comes back."

"Good idea." Jenny took my hand.

We tip-toed across the room and made our way downstairs. The stairwell was covered with cobwebs, and we pushed them out of the way as we descended. The air was hot and musty and full of dust, and we both sneezed more than once. It worried me that we were making so much noise, but it was apparent that with Zilcher gone we had the place to ourselves. Hopefully.

By the time we got to the first floor, our eyes had fully adjusted to the dark. But it still helped that Jenny had thought to bring a flashlight. She took it out of her hip pocket when we stepped off the last step. "Can't be too prepared," she grinned. Then she flipped it on, and our eyes went wide.

"Oh, my, god," I said in amazement as she beamed the flashlight around the room.

I looked at Jenny and she looked back at me, her mouth hanging open. "I never expected this."

Me neither. It was like stepping into the world's greatest candy shop. "It's unbelievable," I whispered, awestruck.

The walls were lined with floor-to-ceiling shelves filled with glass canisters overflowing with candy: there were root beer barrels, lemon drops, and black and red licorice. There were jellybeans and candy corn and sweet tarts and Dum-Dums. That was just for starters.

Jenny wasted no time opening a container and grabbing a piece of pink bubble gum. She unwrapped it and started chewing. "This is incredible," she said, blowing a quick bubble. "This is the best Halloween ever! I could die happy here."

Her words "die happy" shook me out of my wonderstruck mood. "We can look at candy later," I reminded her. "Right now, we've got to find those Sweet Stakes."

"You're right," she said, stuffing a few pieces of bubblegum in her pocket. "I heard they were in a safe in his office. Let's go look."

191

Grabbing a red licorice whip for myself, we prowled around until we found the office. It was through a door at the back of the living room. The room was cluttered but behind the desk, we discovered the safe. "Now what?" Jenny asked.

"We need to find the combination."

I watched as she reached under the desk. She turned to me over her shoulder and said, "I've read about this." Jenny loved mystery books and was a huge fan of Nancy Drew. "Oh, boy," she said, making a face. "It's kind of gross under here." After a minute, she exclaimed, "Hot diggity dog! I found it!" She ripped off a piece of paper taped to the underside of the drawer and showed me, shining her flashlight on it. Bingo! There was the combination.

"Let's get it open," I said. Excitedly, I rolled through the combination and listened to the tumblers clicking. My heart was pounding. Would I be able to open the safe, get the magic candy, and help make Mom feel better? Jenny was beside me holding the flashlight so I could see. Every once in a while she'd dab the sweat off my brow, smearing more shoe polish, but I didn't care. Neither did she.

Finally, I got the safe open. In addition to a bunch of papers and bricks of money wrapped with rubber bands, there was a glass jar. It held what looked like candy canes, curved white sticks with red stripes wrapped in cellophane. Were these the Sweet Stakes?

"It's them!" Jenny exclaimed. "They've gotta be the Sweet Stakes."

"You sure?"

"Absolutely," she said, excitedly. "Grab 'em."

I was still a little hesitant. "All of them?"

"Yeah. All of them." She looked at me with steely eyes rimed in shoe polish. "They're for your mom, remember?"

I mobilized myself. "You're right!" I took the Sweet

Stakes out of the jar and put them in my pack. There were probably two dozen of them. I took all but one which I left in the jar for the heck of it. When I was all set, I said, "Alright. Let's get out of here."

I was closing the door to the safe when we heard the hearse pull into the driveway.

"He's back," Jenny said. "Run!"

We did. We sprinted out of the office and across the living room grabbing handfuls of candy along the way and stuffing them in our pockets.

We ran up the stairs and climbed out the window. "Almost there," Jenny said when we were standing on the roof in complete darkness waiting for Mr. Zilcher to go inside. She turned to me. "You doing okay?" she asked.

I was better than okay. We'd done it. I was ecstatic. "You bet!" I told her and patted my backpack. "I'm great!"

Jenny gave me a quick and surprising peck on the cheek. "Me, too," she said, grinning. Then she winked.

When Mr. Zilcher went inside, we began climbing down the tree to make our final escape. Just then the lights came on both inside and outside the house.

"Who's been in here?" Mr. Zilcher screamed. We could hear him from where we stood out in the yard. "Who's been in my house? Who's been eating my candy!?" We could hear him yelling and kicking things and throwing stuff around in a rage.

He might have said more, but we didn't hear. In the blink of an eye, we ran to our bikes, jumped on them, and sped down the road pedaling for all we were worth, leaving the screaming undertaker to himself. I had the Sweet Stakes safely in my backpack and all was right with the world. By the time we got to my home, we were winded and sweaty but happy. Really happy.

We dropped our bikes to the ground and Jenny hugged me. "We did it, Zak! We did it!"

"Way to go," I told her as we danced around the front yard. "Way to go!"

After a minute the outdoor light came on. "Hey, you two!" Gran called, standing at the door. "What's all that commotion? And more to the point," she looked at her wristwatch, "it's late. The last of trick-or-treaters were here hours ago." She stared at us. "Where have you been?" she demanded.

"You wouldn't believe it," I said.

Both Jenny and I ran toward her to fill her in but before we could say anything, she raised her glasses up on her forehead and frowned. "Wait a minute! What in God's good name do you two have on your faces?"

Oops.

Gran took us into the kitchen, sat us down, and helped us clean the shoe polish off our faces, "tisk, tisk, tisking" all the time. Then she made us some hot chocolate and listened while we told her the story. All of it. She didn't even get mad. In fact, once or twice she even laughed a little.

When we were finished, Gran said, "Okay, let's see those Sweet Stakes."

I took them out of my pack and showed her. "Here. See?"

She laughed. "They look just like candy canes."

Jenny frowned at Gran. "No way. These are definitely Sweet Stakes."

My face turned red. I was right when we'd been back at Mr. Zilcher's, they did look like candy canes. But my Gran was a wonderful person. She took one look at me, recognized my discomfort, and came to the rescue. "Well, maybe there's some magic in them anyway." She looked closely. "They do

194

look pretty special." She turned to us, and then said to me, "Let's go give one to your mom."

So, we did. All three of us trooped upstairs to Mom's room. I tip-toed across the floor to the side of her bed. She was resting but her eyes came open when she sensed my presence. She smiled. "Hi, sweetie," she said. "How are you?"

"Hi, Mom." I smiled at her. "I'm good," I said. "I've got something for you."

I gave her the Sweet Stake. To make a long story short, she loved it. She unwrapped the cellophane, put the candy in her mouth, and took a couple of minutes savoring it. We waited in anticipation. Would she like it? More to the point, would it work its magic and help her to feel better? Finally, she removed the Sweet Stake (I refused to call it a candy cane) and said, "Best candy cane I've ever had."

Jenny and I both coughed at the same time and said, "Ahem."

Mom smiled. "I mean, Sweet Stake." She reached out her arms and gave me a hug. Then she hugged Jenny. Then she hugged us both in between licking and savoring every last bit of her candy. "Thank you both so much."

After a few minutes, Gran said, "Alright, you two." She looked at me. "Let's let your mom rest."

"Okay," I told her.

We both hugged Mom again and then went downstairs and out onto the porch. Once outside, Jenny took my arm and smiled. "She really liked that Sweet Stake, didn't she? You think she's going to get better?"

I tried to be confident. "I'm pretty sure, yeah. She seemed to perk up a little after eating it."

Jenny was quiet, thinking. We sat down on the steps. Then she said, "It was fun, wasn't it? Getting all that candy from old man Zilcher?"

I grinned. "It really was."

We spent the next hour talking. Finally, Gran came out and told us, "Jenny your mom called and said you had to go home."

"Okay." She stood up, dusted off her tights, and gave me a quick hug. "See you tomorrow."

"Okay, see ya," I said and watched her pedal off.

Gran put her arm around my shoulder and led me back inside. "Your mom's feeling lots better, Zak." Then she looked me in the eye. "I'm not sure I can condone what you two did tonight even if it was Halloween, but I have to say that you did a good thing. I think your mom's going to be alright."

I wiped a sudden tear of joy from my eye. "I'm so glad to hear that, Gran." I really was, too, but I didn't know what else to say. Gran seemed to understand. She didn't say anything else, just hugged me tightly. I hugged her back, just as tight, if not tighter.

We went inside, sat at the kitchen table and Gran scooped each of us a bowl of ice cream. Halfway through she pulled out a Sweet Stake, broke it in half and we shared it with each other. It tasted great.

The next day Mom was one hundred percent better. I had an idea and rode my bike over to Jenny's and gave her a Sweet Stake. "For you," I said. "Thanks for everything." She smiled, gave me a big hug and said, "Anytime, Mr. Ninja."

She was a great friend, my best friend. I don't know when I'd ever been happier. It was the best Halloween I ever had.

The Resolution

I was perched in an uncomfortable plastic chair in a cheap plywood-sided cubicle along with maybe a half dozen other cubicles in the row. Mine was the only one occupied. I tried without much success to control my breathing. It was about ten degrees outside in the middle of January so why did it all of a sudden feel like a hundred degrees in here? Sweat was running down my sides, under my flannel shirt, like a river.

My senses were super aware of my surroundings, probably caused by the adrenaline blasting through my veins like a flash flood. The florescent lights were yellowish blue and too bright. I took off my glasses, rubbed my eyes to give them some relief (it didn't help), and put them back on. My nerves were on edge, so I held my hands together in my lap to keep them from twitching. The room smelled of lemony chlorine disinfection, and there was a hint of stale body order mixed in. Not the kind of aroma you'd get from an artisan bag of potpourri, that was for sure.

A thick pane of glass separated me from the other side, the side where my older brother now sat. The brother who I didn't remember. The brother who was serving a life sentence for murder.

There was a low rumbling din of the prison's mechanical system in the background making me wonder what it must be like to live in a place like this where there was never ever complete silence. As a person occasionally drove to the country just to hear nothing but the sounds of nature, my thought was that I'd probably go nuts in about a day if I had to be incarcerated.

Speaking of which, nervous as I was, I made myself look at my brother. He was a huge man, probably six feet four and at least two hundred and sixty pounds with muscles bulging out of his tight black tee-shirt that said *Have a Nice Day* on it. His head was shaved and he wore about a foot-long Billy-goat bead that was pure white. His dark brown eyes were veiled and his fingers on his right hand were stained yellowish orange with nicotine. To be honest, even though he was my brother, he still looked like the murderer he was which frightened me. Not for the first time did I rethink my decision to come to the maximum-security prison here in Dickenson, North Dakota.

Zach was twenty-one and I was five when he shot and killed a husband, his wife, and their two kids in a failed burglary attempt in rural Wright County, just west of Minneapolis where we grew up. He was high on amphetamines at the time and still tearing the farmhouse apart looking for money when the highway patrol, sheriff's department, and local police showed up, sixteen law enforcement officers in all. Neighbors had called it in, having heard the barrage of gunshots coming from the Atkinson family's farm. "Those poor people were surprised in their sleep and never stood a chance" is what everyone said. The trial was short, and my brother was sentenced to life without parole.

I knew nothing about Zach's crime. He was so much older than me that if it did register in my five-year-old mind what was happening, it certainly didn't stick. And it was never talked about in our house afterward, either. The murder and the trial ruined my parents' marriage and Dad left the next year taking my next oldest brother, Paul, with him. I never saw either of them again. Mom told me that they moved to Alaska and wanted to be left alone. I guess there was a lot of bitterness between Mom and Dad. I was still young and never close to Paul who was three years older than me, so I didn't really care one way or the other if he left with Dad.

Mom just got on with her life. She raised me and my younger sister, Savannah, and as far as I was concerned did a great job. We were always close. She moved us from our small rambler in the suburb of Richfield to a tidy two-bedroom apartment in south Minneapolis near a park. Mom worked, didn't drink much or smoke too much, and made sure the bills were paid on time.

Even though I was quiet and withdrawn and a passably mediocre student in high school, I got by just fine and compensated for being occasionally lonely by playing video games. To this day, I still love them.

I started working full-time for Clean-Rite cleaning services after I graduated high school and I found an apartment within walking distance of Mom and Savannah. For the rest of her life, Mom and I visited at least twice a week and talked on the phone every day.

But she never talked about my brother, the murderer. Not until she was dying, that was.

"Darren, I've got something to tell you," she told me in the last days of her life. The cancer had gotten to her bad and me and Savannah were watching over her along with a nurse and one of the good folks from the hospice.

"What is it, Mom?" I pulled my chair up closer to her. We had moved her bed into the living room of the same apartment where she'd raised us. Even though the end was near this was hard. I was going to miss her. I took her hand and said, "Tell me."

She told me then about Zach and the murders and the trial and how it affected my dad so badly that he'd taken Paul and left the state for good and on and on. I have to tell you, I'm not an emotional guy, but even I got a little emotional listening to Mom tell her story. Finding out I had a brother, even though he was an infamous murderer, was a little hard to get a handle on.

"Why didn't you tell me this, before?" I tried to keep my voice down but didn't do a very good job. I was shocked and it was the first thing I could think of to ask.

Mom smiled a weak smile and said, "I didn't want to worry you."

I coughed out a laugh. "What'd you mean? Worry me?"

"Well, I know how you are."

She had a point. Maybe it was because I was the oldest after Dad left with Paul, but I did always have what I'd call a bit of the worrier in me. Growing up, I worried about mom, for sure and how she was doing, making sure she wasn't working too hard and eating right. I worried about Savannah as she got older, especially when the boys started coming around. And, later, after she moved to St. Paul and got married and had kids, I worried about her and her husband and her family all the time and called her every other day or so to chat and see how things were going. (She makes it a point of reassuring me on a constant basis that she doesn't mind.)

I worried about my job working for Clean-Rite and whether or not tomorrow was going to be the day I'd get fired even though I'd worked for them for over twenty-five years and was as loyal and reliable an employee of the top-rated building cleaning service company in the metropolitan area that they could ever want, and there was no reason why I shouldn't keep working for them for another twenty years at least. But, still, I worried.

I worried about whether or not I'd ever get married. (At forty-four years old, the answer was getting clearer every year and that answer was this: probably not.)

I worried if I'd be able to pay my bills. (Which I always did, thank you very much!)

Stuff like that was what I worried about. So, Mom had a point. But I didn't want that to be her last mortal thought on her death bed. "Mom," I said, caressing her thin hand, "I can handle it." I tried to sound convincing, and Savannah told me afterward that she thought I did.

"Good," Mom said, wheezing, out her last breaths. "Because there's more."

"More?" What more could there possibly be? I had no idea, but I was about to find out. "What is it, Mom?" I leaned even closer. Savannah pulled up a chair sat next to me and put one hand on my arm and one on Mom's.

"I want you to go see him," she said. "I want you to go see your brother Zach."

Those were the last words she ever spoke. A few minutes later she inhaled her final breath and passed on. Pretty peacefully, I have to say.

But what the hell? Me go and see the brother I just found out I had? I looked at Savannah and she looked at me. She was crying over the loss of our mother, but she still had enough in her to say, "Good luck with that last wish of hers, Darren. Good luck."

I knew what she was getting at. She knew I'd abide by Mom's last request because of how close we were and she was right. It was in the cards. It was the way I was made. So, I made a resolution right there on Mom's death bed to follow through, make the trip across the frozen North Dakota prairie and see the brother I didn't even remember I had. I had no idea was I was getting into.

A tapping on the cubicle window broke into my thoughts. Zach had his phone in his hand. He pointed to it and to mine and made a "pick up" motion.

Oh, right, I thought to myself. *That's why I'm here.* The black, scarred phone was attached to a two-foot-long metal cord that bolted to the plywood on the side. I reached for it, my hand shaking. *What was wrong with me?* Well, it was obvious. I was going to talk to my brother, a guy who I knew nothing about other than that he had murdered four innocent people. I consoled myself by thinking anyone in my position would be freaked out. Not to mention a thick pane of glass separating us.

I reached for the receiver but before I could say "Hello" Zach beat me to it and said, "Well, well, well, little brother. I never thought you'd show up. How was the drive?"

Based on what Mom had told me I knew where he was serving his sentence, so I'd sent him a letter asking to see him (which was a weird experience in and of itself.) I have to say I was frankly shocked that he replied. We went back and forth a few times and finally agreed to meet. We set up a time and here I was.

In my imagination, he was a gruff, sub-human who probably couldn't string three words together in a coherent sentence. Boy was I wrong. This guy across from me, my brother, sounded… what's the word? Normal, maybe? Nice, even. Polite. I don't know. The gruff voice I expected grunting out one-syllable words wasn't there at all. His was deep and resonant, like that of a person who gave classes on public speaking. Or an ivy league college professor who taught philosophy. He also sounded confident, something, I'd have to say, I was not.

My throat was so dry that when I went to speak, I started coughing. I covered the receiver as my body was wracked with spasms. He just sat watching me, waiting patiently, a skill one develops in prison, I guess, especially if you're sentenced to life without parole.

When I finished my coughing fit and was wishing for a drink of water he said, "So, are you going to say anything, or are you just going to sit there all day and cough?" He smiled. Was he making a joke? He glanced at a clock on the wall. I did, too. It read 10:30 a.m. "I haven't got all day, you know."

Time to get to it. "Yeah. I'm mean, no," I stumbled over my words. Get a grip, I told myself, taking a deep breath and admonishing myself to "start over". Then I did what Savannah told me to do and that was to just be myself.

"I guess I told you in the letter that Mom died," I said to him and watched carefully. There was no reaction so I went on, "She wanted me to come and meet you."

He laughed. "Now why the hell would she want that? The whole time I've been here she's only sent me cards at Christmas. I've got all thirty-nine of them. That's it. No letters, nothing, and certainly no phone calls or visits. I used to write but she never responded so I just gave up. She obviously didn't want to have anything to do with me. Why would she put seeing me on you?"

"I have no idea. Maybe because we're brothers?"

"Brothers, huh?"

I didn't know what to say so I didn't say anything.

Zach set the phone down and sat back in his chair. He put his muscular arms up, locked his hands behind his head, and stared at me. His arms were covered in tattoos. I couldn't make out anything distinct, but I will say this: sitting like he was and looking directly at me, he was one intimidating guy. I started sweating again and wiped my brow with the sleeve of my shirt.

Finally, he picked up the phone and said, "So you didn't know anything about me?"

"No." I wiped some more sweat off my forehead. "I mean I now know about the mur... the killings," I said. "I read up on them online." He nodded. "I read about your trial and all that." He nodded some more. "I know about your sentence."

His eyes softened and leaned forward, picked up the phone asked, "You don't remember anything about us as kids?"

203

"No. Not a thing." Then I added for some reason, "Sorry."

His reaction was unexpected. He yelled into the phone, "Sorry!? You're sorry?"

"Well, yeah." I was thrown off. Why was he so mad?

"You don't remember me or us growing up or anything like that? Nothing?"

"No. I was just a kid," I said, and added, again, "Sorry."

He leaned close to the glass. I could see his teeth which were remarkably white. "Quit saying that." Then his look softened. "Look, I'm the one who should apologize for the outburst. Sorry about that."

"That's okay."

"Look, kid. There's nothing for you to be sorry about. It was Mom's decision and that's just the way it is. I mean was."

I nodded my head. "Okay," I said, and had to bite off the urge to say "sorry" again. That seemed to satisfy him.

One thing was certain, though, there was a lot of rage there. Anger. But I have to say, I was enjoying being with him. Kind of secure in a weird way. And it wasn't just because there was a guard nearby and a thick sheet of glass separating us. I was only seven when Dad left with Paul, so having a brother (even one who was a murderer) to talk to wasn't as strange as I thought it was going to be. I felt a connection with him somehow, like some kind of genetic thing, I guess. It didn't feel all that bad, kind of good, in fact.

We were quiet for a minute or two before he switched subjects and asked, "So what do you do?"

"What'd you mean?"

"You know, work, free time, girlfriend. Your life. What's it like?"

I told him about my job at the cleaning services company, Clean-Rite. "I've been there for almost twenty-five years."

He laughed. "We've got something in common. I work in the laundry. Been doing it since I got here." He paused and went on, "What else you do? Like for like a hobby?"

"I play video games. I'm in some online groups. It's fun. How about you? Do you play?"

"No," he said, with kind of a grim look on his face. "I kind of shy away from anything that's got violence associated with it." Seemed like a good idea to me, but I didn't say anything, just nodded my head, and he continued, "I take online classes. I've gotten a BA in Sociology from the University of Minnesota. I do some counseling here in the prison. I read." He laughed. "You'll never believe it, but I write poetry and send it out. Some of it's been published." He shrugged his shoulders. "I work out." He looked off into the distance. "Chit-chat with my friends. Stuff like that." He looked at me. "I try to stay busy."

Man, I couldn't help comparing Zach's life to mine. He was in prison and living a rich and rewarding life and I was kind of doing the opposite, going to work and playing video games. By myself. I really had no friends, especially now that mom was gone.

"I miss Mom," I suddenly blurted out. "I miss her a lot."

He stared at me, picking up on my loneliness. His voice softened. "I can tell." Then he said something that shocked me. "You know, you and I were close once. You don't remember that do you?"

I had no idea. "Ah, no, I didn't know that. Until recently I didn't even know you existed."

He grinned, spread his arms wide, and made a little joke, "Yet, here I am." I smiled back. I was getting to enjoy talking to him. He leaned forward. "Yeah, I used to take you fishing in the lake by where we lived. He shrugged. "Dad couldn't take the time," he said, sarcastically. "I used to buck you on the back of my bicycle bike. You loved getting a bike ride and laughed the whole time." He smiled. "We built model airplanes together. We were pretty close."

"What about Paul?" The brother between Zach and me was always a bit of an enigma.

"Paul and Dad were close. That's all I know. Dad didn't care much for me or for you, but he and Paul had a thing." He paused and added, "You said they were in Alaska?"

"Last I knew."

"Well, I hope they're happy."

It seemed there was a lot more there, but I just let it go. Maybe some other time. Wait a minute. Some other time? Would I be coming back?

Zach was suddenly in a reminiscing mood. "I remember once you and I were down at the park a few blocks from where we lived. There was a small pond there and we were walking barefoot along the shore. It was a hot July morning and the water felt cool. So did the mud. We were just talking, joking around. You must have been four at the time. We found a frog that you liked. I remember. You picked it up and carried it, cradling it in your hands for a while. You named him Felix, I think after that *Felix the Cat* cartoon show you liked to watch." He looked at me. "You remember any of this?"

I wracked my brain thinking but came up with nothing. It was all a blank. "No. S…" I caught myself from saying "sorry" and said, "No. I didn't."

Zach smiled at me. "That's okay. We walked along for some time and you decided to let the frog go. 'It should be free' is what you said. And, given all of this," he made a motion with his arm encompassing the room, "I couldn't agree more." He grinned, both at the memory and maybe at his little joke. I grinned back at him. It was nice to hear him talk. "Then we stepped out of the water to sit on the bank and dry off. But that didn't happen."

"Why?" I asked, intrigued by his story. I remembered none of it. "Why not?"

"Your feet were covered in leeches. Like in that movie *Stand by Me*. Man, you were freaked out and crying, but I took you in my lap and calmed you down and pulled those leeches off one by one. There must have been about a dozen of them. You were pretty scared."

Well, I never. Listening to him talk I realized that after all these years of not knowing that I had one, I really did have an older brother after all. One who liked being with me, at least back then, maybe even loved me, at least enough to pick those leeches off me and spend time with me.

"I kind of remember," I said.

He laughed. "You liar. You don't remember a thing, do you?"

"Well… I'm sorry. Oops. But I don't."

He smiled, letting it pass. "That's okay. I've got tons of stories to tell you." He watched me carefully. "If you want to listen to them that is." Which would mean coming back and we both knew it.

I thought about it while Zach set the receiver down, sat back, took a cigarette out of a pack, and twirled it in his fingers. He glanced at the guard who'd been watching us and put the cigarette away. No smoking, I guess. He folded his arms over his head and looked off into space, giving me time, I figured, to think. After all, he had a degree in Sociology and was a counselor; kind of a professional in one sense, if you know what I mean, and knew what he was doing. So, that's what I did. I had a think about what he'd said.

I know what you cynics out there are thinking. "This guy is just making all this up because he's lonely and wants someone to talk to. After all, he's a criminal. A murderer." And that's a plausible thought. And it makes perfect sense, but I'm going to have to disagree. Here's why: It was the leeches. Yeah, they did it. How could someone make that up? And Felix the Frog? Come on. It's got to be true. At least to me.

So, I decided that I was going to be coming back. In fact, I made my own resolution right then and there. I was going to come back at least once a month to visit with my brother in person, not because Mom wanted me to, but because I wanted to. Maybe for the rest of our lives. I want to a lot. I think there's a lot I can learn from him because despite his past, he seems like a good guy. Plus, you know, he is my brother. And more than that, I like him. He might be the only friend I'll ever have. And that would be all right with me.

I made a motion for him to pick up the phone and he did. I said, "How about if I come back next month and we can talk some more?"

He grinned and said, "I'd like that. I'd like that a lot."

"Okay," I said and put my hand up on the glass. He put his up, too, right on mine. "I'll see you next month."

"I was hoping you'd say that," he said and wiped away some tears from his eyes.

I couldn't help it. I blinked back my own tears and wiped them away, just like he did.

Whatever Works

We were walking along a favorite woodland path when I turned to Mom and asked, "Say, I was wondering. What's your favorite memory?"

Even though she was slightly hunched over and walked with a cane, she was still a spry lady. She also had a wicked sense of humor.

"At my age, too many to mention," she grinned. Then she winked and added, "But, I'll tell you this, Jack. Walking in the woods with you is among my all-time favorites."

Mom always had a way of making me feel good. Wanted. Something that meant a lot to me since I was one of those guys who was quieter and more withdrawn than most. Expressive and outgoing I was not. Not like my other brother Marc for instance, a successful insurance salesman with friends galore.

I lived by myself in a single-bedroom apartment with my cat Ralph near where I worked stocking produce at a local grocery store. A job I liked. I must have, since I'd been hired in high school and now, fifty-three years later, I was still there.

I liked routine. Walking like this with Mom had been a Sunday tradition for us ever since I'd left home and moved into my apartment. We used the time to get caught up. It was when Mom told me she was leaving Dad because, as she put it, "I'm sick of his fooling around and womanizing." It was when she told me she had earned a BA degree in early childhood education and was going to begin working with at-risk preschoolers. It was when she told me she was moving into the Lakeside Senior Living complex. And it was where she told me she had an inoperable brain tumor.

I was on my way back to the car when my phone buzzed. I grimaced. I had a feeling who it was. I looked at the screen. I was right.

I picked up. "Hi, Marc. How's it going?"

My older brother had strong opinions. One of them was he didn't agree with me "communicating" as he called it with our dead mother. Especially out in public on my woodland walks with her. Too bad. It worked for me.

"Just fine, little brother," he said. I waited for a biting retort but none was forthcoming. Instead, Marc asked simply, "Are you still coming for lunch?"

I metaphorically wiped my brow, glad the two of us would not be arguing, especially on this day, the tenth anniversary of our mother's passing. "Yeah," I said. "For sure. Wouldn't miss it for the world."

I liked seeing my brother. Plus, Marc was a great cook. His nod to the anniversary of our mother's death was to prepare her favorite meal, chicken and rice casserole. He'd fix a simple salad to go with it, and he and I would share a glass of her favorite wine. "Still on for 1 p.m.?" I asked.

"Absolutely. Like always."

"Sweet. See you then."

A pause on the other end of the line. Then, "Out communing with Mom?" he asked. Then, without missing a beat, he chuckled.

"Yeah, I was."

"Thought so." Another pause, then, "Well, whatever works."

Interesting, I thought to myself. My older brother must be mellowing. Not wanting to break the ice of this delicate détente' I said, simply. "Exactly."

He chuckled again, then said, "Okay. See you at one."

"Sounds good," I said, glad to have dodged a potentially brotherly bullet. My stomach suddenly growled. I hadn't realized how hungry I was. "See you then."

With the chicken casserole baking in the oven, Marc went into the dining room and set the table with cream-colored

Spode plates accented by an ivy boarder, his mom's favorite. He put down a setting for him and one for Jack: a knife and spoon, a dinner fork and a salad fork, linen napkins with wooden napkin rings, just like his mother always liked.

He thought of his mom as he finished setting the table. The divorce so many years ago had been hard on everyone. He'd sided with his father, his brother with their mother. It was just the way things went. Their father had remarried only a week after the divorce was final and within a year, he'd died of a massive heart attack. Their mother stayed happily single for the rest of her life. He smiled. She'd been a teacher, a wonderful grandmother to his kids, and when it came right down to it, a really good person.

He wiped an unexpected tear from his eyes. Honestly, he did miss her.

A sudden urge came over him. He went to the cupboard, took out another plate, and made up a place setting for their mom, right down to the linen napkin and wine glass. When he was done, he poured a glass for her and one for himself. Then he raised it in a toast.

"Here's to you, Mom. Thanks for everything."

He took a sip and was turning away when he thought he heard something. What was that?

He turned to the table. *Oh, my lord.*

"Mom?"

"Hi, son."

"What are you doing here?"

She smiled. She always did have a nice smile. Open and honest.

"I just wanted to thank you."

"For what?"

She cast her hand over the table. "For including me," she said.

Wow! This is crazy.

It was, too. Nevertheless, it was great to see her. He smiled. "I'm glad you could make it."

She grinned. "I wouldn't miss it for the world."

So, this was what Jack was talking about. *Communing with Mom.* It felt good. He made a snap decision. "In that case, how about Sunday I'll join you and Jack on your woodland walk?"

"Your brother would love that." Then she smiled. "So would I."

"All right, then," he said, and sat down next to her. They had a lot to talk about. "It's a date."

Originally published in *Pure Slush Lifetime Series – Loss*

Where the Heart Is

"Daddy! Daddy, watch!"

"I am, sweetheart," I said. "You're looking good."

Janey, my five-year-old daughter was flinging herself back and forth on the swing set with courage I never had, pumping her skinny legs for all she was worth.

"Just be careful!" I called out to her, imagining all sorts of horrors if she crashed.

Janey's mind was not on crashing. "Wheeeeee," she called out. Then she leaped into space while I watched, frozen to my spot, as my daughter sailed through the air, her pigtails trailing behind her. She landed expertly in the sand and executed a perfect somersault before popping to her feet in front of me. "Ta-da!" She said and ran off giggling to grab the swing and do it all over again.

We were in a small park, two blocks from our home. I glanced at my wife Lesley sitting next to me, calmly nursing our three-month-old son, Aaron. She smiled. "I like her style," she said. Then went back to gazing lovingly at Aaron.

I grinned and turned my attention to Janey. She was wearing pink tights and a dark blue tee shirt that said *Girl Power* on it. She waved. "Come join me, Daddy!"

I waved back. "In a minute!"

I turned to Lesley and kissed the top of her head. Her short-cropped auburn hair had the aroma of the strawberry shampoo she loved. Then I kissed Aaron, reveling in the sweet scent of milk and baby powder.

Lesley mussed up my hair and pointed to where Janey was back on the swing set, pumping her legs and soaring ever higher. The summer sky was blue. Nearby a robin was singing. "Your daughter's a real daredevil," she said.

I grinned. "Takes after her mother."

Lesley smiled back at me. "You got that right, Big Boy."

Just to be clear, my name's not Big Boy, it's Frank. And, I have to say, I'm happy to be here.

I was wounded some years ago while fighting in Afghanistan. At the exact moment the IED exploded, I was sure I was going to die. I didn't. I lived (obviously); however, the shrapnel messed up my leg badly. I returned to the States with not only a limp but a bad attitude. I drank a lot. Did drugs. And when it came to being with women, let's just say I was not the most fun to be around. In short, I was not a nice human being.

What changed my life was my grandparents. I began living with them when my parents divorced when I was ten years old. My dad wanted nothing to do with me, and, it turned out, neither did my mom. She left me with Grandpa Jack and Grandma Helen and took off with a boyfriend to California. I never saw her again.

They were the kindest people I've ever met. Grandpa worked at the local creamery and Grandma was a science teacher at the high school. The name of the town was Ester. It had a population of about five thousand and was located in southern Minnesota close to the Iowa border. It was a close-knit farming community and at first, I fit in like a pimple on a forehead. But, I adapted. Grandma and Grandpa were patient with me, taught me right from wrong, and didn't berate me for the many mistakes I made growing up. They had a saying for everything, one of the most common was, "You live and learn, Frank. Learn from your mistakes. That's the main thing." And I did. I had ample opportunity, that's for sure.

I met Lesley at Alcoholics Anonymous and we've been together ever since. We were living in Minneapolis, she was working as a cashier, and I for a landscaping company (we plowed driveways in the winter), when I got word that my grandparents had been in a horrific car accident. I didn't hesitate. I hurried down to Ester to be with them and help with their recovery. Unfortunately, there wasn't much either me or the doctors could do. After a week Grandpa died, and a few days later Grandma passed away. Her final words to me were, "Live life well, my son. Love who you love."

Lesley was by my side when Grandma spoke those words. We married a week later.

My grandparents left their home to me. The move from our apartment in the big city to this small town was easy. A year later Janey was born. Then Aaron.

When I was growing up, before my parents split up, there was a saying my mom had on a framed piece of embroidery. It read "Home Is Where The Heart Is." At the time, with all the issues I was subjected to by my parents, I thought the saying was a load of crap. But, later, I found out that Grandma had embroidered it. She had one up in her and Grandpa's home when I moved in. There it took on new meaning With them as my parents, I eventually realized what it truly meant.

Lesley and I work hard to keep Grandma and Grandpa's home like it used to be. What others call "possessions" we call "keepsakes", and our home is filled with them.

I think of Grandma and Grandpa all the time. They gave me a chance at life when my parents left, and they loved me until the day they died. I'll never forget them.

My thoughts were brought back to the present by Janey. "Daddy! Daddy! Look at me!"

She was swinging as high as she possibly could. "Looking good!" I called to her.

She giggled. "Come swing with me, Daddy!"

I looked at Lesley. Aaron was sleeping peacefully in her

arms. My wonderful wife smiled at me. "Go for it." She nodded toward our daughter. "Have fun."

I kissed her and used my cane to get to my feet. I limped over to join Janey. Nothing was going to stop me.

Originally published in *Pure Slush Lifetime Series – Home*

The Winnewacko Lodge

As they boarded the launch, Curly noticed the driver was an unkept, bearded man who wore an old, "seen better days" captain's cap and stank of stale beer. He also smoked the raunchiest cigars Curly had ever smelled in his life.

Giving the man what he hoped was his dirtiest look, the detective took his assistant Wanda by the arm and said, "Let's get out of this pollution. I think I might be sick."

"Fine with me," she said, not caring one way or the other about the smoke. At least it kept the bugs away.

They moved to the stern of the *Northern Belle* and Curly held on to the railing tightly as the captain jammed the throttle lever forward. The twin inboard motors roared as the thirty-foot wooden cruiser took off like a shot from the town dock of the little village of Granite, Minnesota. Thus began an hour of what was soon to be one of the worst experiences in detective Curly Knucklewad's life. Up and down the boat rose and fell as it crashed through the five-foot waves making him feel like he was in an out-of-control circus ride. Then there was the relentless rolling back and forth, back and forth, like he was in a tumble dryer that couldn't make up its mind which was to spin. It was a nauseating experience designed to make one lose one's stomach and it was all Curly could do to keep from losing his.

Then there were the bugs. Insects of all types, mosquitoes, black flies, horse flies and deer flies, not to mention your garden variety blue bottle flies. Buzzing and blood sucking insects that flew around his head in hordes, attacking him and never giving him a moments peace, no matter how much he madly waved his arms to drive them away.

It was a horrific experience for Curly, a dyed in the wool, confirmed city dweller if there ever was one. If he and Wanda weren't on the hunt for the Limp Noodle Sauce recipe, he'd be back in his downtown condominium sipping a martini and watching anything sports related on television, preferably something sedate, like golf.

Curly slapped at a huge horse-fly that had landed on his nose and said to Wanda, "Why did I ever let you talk me into this?"

His mild-mannered and sometimes (to Curly's way of thinking) over-achieving assistant adjusted the netting on her pith helmet and said, "Look. We're being paid to track down that recipe and I've got a good feeling about the Winnewacko Lodge. Remember I did that google search for famous spaghetti dishes two weeks ago? I found that article written in the North Country Herald about how this Minnesota resort on an island out in the middle of nowhere all of a sudden had become known throughout the Upper Midwest for its spaghetti and its "out of this world sauce" to quote the article." She gave Curly a pointed look. "It sounded suspicious so we had to investigate. Remember?"

"Yes, yes, I remember. I understand at that," he said testily. "I know we need to check it out. But, really, for the life of me, Wanda, not to change the subject, but these bugs are eating me alive."

"I can see that," she said, swishing away a horde of black flies. Sometimes known as gnats, they were swarming around them in voracious clouds. Wanda's pith helmet and mosquito netting helped, but Curly had declined her invitation to purchase one back at the dock when they'd been in the gift shop waiting for the launch to leave. *His tough luck,* she'd thought at the time. "Here, this'll help." She took a can of insect spray from her tote bag and without warning sprayed Curly liberally.

"Hey, cut it out," he yelled, waving his arms in surprise. He'd been looking out across Lake Winnewacko to the huge lodge on the fast-approaching shoreline, and although he appreciated the gesture, he didn't appreciate sucking in a nose full of *Northwoods Off with Deet*. The chemicals that had just entered his body made him grimace with repulsion. The spray did, however, have its desired effect and immediately kept the insects at bay. Chagrined, Curly reached out his hand. "I guess a little more won't hurt."

Wanda handed him the can. "Here's the tip of the nozzle," she said. "Point it toward you."

Curly shook the can vehemently. "I know that" he said, and promptly sprayed the spray out over the side of the launch into wind.

Wanda rolled her eyes and turned away to let Curly figure the can out on his own. After all, he was the detective and supposed to be the brains in the outfit. Right?

She looked across the sunlit sparkling waters of the huge lake. The Winnewacko Lodge had been built in the early part of the twentieth century and ever since the 1920's had been the "go to" summer vacation spot for the rich and famous. She was looking forward to checking it out.

Fifteen minutes later, and after a nearly one-hour ride, the captain throttled back on the engines and carefully brought the *Northern Belle* up to the dock. A dock boy from the lodge ran out to greet him. "Hey there Jessup," the young boy said. "How goes it?"

Curly watched the interaction with interest. What he lacked in savvy, north woods survival skills, he made up for with his powers of observation. After all, he wasn't a well-known detective for nothing.

He turned to Wanda. "See that? The captain's name is Jessup."

Wanda was looking through her tote bag to make sure she had her notebook. "Yeah, I heard."

"You should write it down."

"You got it boss." She took out her notebook and made a notation. It read, *Make sure to call Mom for her birthday.* "I'm on it."

"Good," Curly said, and turned to get off the boat, declining the outstretched hand of the dock boy. "That's okay, son, I've got it," he said stepping onto the dock, where he promptly slipped in a pool of water and fell on his rear end. Muttering under his breath he got quickly to his feet. "Dang dock," he said, bushing himself off.

Wanda rolled her eyes and checked her wrist watch. It read 10:30 a.m. She sighed. It was going to be a long day.

"Let go to the lodge," she suggested, jumping lightly from the boat to the dock and hoisting her tote bag onto her shoulder, "and see what we can find out."

"Good idea," Curly said, hurrying to get as far away from the boat and the dock and onto dry land as soon as possible.

The Winnewacko Lodge was on the National Historic Register. It was made of massive white pine logs that were among the last of those harvested from Minnesota. They had been stained deep, dark brown and the windows had white trim. All fifty-five rooms were on one floor.

The entrance to the lodge was a short walk from the dock, across a sandy beach and past a large patio where some of the guests were sitting in the sun, talking, reading or having a bite to eat. Curly eyed them suspiciously as he and Wanda walked past. In his world everyone was a suspect.

Wanda held the massive wooden front door open for him. "Okay, boss. Let's see what we can find." She pointed to the dining room, to the right of the front desk through two large doors propped open by what looked like huge fireplace logs. "How about there?"

"Good idea."

They were greeted by a young man dressed in a dark suit, white shirt and a tie. "Hi." He smiled. "My name's Soren. Welcome to the Winnewacko Room. Table for two?"

"Actually," Curly said, cutting off Wanda who seemed more than willing to get a table, sit down and have something to eat, "we're here for some information."

Soren's smile vanished and he turned serious. "Oh, I see. Are you here for the spaghetti?"

"Sort of," Curly said.

"Well, in that case you'll have to talk to the manager. I'll go get her for you."

And with that he walked briskly through the dining area and into the kitchen.

Curly turned to Wanda. "What was that all about?"

"I don't know. But I will say one thing," she said taking in a deep breath of the aroma of eggs and bacon and toast. "I could go with something to eat. I'm kind of hungry."

Curly glanced at his thin assistant who ate like a horse and never gained an ounce and snorted, "You're always hungry."

She batted her eyes at him. "I can't help it boss. I've got a high metabolism."

Curly snorted again and turned away just as Soren was coming back with a tall, heavy-set woman following close behind.

"Hi. My name's Margaret," she said, coming up to them and stretching out a hand in greeting. "But you can call me Margie. What can I do for you?"

"Hi Margie," Curly said, shaking her hand. He introduced himself and Wanda, then said, "I'm a detective working on a case. Could we go somewhere and talk?"

"Sure," Margie said. "Let's go to my office."

Margie's office was in the back of the lodge with a

221

window overlooking a pine forest stretching for as far as the eye could see. Curly had to admit, in its own North Woods way, that the setting was kind of pretty.

Once they were seated, he filled her in on the case. "The Limp Noodle Sauce recipe was stolen from its vault in San Francisco and Wanda and I have been on the hunt for it ever since. Wanda found an article in the North Woods Herald that was interesting to us. So here we are."

Margie smiled. "Oh, yes. That cook of ours made the best spaghetti and sauce I'd ever tasted. It got rave reviews as soon as it went on the menu. A food critic from Minneapolis happened to be vacationing with us. She sampled it and said that…"

"It was out of this world?" Wanda interjected and smiled at Curly.

Margie grinned. "Yes. 'Out of the world'. Those, I believe, were her exact words. Business really picked up after that article."

"That sounds very interesting," Curly said, making a "hurry up" motion with his hand for Wanda to start taking notes. She sighed and took out her notebook and wrote down, *don't forget to call Mom.*

"Yes, for that month, we did bang up business."

Curly was confused. "A month? What do you mean?"

"Well, he was only here for four weeks. A little less, actually."

"You mean he's not here now?"

"Oh, no. I'm afraid as soon as the article came out, he gave me his notice. Said something about not letting the grass grow beneath his feet or something to that effect. Left a few days ago."

"What?!"

"Yes, he's been gone, let's see, two, maybe three days now."

While Curly tried to process this information, Wanda asked, "Do you know where he might have gone?"

"Well, when the maid cleaned his room, she found some brochures."

"For where?"

"Canada."

"Canada?"

"Yes," Margie pointed over her shoulder. "Lake Winnewacko is a huge lake and goes all the way north to the border and into Canada."

"Wow," Wanda said, "I had no idea." She made a note in her notebook. A real one this time, *Suspect may have fled to Canada.*

Curly spoke up, "Could you give us a description of the cook please?"

"Sure. He was kind of surly if you ask me. Not a lot of people skills that was for sure. But, boy could he cook. That spaghetti and sauce was out of this world."

"Right. We've established that. But what did he look like?"

"Well, he was about your height, Mr. Knucklewad. He always had about a three-day beard."

"Really," Curly said, the wheels in his mind turning. "Anything else distinguishing?"

"Yes, there most certainly was. He smoked the vilest cigars I've ever smelled in my life."

Curly's eyes went wide. "Cigars?"

"Yes. The vilest…"

"Yes, I heard you the first time." Curly cut her off and turned to Wanda. "Jessup," he said.

"Exactly," Wanda responded, nodding in agreement. "At the dock."

Margie spoke up. "Why yes, his name is Jessup. I heard he was driving the launch between here and the mainland in Minnesota."

Curly jumped to his feet and shook Margie's hand. "You've been very helpful." And he took off running. Wanda turned to Margie, shrugged her shoulders and said, simply, "Men." Then she shook the manager's hand and jogged off after Curly.

She quickly caught up to him and they ran across the lobby, out the front door, across the patio and the beach and down to the dock. The *Northern Belle* was nowhere in sight. Soren, the dock boy, was coiling up some rope and Curly ran up to him.

"Where's the boat. The launch or whatever you call it?"

Soren stood up. "You mean the *Northern Belle*?"

"Yeah, that's it. Where is it?"

"I don't know."

"You don't know?!" Curly yelled, waving his arms. "What do you mean you don't know? Aren't you the dock boy? Aren't you supposed to know these things? How can you…"

Wanda gently moved Curly aside and took over. "Hi Soren. Don't mind him, he gets a little excited sometimes. Hopefully, you can help us. We're very interested in talking to Mr. Jessup," she smiled. "Is there anything you might be able to tell us?"

Soren seemed to appreciate Wanda's calm demeanor. He grinned at her. "Well, after Jessup dropped you both off, he got a funny look on his face and said to me, 'Watch out for those two. They might be trouble.' Then he had me fill both gas tanks on the launch and he took off."

"Back to Minnesota I presume."

"No, ma'am. That way," he pointed. "To Canada."

Wanda looked at Curly who was standing at the end of the dock swatting mosquitoes. She took her pith helmet out of her tote bag and put it on. "Did you hear that boss?"

"Yeah, I heard," he said glumly.

"Canada."

He turned to her. "Yeah, like I said, I heard."

"What are we going to do?"

"We've got to go after him."

Wanda turned to Soren. "Can we get a boat and go find Jessup? He's wanted in a case we're investigating."

Soren shrugged his shoulders. "The only boat here is my little fishing boat. I could take you. He's got a head start on us though.

Wanda looked at Curly who nodded at her glumly. "Okay, Soren, let's do it."

"Okay," he said. "Give me a few minutes to get ready."

"Sounds good."

Curly stepped forward and said, "Say, Soren, I've got a question for you."

"Sure. What?"

"Is there a gift shop in the lodge?"

"Yeah, there is. Why?"

Curly looked at Wanda and pointed. "Do they carry pith helmets?"

"Yeah, they do."

"With the mosquito netting?"

"Yeah. Everyone wears them up here. The bugs you know."

"Yeah, I know," he said waving a swarm of deer flies away from his face. "Believe me, I know." He watched as Soren ran to shore to get some provisions, then turned to Wanda. "I'm going to get one. A pith helmet. Want to come with?"

"Sure. Maybe we can get something to eat."

"Might as well," Curly said, looking out across the huge expanse of water toward Canada. "It looks like it's going be a long day." He paused and then added, "A real long day."

225

There's More

Talk about the dark side of serendipity. With my visit to the cemetery over, it was time to go home. I was in a super good mood, finally having resolved my memorial issue, knowing my saying, *it was a great life* succinctly summed up what I wanted etched into my memorial stone. It was time to move on.

I hurried to get on the highway and drive home to be with Annie, my lovely wife of so many years. I couldn't wait to see her.

As my speed increased down the hill my car was suddenly flooded from behind with light. My eyes flicked quickly to the review mirror. Way too fast, a huge bank of headlights was speeding at me. In a panic, I jammed my accelerator to the floor. The engine revved to over six thousand rpm, but nothing happened. My car seemed to float. Time went into slow motion. In an instant a wave of intense brightness overtook me, running right up and over me, blinding me and filling the inside of my car with exploding, brilliant light. The last sound I heard was a sustained air horn blasting, filling my ears with thunderous noise until my eardrums burst; then a cacophony of metal whining and twisting and crunching along with windows exploding and glass shattering as a huge semi-truck ran right over my car, crushing it and me.

Then, merciful darkness.

The next awareness I had was that the darkness started to swirl and take form like some scientists think the earth came together back in the dawn of time. Out of that inky black night, white and gray clouds took shape, slowly floating and undulating. Blinking flashes of light started to irregularly pulsate before becoming more and more regular.

Eventually, the first scene came into view. It was my granddaughter's soccer game. She and her team were dressed in colorful red and black jerseys and were playing on a lush, green grass field. I could tell it was fall because the trees in the background were changing colors; the orange and red leaves were brilliant under a bright sun shining warmly in a robin's egg blue sky. In the scene, she looked to be six years old. That would have put it a year after my car accident and death.

She must have been thinking of me. That's how Memory Recall works. It's a give-and-take kind of thing. If she thinks of me, I can appear to her in her memory. And the cool thing is that it *really* is me. Seriously. In the world I left behind, I always thought that my memory was just that – a recall of a loved one, person, place, or whatever, and it was really just an image in my mind.

But I'm here to tell you that it's much, much more than that. I'm out there all of the time existing in a sort of dream-like state. You know how sometimes you're lying in bed half awake and half asleep? That's how it is where I am now. When you think of me, I can almost materialize right there beside you.

"Almost" is the keyword here. When you think you feel the presence of a loved one who has passed over (that's what we say here, passed over) it's a true fact because we *are* right there, but in a dimension just outside the reach of you guys. I know it sounds crazy, and you probably think I'm nuts, but it's true. Believe me. Just read on before you chalk it all up to the ravings of a delusional nutcase.

The next time it happened was when there was a special dinner for my son's promotion to regional manager for the company where he worked. His wife Lynn had organized it and guests were gathered in the dining room of their lovely home. The promotion was a very big deal for my son, and

I got to be right there with him for the celebration because he was thinking of me at the time, wishing I was there to share it with him. He didn't know it, but I *was* there. The way it works is that your thought or memory of me opens a door and lets me in. Because, like I said, I'm there anyway.

Oh, I almost forgot. You're probably wondering how I could write this if I'm gone from your physical world. I have to say that it's a really good question, and I wish I had an answer for you. But I don't. It's a mystery to me, but I'm glad I can do it, though, aren't you?

Let me tell you, this whole thing took some getting used to. When I was alive, I never thought much about what happened after a person was gone. I had no reason to, other than idle speculation. But now I have plenty of time and I'm kind of into it. Figuring out how things work here is a great experience.

And I'm still learning. There's a lot to find out about, I know that for sure. But I do know one thing: there's a whole other world out here beyond what I used to think of as the physical world. It's taking me some time to get used to it, to understand it, and I guess this is the way to put it – to live in it. But, hey, I've got all of eternity to figure it out and that's just fine with me.

So, remember – when you find yourself missing a loved one, just think of that person and don't worry about a thing. They're right there, right beside you. There's no place they'd rather be. You can bet your life on it. I sure do.

Originally published in *Pure Slush Death Anthology*

The Loch Ness Monster

"Oh, my goodness, I'm stuffed," Barb said, undoing the top button of her slacks. She took a sip of wine and pushed her feet closer to the fire. "But don't get me wrong. I'm glad we had a nice dinner at Galvin's." She smacked her lips. "Those ribs are to die for."

"No kidding. But you better be careful. With the way you were chowing them down, you probably will." Elizabeth chuckled, and sipped from her own glass of Merlot.

Barb raised her glass in acknowledgment. "Noted," she said. Then she took a healthy swig. "But, like I say, you only live once."

Elizabeth reached over and patted her best friend on the arm. "And I want to keep you around, for a few more years at least."

Barb laughed. "No problem with that, girlfriend. It's me and you to the bitter end."

Elizabeth raised her glass in a toast. "I'll drink to that."

Barb got out of her chair and sat on the floor close to the fire. As she got settled, Elizabeth's calico kitty cat Daisy trotted up, jumped her lap and started purring. Barb petted her and rubbed her nose between the ears of the small white, tan and black kitty. "Hi there, girl. How are you?" Daisy purred even louder. Then she turned around a few times and curled up on Barb's lap, closing her eyes in feline bliss. Barb petted her some more and looked at Elizabeth. "Anyway, don't get me wrong. Dinner was great." She wiggled her butt on the rug. Daisy didn't budge, just purred softly. "But this is the best." She smiled at Elizabeth and pulled out a cigarette. "Mind?"

Elizabeth shook her head. "Not at all. Just blow the smoke up the chimney."

"Got it."

Barb lit her Marlboro and blew the smoke at the fire. Both women watched as it swirled up the flue. Elizabeth had quit smoking years earlier in 1983. Now, sixteen years later she still missed it. Oh, well. She'd stopped because of her upcoming lumpectomy and was glad she did. Even though the operation had resulted in a single mastectomy and the loss of her right breast, she was still glad she'd given up the habit and had never gone back. She'd been cancer free ever since. As she put it to Barb, I'll just smoke vicariously through you.

They were in Elizabeth's cozy cottage style home in southwest Minneapolis. She'd lived there for nearly thirty years, ever since her divorce in 1970 from her husband Jerry. Jerry. She took a sip and gave a silent toast to him. After the divorce, he'd become a high-powered executive for an electronics control manufacturing company. The work pace was relentless, but he loved it (more than his family, Elizabeth had realized early on) and had died of a massive heart attack in Singapore where the company had its East Asian Headquarters. That had been, what? Twelve years ago. Where did the time go?

"Penny for your thoughts?" Barb asked. She leaned back against her chair, making sure not to disturb the sleeping Daisy, and stretched her long legs so her feet were close to the fire. She was wearing black slacks and a pewter silk blouse. Her once blond hair was now a soft yellow which Elizabeth knew was the result of regular sessions with her stylist.

"Actually, I was thinking about Jerry."

"Really? He's been dead twelve years hasn't' he?"

"Yeah."

"Don't tell me you miss the SOB?"

"No. No, I don't. I was just thinking about my life." She raised her glass again in a toast. "After all, it is the coming of a new year."

230

Barb raised her in return. "Well, if that's the case then I'll tell you. I don't miss that SOB I was married to one bit." Alan, Barb's successful attorney husband had died of a massive heart attack five years ago in the mid 90's. "Don't miss him at all."

Elizabeth nodded. Her friend had not had a happy marriage. "But at least you got to keep the house, right?"

Barb now lived alone in the big mansion she and Steve had purchased when her husband's law practice had taken off.

"Yeah, right. All by myself."

Elizabeth looked closely. Was it self-pity she detected? "You thinking of moving?"

"No way Jose'," she said. "I love that place."

So, not self-pity then.

"More wine?" Elizabeth asked.

Barb took a final drag and blew the smoke at the fire. "Absolutely," she said, snubbing her cigarette out in a nearby ashtray, one of many Elizabeth kept scattered about for her friend. "I'm staying here tonight, right?"

"Absolutely."

"Well, in that case, let's put on a little Prince and, as they say, 'Party Like it's 1999'." She giggled. "Cuz it is!"

Elizabeth poured more wine and brought out a plate of ginger cookies for them to munch on. The two friends continued to chat and talk about their lives, reminiscing, as the clock on the mantel ticked ever closer to midnight. With her husband being very rich, Barb had no need or reason to have a job, but she liked being around people so over the years she had occasionally worked part-time at one of the many boutiques in the area. She had two girls, Erin, a public defender, and Mona, a nurse in the burn unit at Hennepin County Medical Center, the huge regional hospital located in downtown Minneapolis. They were both married and were raising their children with their husbands in nearby suburbs. They saw their mother on a regular basis.

Elizabeth had two boys. Eric, taught gym and history at the junior high school in Bemidji, a three-hour drive north of Minneapolis. His wife Bonny worked in admissions at the college town, the largest city in that part of Minnesota. She had been diagnosed with MS in 1980, but it had been in remission for the last ten years and everyone had their fingers crossed her health could continue to be stable. They had two kids, Allie twenty-seven who had moved to Seattle with her boyfriend and worked in a restaurant, and Brittany twenty-three who was going to the University of Minnesota and writing a thesis on the effect of fertilizer runoff on the streams and lakes in northern Minnesota. She lived with her friend Jen in Dinkytown near the University campus.

Elizabeth's youngest son Ben and his partner Quinn lived only a few miles away from her. Ben taught music at Southwest High School and Quinn was an instructor at the University of Minnesota specializing in Native American studies. They had adopted a young boy from Korea named Kim when he was six months old. He was now seven and the pride of their lives. And Elizabeth's. She helped out taking care of the rambunctious little guy as often as her son and Quinn needed.

Elizabeth had had the entire family over for Christmas and she'd been in seventh heaven. Eric and Bonny had driven down Christmas Eve day from Bemidji. Ben and Quinn and Kim came over that same afternoon. Mona and her friend Jen were there. Even Allie and her boyfriend Noah had flown in from Seattle. She loved the gaiety and laughter and having the house full for Christmas Eve and Christmas Day had been the highlight of her year.

But Elizabeth had to admit it was nice to relax tonight on New Year's Eve with her best friend, a fire in the fireplace, and Prince on the stereo. And Daisy, of course, who was still purring softly on Barb's lap.

Elizabeth was smiling to herself when she felt a nudge. She glanced at Barb who had poked her for not the first time that evening. "There you go drifting off again. Are you sure you're okay?"

Not really, but she didn't want to get into it just then. She smiled to change the subject and told a white lie. "I am. I really am. I'm just thinking about the way things have worked out. Mainly with the kids."

Barb nodded and thought to herself, *Hm. I wonder what's going on?* She knew there had to be something. She'd known Elizabeth long enough to be able to read her, but couldn't quite put her finger on it right now. She glanced at her friend, who was now staring pensively into the fire. Well, for now she would just let it go and play along. After all, it was New Year's Eve. No sense making a big deal if she didn't have to. Besides, it was probably nothing.

In her lap, Daisy stirred, stood up and arched her back. Then she yawned, lay down and curled up again. In a moment the little kitty was fast asleep and purring. Barb smiled and petted her. She turned to Elizabeth. "I get it," she said, sipping from her wine. "I think about my girls a lot." She tapped out another cigarette, looked at it and put it back. Instead, she reached for a ginger cookie, took a bite, and munched thoughtfully. "I'm just happy they're doing alright."

Elizabeth nodded. "I know. They're good kids." She reached for her own cookie. She'd made them that afternoon. She had to admit, they were awfully tasty. "Same with Eric and Ben and their kids. I couldn't ask for more."

"And the grandkids," Barb interjected. "They're good, too, right?"

"Right." Elizabeth was quiet. What was with this mood that had suddenly come over her?' She broke eye contact with Barb and stared into the fireplace some more. She'd had a good life. She'd raised two good kids. She had three wonderful grandchildren. Her marriage hadn't worked out, but she had made peace with that. Sure, she'd dated some afterward, but soon realized she didn't need a man in her life. As she'd told Barb once, "They're just too much trouble." To which Barb had raised a glass in agreement. "I'll drink to that."

She'd had a good job working in the office at the garden center, eventually becoming manager. She made good friends there and had retired six years ago with a nice pension, enough so she didn't have to worry much about money.

She was seventy-five years old. She was in good health. She'd survived cancer. Why was she feeling this New Year's Eve angst?

She looked at Barb, who had her eyes closed and was humming along to *Little Red Corvette*. She smiled. Her friendship with Barb meant the world to her. Without her…

Suddenly, she got to her feet, feeling the bones in her joints cracking, but she didn't care. Barb's eyes popped open in surprise. "Hey, there girlfriend. What's going on? You're interrupting my mellow mood."

Elizabeth grinned. "I just had an idea."

"What?"

She looked at the clock. They still had time. "If we hurry, we can still see them."

"See what?"

"Fireworks."

"Fireworks?"

"Yes. Downtown. If we step on it, we can get to the lake. We'll have a great view of them."

Barb looked at her friend. At least she wasn't maudlin anymore. She didn't have to think. "Okay! Let's go!"

They bundled up their heavy jackets and stocking caps and scarves and boots and mittens and hurried out into the cold night. Cold but exhilarating. Elizabeth couldn't remember ever doing anything so spontaneous before. Neither could Barb. The two of them giggled and held onto each other's arms as they made their down one street and over two others and down two more until they came to Lake Harriet. There they stood on the snowy shoreline of the ice-covered lake with maybe two dozen other hardy folks and watched the annual New Year's Eve fireworks display arcing over downtown Minneapolis five miles away. It was, as one young boy said, "Spectacular."

Spectacular and cold. But both the fireworks and the frigid air seemed to revitalize Elizabeth and shake her out of her funk. On the way home, hurrying along the snowy sidewalks, Barb noticed a spring in her friend's step that was good to see. She smiled to herself. Whatever had been bothering Elizabeth, it had seemed to fade like the smoke from the last massive explosion of cascading rockets at the finale of the fireworks show.

It was true. Elizabeth's mood had brightened considerably. Once back in her snug home, she made hot chocolate in the kitchen while Barb petted an appreciative Daisy in front of the fire. When the hot chocolate was done, Elizabeth brought a tray out to the living room and set the two mugs between them on the coffee table along with a fresh plate of cookies, chocolate chip this time. She gave Barb a friendly kiss on the top of her head and said, "You know what?"

"What?" Barb smiled at her and squeezed her hand appreciatively, happy beyond words with their friendship.

"Let's do something special." She sipped from her mug.

"Special? What do you mean?" Barb took a cookie and bit into it. It was delicious.

"Let's each pick a place we've always wanted to go and then let's go there."

Barb looked at her friend with her eyebrows raised as she munched on her cookie. Elizabeth was a stay-at-home person if there ever was one. Going on a day trip antiquing an hour's drive away in Northfield and back was a big deal for her. What was with her tonight? Well, whatever it was, it was good to see her excited about something and not down in the dumps anymore. "Okay," she said, joining in the spirit of the occasion. She picked up her mug and tossed her. "You're on."

Elizabeth returned the toast. "Great! You pick first."

Barb laughed. "Girlfriend, I've been able to go anywhere in the world I've ever wanted my entire married life. Don't forget. Alan was rich."

Elizabeth nodded. It was true. She remembered Barb going to Europe on numerous occasions. She had a special fondness for Barcelona.

"Hm. That's true."

Barb didn't want Elizabeth to lose the buzz of her good mood. She looked at her and grinned. "It's a great idea, though. Where would you go?"

Elizabeth set her mug down. She smiled and closed her eyes seeing a land she'd always dreamed of going to; a place of rugged mountains, rushing rivers, and long deep fords. It was a place she'd wanted to see, ever since she was a little girl, and read about it once in a magazine.

"Okay," she said. "Here goes."

Barb grinned. "Fire away."

Elizabeth leaned forward and said, "I've always wanted to go to Scotland."

"Scotland?"

"Yep. I always wanted to go and see the Loch Ness Monster."

Barb frowned. "You know that's been proven fake, right?" Elizabeth stared unblinking right back at her friend as Barb realized what she'd just said. "Oh, yeah, right. You know that. Right?"

Elizabeth nodded. "I do. But the point is a I've always really wanted to go."

Barb smiled. Elizabeth was a good person and a great friend. She had given a lot of herself to others in her life. Why not do something she'd always wanted to do?"

Barb reached over and hugged her. "I think it's a great idea."

The next day was a new year. Barb stayed over and they began making plans for their trip to Scotland. And while they did, Elizabeth told her friend what she'd only found out just a few days before. Her cancer was back. Her doctor told her it was treatable and she believed her. Still, you never knew.

Barb cried with Elizabeth as they held each other. Then Barb said, "Girlfriend, we're still going to Scotland. Right?"

"Absolutely," Elizabeth said. "We are going, and we are going to make it the best trip ever."

"That's the attitude!" Barb said.

They hugged each other again.

A few months later, they took their trip to Scotland. Barb had been right. It was the best trip ever.

Originally published in *Holiday Stories*

Acknowledgments

First of all, I'd like to thank the incomparable Gill James and her team for continuing to support my writing. Gill published my first story on *CaféLit* in March 2018. Her confidence in my writing has been extraordinary. My first collection *Resilience* was published by her and Bridge House Publishing and my collection of flash fiction. *Short Stuff* was published by Chapeltown Books. More recently, *Old Man Jasperson and Other Stories* was published by Bridge House. In addition, she and her team have included my work in many *The Best of CaféLit* anthologies as well as themed anthologies such as *Mulling It Over*, *Nativity*, and *Aftermath*. Again, Gill, thank you so much.

Special thanks go to editor Fatima Khan for her sharp eye and constructive comments. Fatima, your input is greatly appreciated. You've made this collection the best it possibly can be. Again, thank you so much.

I'd also like to give a shout-out to some of the people who have supported me over the years. I'll pick out two: author PC Darkcliff who has written the esteemed *Magic Circle* series, and poet Christine Tabaka whose most recent book is *Favorite Child*. You are both not only amazingly gifted and talented writers but also wonderfully kind and caring people. It's a pleasure and an inspiration to know you both.

Next, I like to acknowledge my brother Tom who serves as a benchmark for much of what I write. He gives his advice freely and honestly. I really appreciate that.

Finally, many heartfelt thanks to Debra for being with me. My life is immeasurable richer with you in it.

About the Author

Jim lives in a small town in Minnesota. He loves to write! His stories and poems have appeared in over five hundred online and print publications. His collection of short stories, *Resilience,* is published by Bridge House Publishing. *Short Stuff,* a collection of flash fiction and drabbles, is published by Chapeltown Books. *Periodic Stories*, *Periodic Stories Volume Two*, *Periodic Stories Volume Three – A Novel*, and *Periodic Stories Volume Four* are published by Impspired. *Dreamers,* a collection of short stories, is published by Clarendon House Publishing. *Something Better,* a dystopian adventure novella, and the novel *The Alien of Orchard Lake* are published by Dark Myth Publications. In the fall of 2022, his collection entitled *Holiday Stories* was published by Impspired as was his collection of poetry, *Haiku Seasons*. In February 2023, a collection of flash fiction, *Dancing With Butterflies,* was published by Impspired. In July 2023, his YA novella *The Battle of Marvel Wood* was published by Impspired. In July 2023, his collection of poems, *The Alchemy of Then,* was published by Impspired. In August 2023, his novel *Conversations With the Dead* was published by Impspired. In September 2023, his collection of poems,

The Metaphysics of Now, was published by Impspired. In October 2023, his collection of short *stories, Old Man Jasperson and Other Stories,* was published by Bridge House Publishing. In January 2024, his collection of poems, *The Evolution of Tomorrow,* was published by Impspired. In January 2024, his novella *Eye of the Beholder* was published by Dark Myth Publications. In March 2024, his collection of poems, *The Science of Forever,* was published by Impspired. In August 2024, his collection of long short stories, *The Stargazer and Other Stories,* was published by Jim. In November 2024, his collection of long short stories, *On Rainy Lake and Other Stories,* was published by Jim. In January 2025, his YA adventure/fantasy novella *The Time Traveling Healer* was published by Jim. In March 2025, his YA adventure/dystopian novel *The Defectives* was published by Jim. His short story "Aliens" was nominated by The Zodiac Press for the 2020 Pushcart Prize. His story "The Maple Leaf" was voted 2021 Story of the Year for Spillwords. He was voted December 2022 Author of the Month for Spillwords. He also reads his stories for *Talking Stories Radio* and for *Jim's Storytime* and *Jim's Poetry Corner* on his website. He lives in a small town west of Minneapolis, Minnesota. All of his work can be found on his blog at
www.theviewfromlonglake.wordpress.com.

Like to Read More Work Like This?

Then sign up to our mailing list and download our free collection of short stories, *Magnetism*. Sign up now to receive this free e-book and also to find out about all of our new publications and offers.

Sign up here:
   http://eepurl.com/gbpdVz

Please Leave a Review

Reviews are so important to writers. Please take the time to review this book. A couple of lines is fine.

Reviews help the book to become more visible to buyers. Retailers will promote books with multiple reviews.

This in turn helps us to sell more books… And then we can afford to publish more books like this one.

Leaving a review is very easy.

Go to https://amzn.to/4lktkOO, scroll down the left-hand side of the Amazon page and click on the "Write a customer review" button.

Other Writing by Jim Bates

Old Man Jasperson
Published by Bridge House

In this collection, Jim looks into what it means to be human in this day and age. How do we cope with the loss of a loved one? What brings us joy? How important is friendship? Can Nature heal?

These are heavy questions, and Jim tackles them head-on with stories that are both intriguing and entertaining. He is not afraid to delve deep into life's challenges. He looks at love and loss, our hopes and dreams, and our own inner fears. Ultimately, his stories show us the strength of the human character.

These stories are heartfelt, and told with quiet passion and a gentle touch. In the end, they resonate with Jim's appreciation for the challenges we all face and, ultimately, the beauty of what it means to be truly alive and to live in this world.

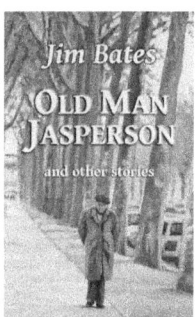

Order from Amazon:

Paperback: ISBN 978-1-914199-46-2
eBook: ISBN 978-1-914199-47-9

Short Stuff
Published by Chapeltown

This is a short sharp collection of well-told stories by Jim Bates who once again brings us some evocative writing with a strong literary voice. We meet a plethora of characters, each with their own concerns and triumphs. They face life's challenges and often have to turn situations around. Will they succeed? Will they make life good again?

In this collections of flash fiction, Jim Bates packs a lot of story into a few words.

"You will not want to put this gem down." (Amazon)

Order from Amazon:

ISBN: 978-1-910542-78-1 (paperback)
978-1-910542-79-8 (ebook)

Chapeltown Books

Resilience
Published by Bridge House

Remembrance Day is special for one grandfather. Which story of him and his brother at the lake will John remember today? Blake loves his garden but he's not so sure about the rabbit. Tyler stands up to his dad while hunting crows. What really did happen in the room at the Inn on the Lake? Why doesn't Quinn run away anymore?

"Resilience is an absolute gem. A collection of twenty-seven beautifully written short stories that deal with the central theme of its title." (Amazon)

Order from Amazon:

ISBN: 978-1-914199-00-4 (paperback)
978-1-914199-01-1 (ebook)

Other Publications by Bridge House

White Moon
by Mehreen Ahmed

White Moon is a collection of avant-garde short stories, micro and flash fiction.

Together they bring a stronger message than they do individually. The incidents in this book depict imaginary characters and events underpinned by dreamlike, strong surrealistic, even esoteric connections. The narratives bring together a unique blend of absorbing, entertaining and otherworldly experience.

As ever Mehreen Ahmed brings a strong and convincing voice to all of the texts. Enjoy the surreal and dreamlike quality of these stories.

Order from Amazon:

Paperback: ISBN 978-1-914199-90-5
eBook: ISBN 978-1-914199-91-2

Between Worlds
by S.Nadja Zajdman

We all inhabit multiple worlds and the real person lives in the liminal space between them.

In this fascinating collection of vignettes and creative memoir, we are invited to explore several constructs of the times and places defined by the narrator, and also envisaged by those around her. These accounts have appeared in other publications, but gathered here the whole becomes greater than its parts and tells a larger story.

S. Nadja Zajdman brings her rich and unique voice to this story: *Between Worlds*.

"This collection will not disappoint…! Bravo!" *(Amazon)*

Order from Amazon:

Paperback: ISBN 978-1-914199-84-4
eBook: ISBN 978-1-914199-85-1

Once We Were Heroes
by Henry Lewi

Where do the gods of Olympus do their shopping?

Do the Old Gods live amongst us, and if so where? And which jobs do they do? Where do the Old Gods shop, or do they do it online? Which football clubs do they support? When Angels are sent down to Earth, how do they get home? How did Vampires cope with Lockdown during the pandemic? And finally, are Extra-Terrestrials dangerous, or do they just want to speak to us?

"Henry Lewi writes with confidence and with imagination. The story about the gods moving to North London provided an interesting opportunity to comment on modern times. The Pandemic features in many of the items in the collection."
(Amazon)

Order from Amazon:

Paperback: ISBN 978-1-914199-82-0
eBook: ISBN 978-1-914199-83-7

www.ingramcontent.com/pod-product-compliance
Lightning Source LLC
Chambersburg PA
CBHW072221170626
46813CB00003B/1037